A SUDDEN GUST
OF GRAVITY

A Sudden Gust of Gravity
Published by Laurie Boris

© 2015 Laurie Boris
Cover design and illustration: Paul Blumstein
ISBN-13: 978-1519181930
ISBN-10: 1519181930

1

The box arrived on a Tuesday and sat on the kitchen table for three days before Christina could bring herself to touch it. She'd assumed her father's things had been tossed after all these years, but no—*this* remained. Mom had found it in the attic and decided that his last surviving possession would make an ideal twenty-fifth birthday present for his only daughter.

She almost sent the package back. But then she didn't.

"Get it out of here, already," one of her roommates told her. So she took it off the table, stuck it in the corner of her bedroom, and covered it with a green pashmina.

As a child, she'd memorized the contents of the tarnished metal case engraved with her father's initials: three silver cups, a half-dozen red sponge balls, five decks of cards, a few magic quarters, a selection of spring-loaded wands, and various other doodads and thingamabobs handy for a close-up magician to have up his sleeve.

Pick a card, Chrissie.

She itched to hold the decks, palm the tiny objects the way he'd taught her, but another part of her wanted nothing to do with it.

She thought about it on the way to yoga, and on the way home, and after her long shift at the restaurant. And her sleep fractured, leaving her as wide-awake as the thrum of Boston outside her window.

This went on for another week, until she got the call that her boss, Rosa, was in the hospital, and the restaurant was closed. Now there was nothing to think about *but* the box, and what it contained. And the truth was, no matter how great her anger at her father and herself, her desire to open the box was greater. She craved the comfort of those old, familiar objects.

Christina surrendered.

Swallowing the knot in her throat, she flipped the latch. It sounded louder than all the traffic on Commonwealth. Her fingers once again tasted the textures—the foam of the sponge balls, bits of red crumbling into dust; the shiny silver cups; the decks of cards engineered for tricks.

Pick a card, Chrissie.

Shuddering, she snapped the lid shut.

It was too late for her. Too many years had gone by, and her skills were shot. She might as well give the box away—to the owner of the magic store she passed on her way to yoga class. But she didn't.

* * *

A mild heart attack. The words sounded ridiculous, like a teensy war or an insignificant tsunami. Nothing about a heart attack, especially one that required an emergency bypass, struck Christina as mild. Especially when it involved Rosa. The older woman acted as if it had been nothing, like she'd burned her hand taking a pan of lasagna out of the oven. In fact, only hours post-op, Rosa was putting on lipstick and inviting Christina to play a few hands of gin rummy on her hospital bed. Christina accepted, of course. She wanted to. And none of the other waitresses had bothered to visit.

"Your turn, honey." Rosa nodded toward Christina's cards.

"You sure you don't want to try to get some rest?"

"Rest, ha. I don't need rest. I need to cook. And then get a decent night's sleep in my own bed."

She did look tired, though. Her color was beginning to fade; the words were coming slowly, mixed with more Italian than usual. Yet Rosa kept talking, telling Christina the secret of her famous osso buco. She was just winding into her story about the night Joe DiMaggio came into the restaurant when her husband returned to the room.

"Rosabella." Sal reached down to pat her cheek. "It was DiMaggio's son. Remember?"

"I think she needs a nap," Christina said.

Rosa's lovely, limpid eyes were already half-closed. Sal nodded, cupped a hand to Christina's elbow, and guided her out into the hall. "You're a good girl," he said, "like a daughter. But you don't have to stay. Surely you have other things…"

Christina shrugged. "I don't mind." A yawn caught her off guard. "But I need to pop downstairs and grab a cup of coffee. You want anything?"

"Yes," he said. "I would like this never to happen to my beautiful bride again. Maybe you could pop into the chapel and ask the Big Guy to do something about that."

If only she could. If only her father's magic wands were real and she could wave all of this away.

* * *

The cafeteria was somewhere in the basement of the main building. Christina knew that. She'd been there. Several times. But maybe fatigue and worry had disoriented her. Her wall-eyed gaze latched onto a lanky young guy in green scrubs. "Excuse me?"

"Yes?" He looked about as tired as she felt.

"Which way's the cafeteria? Because, seriously, if I don't get a cup of coffee in the next ten minutes, I think I'm gonna die."

A corner of his mouth twitched up, and he gestured that she should follow him. Soon she was standing in front of the mother lode: a bank of coffee carafes and all the trimmings. He grabbed two large cardboard cups, handed her one, and she gave him a weak smile of thanks.

After they'd filled up, he said, "Is that all you're getting?"

She nodded. He went up to a register, swiped an ID card through a scanner, and told the cashier he was paying for two.

"Thanks, but that's not necessary, I—"

She was interrupted by an electronic bleep. He grabbed his pager, and when he glanced at the readout, he sighed. Fatigue reclaimed his face, making him look older. "Sorry, I need to get back to the ER." He lifted his cup. "Good thing I stopped to refuel. You can find your way back, right?"

"I think so. Third floor, Cardiac Care."

"Easy. Make two rights and there's your elevator."

He began to turn, and she pressed a hand to his arm, stopping him. She was surprised at the silky texture of his skin, surprised at herself for liking it.

"Wait…this is stupid, you probably see, like, a hundred people a day, but were you in the ER a couple nights ago, an Italian woman with a mild heart attack, owns Rosabella's?"

"Sorry. I can't really talk about patients."

"Right." She sighed. "Privacy laws and stuff. I understand."

"I hope she's feeling better." Again he apologized and told her he had to go. Christina lingered near the register, warming both hands on her coffee, gaze stuck on where the guy had been standing.

"Park," a woman's voice said.

At first Christina thought someone was asking her to sit down, get out of the way. Then she snapped out of her fog and realized it was the cashier. "That's his name?"

"Yeah," she said. "Nice guy."

Christina thought for a moment. "Yeah, he is."

2

Christina climbed the stairs to the second-floor magic shop, her sneakered feet whispering against the wood. Mingling aromas of mold and the gunpowder tang of burned flash paper beckoned her forward. Behind the counter stood an older gentleman polishing a set of stainless steel cups with a cloth. The tall, slender man's thinning hair was neatly combed, and he held himself stock-straight—confident, but without arrogance. All he needed was a tuxedo and he could be any of the old-school magicians she'd met at her father's club. He flicked a glance at her, maybe meaning only to see who had come in. But then his gaze lingered, and he paused at his task.

"Morning, miss."

Christina stepped deeper into the shop, pulling in a long breath to defend herself against the press of clutter: towering displays, top-hatted foam heads, and stacks of children's magic kits.

"I know." He nodded. "Been meaning to clean this place up. Best you want to set your things down. I can take them behind the counter if you'd like."

His gentle voice soothed away the impending attack of claustrophobia. "Thank you," she said as he took her gym bag and rolled-up mat.

"Now." He pressed his hands to the glass-topped counter and leaned forward. "Anything in particular you need?"

"Just looking, I guess."

Was he worthy of her father's collection? She wanted more time to decide. Meanwhile, the goodies on the display shelves beneath the window caught her attention. Polished to a high shine, they winked at her. Finally she found the illusion she craved. The one her father had; the one that wasn't in the case her mother had sent. Not the cheesy rhinestone version, but the real deal, made from ebony wood and colored crystal. She smiled, remembering the day she could finally make a gem look like it had leaped from one stick to the other. She'd run to perform it for him. He'd acted like she was the greatest show on earth. Now, with dust tickling her nose and fingers pressed against the display's clear panel, the memory of the joy fluttered higher than the pain. It soared above the chatter of the people who tried to discourage her, who tried to tell her that she was too broken to take up magic again. Too traumatized. Too female—

"How much for the Jumping Gems?" she asked over her shoulder.

He called out a price and she winced. "Do you take plastic?"

The man snorted a laugh. "Cash on the counter, that's my policy."

She sighed. "Next time, I guess."

"And we'll be glad to see you." His eyes, a watery shade of green, changed then, softened. "Say. You lookin' for a job?"

She glanced around the store, empty only of customers. "What, here?"

"Naw. Hardly enough business for more than one of me, here. I meant"—he paused to eyeball her—"as a magician's assistant."

Christina barely topped out at five two, but with his last few words she could have sworn she'd jacked herself up taller. "Assistant? Why would I want to be someone's assistant?" She jabbed a fist into her hip. "Because 'woman' and 'magic' only means little froufrou costumes and getting cut in half?"

He put up his hands. "Whoa. Slow down there. You look the part, is all. It was an honest mistake. One of my regulars was just in here, said he needed one, so I thought—"

"You thought wrong." She thrust a palm toward him, gesturing for her things. Tossing her bag over her shoulder, she thumped down the stairs. Good thing she had a yoga class to go to. She had some stress to kill.

* * *

Even though Christina had arrived with ten minutes to spare, only a few spots were available at the back of the dimly lit room. All around her, supine bodies lay still except for the soft sigh of breathing and the gentle rise and fall of breasts and bellies. Readying to immerse herself in the calm, sacred womb of the yoga studio, she slipped off her little white sneakers, and atop the gleaming wood floor rolled out her mat, angling it for a better view of the instructor. But she'd barely settled onto her back in her purple rectangle of real estate when a shadow fell over her. Her shoulders tightened at the intrusion. A quick glance told her that the person crowding into her space was male. Not especially tall, but with broad shoulders and muscular arms bared by a fitted tank top. As he set out his own mat with a deft snap of his wrists and lowered his body into a hurdler's stretch, impressive quads straining against the fabric of his warm-ups, a deeper perusal made her wonder what he was doing in her class. He didn't resemble any of the goateed, soft-bellied guys who occasionally dropped in, mainly dragged by women.

"Saw you going into Herbert's place." He tipped his strong, clean-shaven chin toward the magic shop. "Hope you found what you needed." His voice had the kind-of-sexy cadence of a radio announcer, yet the intrusion made her stomach clench. Had he followed her here?

He hadn't spoken all that loudly, but the woman on the other side of him flashed a sharp, silencing glare. "Excuse me for disturbing your peace," he whispered, pressing a finger to his lips. "Namaste."

He then turned to Christina, gave her a whiter-than-white smile and looked like he was about to intrude further, but then the instructor rang her little Tibetan gong.

She hoped he'd can the chatter. Yoga wasn't a social event for her; it was her island of sanity. Rosa, still convalescing at home, had pushed Sal to reopen with a temporary chef. After class, Christina was working the lunch shift. Sal was bound to be bouncing off the walls micromanaging the poor temp, and she needed all the sanity she could muster.

Thankfully, the dude kept quiet. But with every move, every stretch of her leg, every sweep of her arm, she sensed him watching her. At first it was a little creepy. But after the triangle position, she was finally able to tune him out and focus on her body, her breathing.

She didn't think of him again until, in corpse pose, the gong sounded a return to consciousness. She lay still, eventually becoming aware of the background static of people rolling up mats, putting on shoes, their soft voices an undercurrent of music.

"Man, that was good," he said. "I was so centered I almost fell asleep. How long have you been taking this class?"

Christina let her eyes drift open and, not ready to speak yet, narrowed hers at him.

"Oh, how rude of me." He gave her a slow blink, bringing her attention to irises a deep shade of indigo in the dim light, and he introduced himself as Reynaldo. No last name, like Cher or Beyoncé.

Of course. He's a magician. Who else hangs around a magic store, has no last name, and has time during the day for a random yoga class?

"Christina." He offered his palm in greeting, and she hesitated before accepting, like it portended an agreement that was not stacked in her favor. The hand was warm and strong and lingered around hers. Something inside her fluttered when meeting his now smiling eyes, something she promised to have stern words with later, but for the time being, she shoved it into a corner.

She rose and began rolling up her mat. "I should be getting to work."

He pointed toward her. "Wait, don't tell me. You're a model."

"Yeah, funny."

He closed his eyes and pressed a fingertip to each temple like a sideshow mind reader. "Nope. Not one of those mannequins. An artist's model. Someone should be painting you."

Nice try. "Sorry." She shoved the mat into its quiver and slung it over her shoulder. "Gotta run."

"So what do you do?"

Christina huffed out a breath. "Waitress. I know. It's terribly exotic. But it pays the bills. Speaking of which…"

The dude blocked her exit. "Who do you work for?"

She glared.

"Sorry," he added. "*Whom* do you work for?"

"I just said—"

"No, I mean which magician do you work for?"

Right. He'd seen her going into the shop. "I don't," Christina said.

"So…what were you doing there?"

"I saw something shiny in the window."

"Do you"—his dark eyebrows rose; a small vertical scar parted the left one at the arch—"want to work for a magician?"

What is this, Piss Off Christina Day? "Meaning you?"

The grin, combined with a little shrug, probably practiced in front of a mirror, had an appeal that might have worked on someone else. "Well, yeah. I have a shot at performing a stage show, but I need an assistant."

Like hell she was ever going to do that again. "Look, I can't afford to be late."

Finally he moved out of her way, but after giving the front desk manager the briefest of nods, he followed her through the door. "I'm not pulling your leg, I swear." Then he dropped his voice an octave or so. "Come by and audition for me? Hey, if it doesn't work out, we go our separate ways. But I got a feeling we'd be so good. I'm working on backers, a venue… We could make a boatload."

For a second she allowed herself to imagine what she might do with a boatload. Finish college. Pay her mother back every cent of what she'd borrowed for the few semesters she'd already taken. Walk into that magic store and buy anything she wanted.

She slowed just enough for his smile to broaden. He reached behind her ear and pulled his hand back, revealing a business card.

Christina took it.

And then he bowed. He actually bowed and kissed her hand. "Until we meet again, fair maiden of the strawberry-blond curls."

She almost laughed in his face. But after he left, she took a moment to readjust her gear on her shoulders before heading to the restaurant. What if he wasn't full of shit? She wasn't thrilled about being an assistant again, but she might be able to suck it up and handle a short-term gig. She could wave her arms around and wear a bit of fluff if it meant a few extra dollars and a ticket to something bigger. He had the right package for success in this field: charm, looks, charisma. Probably some talent. Maybe some connections.

If the audition worked out, she could learn from him.

He could be her on-ramp back into magic.

Her step lightened as she made her way to the T stop, fighting the urge to smile at everyone she passed. It was like being handed a gift bigger than anything she could conjure from her father's kit: a chance to redeem herself. A chance to prove her critics wrong. A chance to prove to herself that, despite everything, she had the goods and the drive to become a magician in her own right. To pick up her abandoned dreams and run with them.

3

It had been a slow night in the emergency department, and one of the interns volunteered to make a coffee run because nobody but the third-year medical students and the desperate drank the swill in the waiting room lounge.

After she left, Devon Park leaned back in his chair and closed his eyes, trying to rouse himself with deep breathing. Maybe a fifth cup of coffee was a bad idea, but he couldn't stay awake much longer. The medical dramas on TV had it all wrong. For most of his shift, he battled boredom and paperwork, interspersed with short and sometimes terrifying bursts of activity. Any camera crew following him around would give up after forty minutes.

Suzie, a nurse who'd worked with him since he'd started his residency at Mass General, nudged his shoulder. "Hey. Dev. Wake up."

Her voice snapped him back to attention. "I'm awake," he said, much too loudly, which probably meant that he hadn't been.

Suzie gave him the hairy eyeball. "How many hours have you been on?"

"I think the little hand was on the two." He'd spent most of the morning in a blanket fort, teaching his young nephew how to tell time.

"Go home."

Devon shoved thick, almost-black hair off his forehead. "Can't. I need to go on rounds in"—he checked his watch—"two hours and thirteen minutes."

"Then grab a few winks in the on-call room. That's why we have them, right?"

He thought about it. He'd just decided a catnap was a good idea and hauled himself to his feet when the phones started going crazy. "Multiple GSWs," an ambulance dispatcher said and, as if someone had flipped a demonic switch, everything went from zero to crazy. Soon the doors flew open and the place boiled with EMTs and cops and screeching women and teenage boys who had to be pulled apart.

Gang shootings? In this neighborhood?

Adrenaline zapped Devon awake faster than a gallon of coffee, and he was moving as fast as his long legs would take him. He did what he'd been trained to do, what generations of Park men had been trained to do. Make decisions. Fix people. Save lives.

Suzie called for security and yelled at two boys throwing punches at each other. Amid the chaos Devon heard a woman crying for help.

"Holy Mother of God," the nurse muttered. "Dev, you get that one. I'm paging everyone down here."

He narrowed his focus past the anger-contorted faces of the rival gang members to an EMT crew. He couldn't see beyond them to the patient on the gurney, but he found the woman. A girl really, with blood on her face and arms, blood staining her flowered summer dress. She looked at least seven months along and couldn't have been more than fifteen.

"Please," she wailed. "Please, my baby…*ese bastardo le disparó a mi bebé*."

What? They shot her in the abdomen? Or was that a baby on the gurney? Devon didn't know how it happened, but they parted to make way for him. He ushered the crew back into a booth, knowing he was breaking the rules by not getting someone to do the full intake, but he didn't care. It *was* a baby, for Chrissakes. There was no time for paperwork. Suzie tried to take the mother away, but she was having none of it, crying and cursing in Spanish. Whether the blood had come from her, the baby, or another injured party, he couldn't tell. But color was draining from her face.

"Need help here!" He hoped Suzie's backup had arrived. From all the testosterone-juiced shouting in the lobby, he assumed it hadn't. *Where is everyone tonight?*

"I'm not shot bad," the girl said. "Just my baby…"

"It's okay, it's okay." Devon tried to keep his voice calm despite the panic hammering through his body and the fright in her eyes. "We're gonna fix her up, we'll fix you, too, let's just have a look."

He peeled back the bloodstained blanket and nearly vomited. No way. There was no way to save the baby. Even as a first-year resident, he knew that. Yet he had to turn back to this girl, this mother, this *child*, and tell her what he knew.

"Doctor, Doctor, please." She grabbed at his scrub top, her eyes huge and wet.

Even though he knew, he made himself go through the paces. *Never assume*, his uncle had always told him. *Pulse, none. Pupil activity, none.*

He lifted the baby to his chest and cradled her. Tears and blood mingled on the young mother's cheeks as she touched the small head and began to pray in Spanish. He prayed too, feeling her swollen belly pressing into his side. The girl's perfume, something sweet and fruity, floated under the copper reek of blood, and the juxtaposition tightened his throat. But he swallowed his feelings; he had to. Then he spied the flash of a white coat flying past the booth. He called out. The doctor caught the mother just before she fainted and grabbed an orderly to help take her away.

Which left Devon alone with the baby in his arms. *Pretty little girl.* He didn't know how long he stood there, rocking her, singing lullabies in English and the smattering of Korean he'd learned from his mother and his aunt. Finally Suzie, with soft words of encouragement, persuaded him to put the body down and step away. He set her on the gurney and touched the small forehead, sticky with blood, before he walked out. And kept walking through the ongoing chaos straight to the staff locker room, where he tore off his scrubs and hit the shower.

As blood spiraled down the drain, Devon leaned against the wall. He caught the tail end of the tattoo on his bicep—a black serpent etched into him ten years ago by the flickering light in some Seattle biker's garage. In that moment, he could have shredded it off with his teeth. But it was a reminder of what he'd escaped, and a memorial to those who hadn't.

Finally, with most of his energy spent, feeling suspended in an eerie, disembodied calm, Devon toweled off, dressed, and clocked out.

Two days later, he still hadn't returned.

4

The trip to the address on Reynaldo's business card required an outbound T ride and a bus transfer. The scenery changed from the row houses of her neighborhood to edgy student slums to a gentrified shopping area to...this—a sliding-down block of boarded-up businesses, auto repair shops, and the two-story wood-shingled building she now stood in front of, a growing feeling in her gut that she'd been duped. Or was about to be cold-cocked and carted off by organ traffickers. The number matched what he'd given her. But the place looked more like an abandoned retail establishment than a home where someone would actually live—legally, anyway. To the left was an alleyway, occupied by an old brown pickup truck.

As she was wondering whether to ring the bell or run for help, the front door creaked open, and the magician stepped out, shooting her a grin. "First test passed," he said, spreading his arms wide. "You found me."

"So I did." She peered up at the drooping gutters. "Is this place even zoned for human habitation?"

"Be it ever so humble." The smile broadened. "Come on in. I'll make tea."

* * *

The interior décor was a step up from what the exterior promised. His digs were modest and could use a good cleaning, although thankfully clutter was the only problem and not frat-house filth. The main, open room consisted of a kitchen-slash-dining area, a tatty sofa beneath windows dressed in blackout curtains, and a coffee table that might have been rescued from a household of teething dogs. At the back was a closed door, and beyond that, Christina imagined a bedroom and bath.

"Make yourself at home," he said as he set about the tea preparations. Despite his muscular build, he moved gracefully and had a light touch with the cabinet doors and mugs. *Yep. That's a magician.* So he was at least legit on that score.

Satisfied that she hadn't been summoned to this address for nefarious purposes, she headed for a painted chair at the Formica-topped table in the dining area. Before she could sit, he darted over and, with one sweep of his arm, pushed the accumulation of paperwork and books toward the wall, then made a little bow and glanced up at her as if expecting applause.

Also a magician. "Thank you," she said.

He set the mismatched mugs down and slipped into a chair opposite her. She hooked her feet around the rungs and sat up straighter. Her last interview, three years ago at Rosabella's, had lasted exactly thirty seconds. She'd walked in cold, a stressed-out Sal asked if she'd waited tables before, she nodded, and he handed her an apron and a pad. So she wasn't sure what was expected of her here.

"Got a résumé?" he asked.

She shook her head.

"Video?"

Again, she shook her head.

"Performing experience?"

She wondered if waitressing counted. Because she damned sure wasn't telling him about her father.

He leaned back, tapping a pen against his open notebook, and narrowed his eyes at her, grinning a hitch as if she were an intriguing puzzle he couldn't solve. Then he pointed the pen in her direction. "I like you, though. There's something about you. And you're easy on the eyes. I think we can work with that. What do you know about magic?"

Again, not talking about her father. What he'd taught her. The hours she'd practiced. Or why she'd stopped. In case he got the wrong idea about her intentions, Christina decided it was better to plead ignorance. She swallowed and curled a hand around her mug.

"Um…abracadabra?"

"Cute. You're cute." He scribbled some notes. "We can work with that, too." He paused a moment. "What were you doing in the magic store?"

"Like I said. I saw something shiny in the window."

He gave her a long, flat stare. She exhaled and let her shoulders relax. "Okay. I was looking for a present for my little cousin."

He tapped the pen again. "Tyke wants to be the next big thing?"

"I guess."

"Well, tell him to stop it. We don't need the competition."

"Fine," she said. "I'll get him socks and underwear."

"And she has a sense of humor. We'll have to train you out of that. I do the jokes in this act."

"So, I just get to stand there and be easy on the eyes?"

"Depends on the skills you bring to the table. Each one makes you more valuable. You don't have to know how to perform the illusions—I don't require that of my assistants—but if I ask you for a thingamajig and you hand me a whatchamacallit, well, that could suck big time."

"I can learn." She pulled herself up straighter. "I've waitressed in three different restaurants, and I've memorized all their menus, even the daily specials. I pull wicked good tips, too."

"Nice to know. Local flavor with a decent memory and customer appeal. Your stock just went up. Are you claustrophobic?"

Her insides froze. "Why?"

"For the stage illusions, of course. That'll come later. But I don't want to invest my time training an assistant only to find out she freaks when she gets into a box."

"I'm good," she said.

He lifted a brow. "That remains to be seen. You'll need a name."

"Christina usually works."

Reynaldo shook his head. "Oh, you crack me up. What do you think about Teeny?"

She shot him a glare. Then, realizing the reaction might have come off a little frosty and lowered her stock, she said, "Maybe something else."

"No, I like it. It's cute. It's you." She must have looked unconvinced, because he added, "That's showbiz, kid. The crowd likes a little fun. A little flash and dazzle. Think anyone's gonna pay attention to a magician named Ralph?"

He had a point. Reynaldo suited him. With his square, rugged face and movie-star jawline, all that stood between him and the cover of a romance novel was long, flowing hair and a pirate shirt. But now she struggled not to laugh. "Ralph?"

Clearly displeased, he jabbed a finger at her. "Don't ever call me that. Especially in public. And on stage it's 'Reynaldo the

Magnificent.'"

She wrangled back a snarky grin when he speared her with a glare. "Hey, you want this job or not?"

"I'm sorry, I just…Ralph?"

The glare hardened. "Look, Teeny Tiny Tina." He hooked a thumb over his shoulder. "I could go back to that yoga class and find another girl in about five seconds. This act could go big. We could go to Vegas. So can the attitude or get out."

Christina flinched, biting at her lower lip to stay in control, admonishing herself to suck it up. No way was she losing out on this gig over something as dumb as bad acting skills. She could have done a better job, because his face softened, and he extracted a handkerchief from his pocket. "Aw, don't cry," he said.

"I'm not—"

Then the cloth began to dance in his palm. She glanced up at him, confused for a moment before remembering her father teaching her that same trick and how it worked.

Ralph/Reynaldo shrugged. "Simple illusion. I'll show you how to play it." His hand lighted on her shoulder, and his voice was a caress against her ear when he said, "I'll teach you everything. Look, Tee—Christina. I like you. I've seen you in that class before. You're exactly what a magician wants in an assistant. Small. Graceful. Flexible as hell. And like I said, not a bad piece of misdirection. So whaddya say? Work with me. We'll make a mint off these suckers."

He'd been watching her? Something landed in her gut with a thud.

He pressed a hand against the tabletop. "Come on. What's your wildest dream?"

She squeezed her eyes shut for a second. Gathering herself. It settled her rapid breathing. "I, well, eventually I want to go back to college."

"Meh. That's for the other sheep. What do you really want?" He thumped a fist to his chest. "Deep inside, in that hot, beating core of you, what's Christina about?"

"I'm not sure yet." Which was partially true. Yes, she'd wanted to be a magician. When she was eight, she decided that one day she would call herself The Amazing Christina. Mom found out, sighed, and said that magic was no career for a girl—or anyone else, for that matter. And then she'd been sent off to do her homework while her parents argued. But after her father died, she couldn't bear to think about her old dreams. Sometimes when she passed the store near the yoga studio and saw the shiny top hats in the upstairs display window, her heart would clutch and her step would slow, but she forced herself to keep walking, cataloguing the usual litany of excuses. *I've let my skills deteriorate. Too many years have gone by. Magic is a boys' club.* But then the box arrived—

"See, that's the beauty of it," Ralph said. "We'll make money, have some fun, and by the time you figure it out, you'll be set."

She let his words roll over her. *You'll be set.* If she worked with him, she'd have the chops, the connections, enough in the bank to try to go out on her own and maybe finish college on the side. But she drew out the silence, mainly to see what he'd do next.

"What?" His eyebrows rose, mouth turning down. "You want to wait tables forever?"

That much she did know for sure. She didn't completely despise waitressing, but she'd never considered it a long-term career move. It was supposed to be what she did until something else came up, only it never had. Until now.

"Hell, no," she said.

He unwrapped a smile. "Then I have some paperwork for you to sign."

5

Devon woke to a pounding fist at his bedroom door. "Yo, Dev," boomed his roommate's northern English accent. "Wakey-wakey, son. Company."

"Wha...? Who?" He rolled over with a groan.

"Just get out here." Thomas sounded strained. "Now."

Then he heard a second voice. It called his full Korean name, and Devon jumped straight from the bed and nearly out of his skin. He shoved his hair into order and, while grabbing clothing, he called out, "I'm sorry, Uncle. I'll be right there." *Crap. Crap, crap, crap.*

He almost fell over getting into his jeans and was zipping his fly when he stumbled for the doorknob. Sucking in a deep breath, he readied himself to meet his fate.

Uncle stood in the living room, his face unyielding as granite, but as he took in his nephew's appearance, a thick black eyebrow lifted so slightly that few but those closest to him would notice the gesture. "Maybe it's true that you've been too sick to take your shifts. It would explain the grooming."

Devon's hand went to the stubble on his chin. The non-Korean component of his DNA was dominant in the area of facial hair. But in the presence of Uncle Doctor, he could almost feel the hairs withdrawing into their follicles.

The man merely waited.

It had always been Uncle's way to let the silence drag out until Devon rushed to fill the space with admission of his wrongdoings, real or imagined. This patience was what made him such a good doctor, and served him well as chief of surgery at Boston's Brigham and Women's Hospital. He rarely even raised his voice. But when Uncle chose to wield it, his intimidating presence commanded respect. And sometimes fear.

The younger Park felt a nearly uncontrollable urge to empty his bladder.

As if he knew the effect his watchful, stony silence had on his young charges, medical and familial, Uncle Doctor waved a hand and Devon shot to the grubby bathroom, relieved himself, brushed his hair, and returned, heart whumping against his chest, wishing like hell he'd put on a shirt.

Uncle continued his scrutiny, hands behind his back, circling Devon now.

Finally, the man spoke. "A very puzzling thing." He stopped in front of his nephew. "Many a third- and fourth-year student has been under my care during their rotations. If they are to break, that's when they're most likely to do so. For many it's when they lose their first patient. You've passed this mark. That's what I'm struggling with. You've been a model student. You have the potential to be an outstanding surgeon—"

"Uncle, please, let me explain."

Dr. Park raised a hand. "Have I finished speaking, Dae Soon?" His hard eyes betrayed the mild voice.

"No, sir," Devon said to his bare feet.

"Look at me."

Devon swallowed and lifted his chin. Guilt tightened a knot in his stomach. This man had taken him in. Paid for his undergraduate education. Helped him get into Harvard Medical School.

"If I tell you that I understand," his uncle continued, "know that this does not excuse you from my disappointment."

Devon blinked at him. He...understood?

"What?" Uncle Park made what Devon could only interpret as a smirk. "You think I'm made of stone. That I've never wanted to walk out the doors of my hospital and never return, even after all that I've seen?"

"Um, no, sir." He then realized it was the first time Uncle had been to his apartment. Heat rose into his face at the condition of the rooms he shared with Thomas and another Mass General resident. Especially at the empty takeout containers and beer bottles on the coffee table.

"That you walked away from your responsibilities in the middle of your shift disappoints me. That you abandoned your patient disappoints me." He picked up an empty, frowned at it, and set it back down. "Frankly, you were lucky that you weren't dismissed on the spot. But that you didn't come to me disappoints me greatly."

Once again studying his feet, the spindly toes that were another legacy from his American father, Devon said, "I'm sorry."

"It's not me to whom you owe the apology."

Devon whooshed out a breath. To the unasked question, his uncle said, "She's fine, I'm told. But it was your responsibility to see this through. No matter your personal feelings."

"But," Devon lifted his gaze, "you just said—"

The sharp brown eyes cut him off. "Yes. I said I understood. I did not, however, excuse."

"You know why, Uncle," Devon said through clenched teeth.

"Yes, I know why," he snapped back, and then his voice softened. "You're still a young man. And I've learned the folly of telling a young man what to do. This is why I strongly suggest rather than insist."

Devon nodded. Those strong suggestions had always felt like you-damn-well-betters. But he was grateful for his aunt and uncle's generosity and didn't want to imagine where he'd be without them. So he waited for the strong suggestion.

"If you don't cut your ties to your past, it will weigh heavily around your neck."

Devon's eyes widened. His uncle might as well have asked him to sprout wings and fly. Forget his past? Forget his brother?

Uncle lifted a hand. It was a delicate, steady, and deceptively strong instrument. Devon's looked a lot like it—a gift, or burden, depending, from the Park side of the genetic pool. "I don't pretend this will be easy," he said, "but you will be better for it."

Perhaps confident from the slump of Devon's chin that the message had been received, Uncle Park nodded and turned toward the door. Then stopped. "Now. How long do you expect this *illness* to last?"

"I don't know."

The elder Park took another full measure of his nephew's face and nodded again, his expression relaxing into one Devon had seen after family dinners, when they sat, just the pair of them, softened by Aunt Mimi's cooking, talking about what Devon had learned in school. "Two more strong suggestions I wish to leave you with."

Devon glanced up.

"Take the time to ponder very seriously if this is indeed the path for you."

The words were out before he could catch them. "Like I have a choice? I'm a Park. I practice medicine. It's been drilled into me from the day I got off that plane."

"And that"—Uncle stabbed a finger toward him and raised the volume of his voice higher than Devon had ever heard him—"is why you are not dead from some gangster's bullet in Seattle. I taught you to value life! To preserve life! I gave you what I could not give your brother!"

It was then that the ghost of Lee seemed to step between them. Uncle gripped the doorknob. "Make your decision carefully, Dae Soon." He drew in a long breath and exhaled. "One more suggestion."

Devon's eyes burned with the effort to hold back tears. No. He would never. Not in front of this man.

Uncle waved a hand toward the tattoo on Devon's shoulder. "Get that thing removed."

The click of the door resounded as heavily as if it were the slam of a metal barricade.

Devon didn't know how long he stood in the living room, his uncle's words still echoing in his head, but he jumped when he felt the clap of a large hand on his shoulder. Then relaxed when he realized it was Thomas, or Thomas the Tank Engine as some of his young patients had tagged him, because of his size.

"He's right, mate. Damned ugly thing, that."

"Shut up," Devon said, and retreated to his room.

6

On the eve of his college graduation, Auntie Mimi had given Devon a new wallet with a crisp twenty inside. For luck, she said. The next day the bill was missing, and he had a good idea where it had gone.

"I would have given you the money if you'd asked. All you think of is yourself, you don't—" Devon froze in the doorway of the bedroom he shared with his brother. He clutched his empty wallet, the words he wanted to reel back in still hanging like a bitter cloud around his head. Lee was stuffing a handful of clothing into a backpack atop one of the narrow twin mattresses. "Where are you going?"

A fringe of dark hair fell across his sixteen-year-old brother's eyes.

"Tell me you aren't going back there."

Lee shrugged.

"I forbid you from leaving."

Lee merely smirked. "Still think you're the boss of me, huh? Elder brother, get a life. Oh, right. You're one of them, now."

"Ungrateful," Devon muttered in Korean.

"You sound like one of them, too. Watch out, keep making that face and you'll end up looking like Uncle Doctor."

"Say what you want about him, but look at all he's given you." He gestured out the window to the Boston waterfront and the boats rolling against the dock bumpers of Rowes Wharf, as if asking them to chime in. "You have a good home. A chance for a decent education." Devon's mouth settled into a frown. "But you crap on all of it."

"Are you done?"

"Kwang Lee—"

He pointed a balled-up pair of socks at Devon before tossing them into the bag. "Don't start with that. You can't guilt me into this. My friends need me."

"Yeah, which ones? The ones you carried drugs for?"

"Billy Cho. It's Billy Cho, okay, so shut up."

Devon stilled. "Is he all right?"

"Yeah… But he said he wanted out, and a couple of the guys beat him up. Like a warning."

"And you think you can change their minds?"

"I've done it before." He lowered his gaze to the pack and one side of his mouth hitched. "Darcy's gonna love Seattle."

"You're taking Darcy? Almost eight months pregnant, and you're..." Devon reined in the tone of his voice, because he knew from sore experience that getting upset only made his brother more defiant. "They could send the cops after you, bring you back."

"They can bring me back all they want; they can't make me stay."

"But the baby... How are you going to take care of a family?"

"I'll get a job. Stay with friends, save money. I'm gonna do all the right things. Spend time with my kid. Not like Dad."

Devon sighed and watched his brother fling colored T-shirts on top of the socks. "So what am I supposed to tell them?"

Lee waved a hand. "Whatever keeps the precious family honor intact."

Devon pursed his lips. "I'm coming with you."

"Hell, no." He raised his chin toward the tidy row of textbooks on the shelf over Devon's desk. "You gotta go to medical school, march down the runway of the Park assembly line."

"I don't start until September. I'll just stay for a while, make sure everything's okay."

Lee groaned. "Will you stop?"

"What—?"

"I don't need you hovering over me. I don't need to be rescued all the time! It's like some kind of sickness with you. What is that thing Uncle Doctor says? Physician, heal thyself?"

"But—" Devon started reaching for him, but the hard look in Lee's eyes warned him off.

"Believe it or not, there are things I can do on my own." He tugged his pack closed. "And maybe you should start doing some of those things, too."

"Like skipping school? Staying out all night? It must be nice getting away with being so irresponsible."

Lee crossed his arms over his chest and leaned back, the posture reminding Devon of a little bantam who thought he ruled the roost, especially the way he wore his hair, too long and flopping over his face. "Maybe you should try goofing off once in a while. It might take that stick out of your ass. Like, when was the last time you had a girlfriend?"

"We're not talking about me," Devon said.

"Right, what's to talk about? No life. Well, I have one, I'm late, and I'm leaving."

Devon opened his mouth but knew at this point the argument was lost. "Just be careful." His voice sounded small. "Please."

"I'm always careful. Most of the time. Besides"—Lee shouldered his pack, flipped down his shades, and flashed his brother a charming, crooked smile—"I have your lucky twenty, don't I?"

* * *

Less than forty-eight hours after his brother had left Boston, Devon Park was on a plane.

He'd vowed never to return to Seattle, especially the poor, broken corner of South Seattle he'd called home. The cracked sidewalks, the schools, the places they'd hung out in until the police chased them away—they all held too many memories, nearly all of them bad. One of the few bright spots had been visits from Auntie. She brought him and Lee new clothes and treats and sweet, perfumed hugs.

He could really use one of those now.

He dropped his head against the seat in the back of the cab. Rain slid down the window as the remaining light melted into dusk. Instead of filtering the old neighborhood into a time-blurred impressionist painting, the streams of water overtaking the graffiti and trash and homeless men made him feel like he was drowning, and he sucked in a few deep breaths to try to convince himself otherwise.

Soon the streets of White Center grew all too familiar, and the cab slowed to a stop at the curb. The building looked the same. The Chos lived on the nicer end of the block, close enough to an up-and-coming neighborhood that the owners at least made an attempt to keep up with the maintenance. But a closer inspection revealed its tattered underskirts. Baskets of flowers bloomed from barred windows; doors had multiple locks, and the neighborhood watch placards were tagged with gang marks.

He overtipped the driver and climbed the stairs.

Huge blue eyes set into an elfin face greeted him in the crack of a still-chained door; Mrs. Cho scolded in broken English behind her. "You gotta be Devon," Darcy said.

He nodded, recognizing her from one of Lee's photographs.

"Well, the boys ain't here." When Darcy let him in, she glanced at his bag. "Might as well put your stuff down and wait 'em out."

"Will they be back soon?"

Darcy shrugged and curved a tiny, swollen hand around her belly. "Said something about meetin' up with some old friends. Didn't want to drag me around, I guess. Don't blame 'em. I'm like three hundred pounds of beached whale." Her rosebud lips tilted into a smile. "He says I'm beautiful, but you know he's a goddamn liar."

Devon almost grinned back. *Meeting.* "Where?" He grabbed her arm. "Where is this meeting?"

"Ease off." She shook out of his grip. "Probably that old garage, couple blocks down on the corner. Said they played cards there, sometimes, back when."

Alarm pierced him. "Stay here," he said. "No matter what. Stay here."

"Jesus Christ on a Popsicle stick," she muttered. "Story of my life. Sit, Darcy. Stay, Darcy. Screw that, I'm coming with you. I just got here. I didn't ride a bus all the way across the country to sit in some little apartment with a lady barely speaks English."

He blew out a breath. "I don't have time to argue with you." Then he saw salvation in Mrs. Cho, turning into the hallway from the kitchen. Giving her his best Korean apology, he told her to watch out for Darcy. "Please," he added.

* * *

Devon's chest constricted more with each step he ground into the cracked sidewalk. Rap music thumped in the distance like a caffeinated metronome, syncing up with his heart. Lee's words pulsed at him on the backbeat, that he could talk to these guys, that he could change their minds. He shoved his hands into the pockets of his jeans, ducked his head, and walked faster.

Light glowed from the garage's panel of windows, fogged over with cigarette smoke and grime. The music grew louder. The lyrics pumped through, a bunch of noise he'd never liked, about busting skulls and getting women. When he raised his fist to the door, he hated that he remembered the signal. The shadow of a face crossed one of the panels, and he was being ushered in by a kid who couldn't have been more than twelve. Devon cursed under his breath that they'd caught another one.

From the ring of young men playing poker around a ratty folding table, Lee's cocky grin fell a few notches lower than usual. "Damn. That was fast. Thought it would be at least three days before you came chasing after me."

A familiar smooth voice greeted him. "Look, Big Brother's home." Devon's eyes darted toward the fireplug of a dude who still apparently ran the operation. The fitted red tank revealed twin serpents on each huge shoulder, another crawling up his thick neck. "You haven't forgotten us after all. See, I told everyone college wouldn't make you too good to hang with the downtown boys." He laughed and elbowed his second, a pockmarked, glassy-eyed kid, who snickered and said some rude things in Korean about Devon's mother. Devon's fists automatically tightened until he reminded himself why he was there.

"Kwang Lee." His words came out with more of a pleading tone than he would have liked, and he berated himself for showing weakness. "May we speak a moment?"

"Aw, can't it wait? I got a good hand."

Devon forced out a breath. And dared a peek at Billy Cho. He'd filled out some, but his nose twitched like a scared rabbit. One shoulder hiked up higher than the other, as if he were protecting it.

"Buzzkill." Lee slapped down his cards as he rose. "What's so friggin' important?" Then he swept a glance around the table. "This'll only take a second. Maybe he thinks it's time to change my diaper."

The guys laughed. Devon nodded and looked to the floor. He knew Lee had to talk tough around these guys. If it would get his brother free of this place faster, he would take the abuse. But Lee nearly pushed him out of the garage, and that he wouldn't tolerate. As he spun to reprimand his younger brother, Devon was stopped by a quick, low hiss. "Just couldn't stop yourself, huh? Well, fine. But don't blow this."

"You mean about Billy—"

"Things are changing here. So I gotta work this right."

Devon's eyes narrowed. "Changing. Changing how?"

"They're looking at us. Pretend like you're glad to see me."

"I am, but—"

"You were at the house?"

"Yes."

"You met Darcy?"

Devon nodded. Lee's grin broadened. "Nice, huh?"

"Pretty. Very pregnant." He leaned closer. "And very angry."

Lee rolled his eyes. "Women."

"Yes, because you know so much about women. Tell me. What's changing?"

"New guys moving in. Want loyal soldiers, want things their way." And then he shrugged, like it was no big deal.

"What do you mean, their way? Like..." Devon swallowed and lowered his voice. "Organized?"

"No time for this, Dae Soon." He turned back to the door. "Just follow me."

Follow you. He'd been following Lee most of his life.

"Gentlemen." Lee beamed a broad smile at his buddies. "Deal my brother in."

The game went on for what felt like hours, each gesture seeming to communicate volumes of portent Devon didn't understand. A tap from Lee's foot under the table told him to hold on. He was offered a beer, then another, but thought it wise to stop at one. It might have been the jet lag or the anxiety, but with one blink, Devon could have convinced himself that he was sixteen again, sitting at this very table, fear he could not show coiled like the fresh serpent tattoo still burning on his skin. Eventually, the beer ran out and nobody could be bothered going for more, so they called the night done.

The rain had stopped. Their leader locked up and most of the boys fanned out toward wherever they were calling home. Lee and Billy started toward the Chos' place. Devon called out for them to wait, and then a meaty arm was slung around his shoulders.

"Right behind you, boys," the smooth voice said.

Devon toughened his face over.

"Nice to have these little family reunions, huh?"

"It's been a while." Devon wanted to stay closer to Lee but didn't want to blow whatever his brother intended as a plan, so he was careful about his responses, careful to match the man's more leisurely pace.

"So. Off to medical school in the fall, Kwang Lee tells me. When you become a rich doctor, you're not gonna forget your friends, are you?"

"Not likely." Devon narrowed his eyes ahead. The boys were gaining distance. Or he was falling behind. Twenty, thirty feet. Forty. Half the streetlamps were broken. Except for the hitch in Billy's shoulder, from the back he was nearly indistinguishable from his brother.

"Now you say that, but when you have a big house and women—"

The man was still laughing when Devon thought he saw movement ahead, swallowed up by an alley to his left. His heart banged against his ribcage, and he pushed to walk faster. The arm gripped tight, though, and the liquid voice, potent with alcohol, whispered in his ear, "What's your hurry, Big Brother? You and Kwang Lee sharing that sweet little blond? Can't wait to get to her? Something about a knocked-up girl, huh?"

Devon's jaw tightened. *Enough.* But the word lodged in his throat when a hooded figure emerged from the shadows next to Lee and Billy, a glint of metal flashing against the wet sidewalk.

Devon broke free and took off at a run.

Two gunshots popped like firecrackers. One body flew across the other. Both fell.

Billy's voice pitched up three octaves, screaming about the blood.

Devon rocketed toward them, smashing down his pockets for his phone. Damn. He'd left it in his bag at the Chos'. "Get help." He darted glances all around, but the gang leader was nowhere. Like he'd dissolved into the night. He swore again as he fell to his knees before the boys. Half in the trash-strewn alley, half out. One grimy flood lamp above them. But it was enough. Enough to see the blood pulsing from his brother's chest. The disbelief in Lee's eyes.

"Is he...is he...is he..." Billy hiccupped.

The boy, on his knees over Lee, looked physically unharmed.

Devon shook his shoulder. "Billy. Go. Get help." He stared, frozen. "Now! Call 911, anyone, now!"

"Darcy," Billy whimpered. "Should I get Darcy?"

"No!" Lee croaked, his head falling back against the concrete. The alley reeked of vomit and urine and worse. "Man, don't let her see this, swear to me—"

Billy jumped up and fled.

Devon took his spot, leaned in close. A fist of agony drilled through him, and he sucked in a slow breath. *Don't show fear. Don't let him see this on your face.* He felt for a pulse. Weak. Uneven.

"Keep Darcy away."

"Done. Don't worry about that, now. You just stay with me, now. Help's on the way, we'll get you fixed up." Devon yanked off his shirt and pressed it to the wound.

"You stud," Lee wheezed, a corner of his mouth quirking. "Working out, huh?"

"Very funny. And no."

Smile fading, Lee shook his head. "This…wasn't the plan."

"I know," Devon said softly. *No fear. Stay strong. He needs you.*

Lee winced. "Billy?"

"He's okay. Don't worry about him."

"The shooter was…aiming right at him." The pulse was fading. "I tried to push…"

Devon's insides twisted. Imagining Lee shoving Billy out of the way. Not fast enough. "No." His voice dissolved, and he cleared his throat. "You did what you could."

"Not enough. Should have…I should have seen how bad…" Tears slid from eyelids drifting closed.

Devon pressed a hand against his brother's cheek. "Kwang Lee. *Dongsaeng.* Stay with me, now. It'll be okay."

An ambulance siren wailed in the distance. Too late. Pulse, none. Breathing, none. Devon brushed the thick silky hair from his younger brother's forehead, and waited.

7

Three days after her interview, Christina had been officially awarded the gig and was summoned back to the sketchy end of Allston to sew up the details. Reynaldo the Magnificent, in black T-shirt and jeans, greeted her at the door with a flourish of his arm. "Congratulations," he said, "and welcome to our first rehearsal."

"What, already? When's the show?" Stomach knotting and a cold sweat breaking out at the nape of her neck, she peeked over the threshold, expecting a stage illusion that she'd have to fold herself into. But she was relieved to see only the usual clutter, with the addition of a card table in the living room.

He flashed a smile. "We're still working out the particulars. Until then," he added, before she could question the scope of those particulars, "we'll have to make do with the street act."

With a tip of his chin, he gestured her over to the card table. He then produced a large square of black felt, draped it lovingly across the surface, pulled a case from underneath and set it on top.

"This"—he let the intense indigo of his eyes seep across the space between them as a plastic wand appeared in his hand—"is your standard collection of close-up magic suitable for a small crowd at your average tourist-type street venue."

That meant... Happy flutters danced inside her as she remembered her father taking her downtown on Saturdays to watch the street performers. He'd hand her money to put in magicians' hats while the men talked shop and swapped techniques. Her mother had put both feet and a strong hand down about her dad's putting an act together—and warned him not to involve their daughter in what Mom called his foolish, expensive hobby—but that hadn't stopped him from the occasional guest appearance in his buddies' shows. And buying Christina's silence with ice cream afterward. "You mean...like Faneuil Hall?"

Ralph let the wand kiss the top of her head. "Precisely. I won't tell you what I had to give up to bribe my way into the courtyard, but we have ourselves a few weeks on the schedule. You can thank me later. Now, my lovely assistant, if you'll step up to the stage, I'll show you how it's done."

He opened the case. Nestled into little compartments were things she knew well from her father's kit: a variety of cups and balls, coins, cards, other devices. He let her look for a moment, and then he snapped the lid closed. "Wait. Did I have you sign a nondisclosure agreement?"

She swung a glance in his direction. He'd pushed a lot of forms at her during the interview, but she couldn't remember that one. "I don't think so."

"Okay, let's get that business out of the way." He extracted a piece of paper and a pen from the pile of things on the couch. "It's pretty boilerplate stuff. I agree to split the take with you seventy-thirty; you agree not to reveal how the goods work."

Her eyebrows scrunched together. "Seventy-thirty?"

He began withdrawing the paper.

She sighed and stuck out a palm. "No. I'll sign."

"I'm not completely against opportunities for advancement." He cleared his throat. "Once you prove yourself worthy."

She looked up from firing off her signature. *Oh, I'm worthy. Are you?*

"For instance," he said, "here's your first test. We've just blown the crowd away. I bow and they're throwing money into my little chapeau here." He cocked his head, miming the removal of a hat. "Some dude from Southie pushes over to you and says, 'Wicked pissah! How'd that guy *do* that?'"

"Uh, I can't tell you because I just signed a legal agreement in which I've ponied up my first-born child if I blab?"

He grinned. "I like that. Keep proving yourself worthy and I'll think about that split. But no. Here's what you do. You lean in real close. And you whisper at him, 'Can you keep a secret?' Naturally, he'll bite, you being a tasty little dish and all. Then you say, 'So can I!'"

She shook her head. The bit predated mankind's first attempts at humor, but he seemed so pleased with himself and, yes, kind of adorable, that it made her laugh. Then something caught her attention: a grouping of stage-quality juggling clubs in the corner. Had they been there all along, covered by the black felt drape? He caught her looking and pressed a hand to his chest. "I'll knock that split down to sixty-forty right now if you tell me you know how to juggle."

She'd learned the basics, another gift from her father, and taught herself the rest of it, although it had been years since she'd picked up a club. But she felt confident the muscle memory would return. The sixty-forty gave her confidence extra incentive. "A little." She nodded toward the Dubé Europeans as if to ask permission. He responded with a sweep of his arm.

The weight felt odd. The clubs were heavier than the ones she'd practiced with, and as she set to begin a rotation, two clubs in one hand and one in the other, she raised and lowered her arms a few times to get accustomed to the heft. She released the first, attempted the second, and they went skittering across the floor.

So much for my sixty-forty. But he just laughed. "At least you know where to start. We can work with that."

He grabbed the clubs, and with the softest of motions lobbed them up and over, their fat bottoms flicking back toward his face, making it look as easy as breathing. Still juggling, he walked toward her, and even tossed one club beneath a raised knee on one of the rotations.

"You'll pick it up again," he said. "Just like falling off a horse. Or riding a log. Something like that."

It wasn't his graceful skill that caught her attention. Okay, that was impressive, as was the hypnotic pinwheel of the spinning colored panels on the clubs and the flexing of his arm and shoulder muscles. No, something about his demeanor had changed. While he looked almost comically serious when he worked with the close-up magic, juggling brought a kind of childlike glee to his whole body, almost as if he were dancing. And, heart skipping a little faster, Christina wanted to dance with him. To twirl into the center of that playfulness, that joy, and—

Stop it. You're here to learn, not jump the guy. Haven't you had enough of guys like this? Although, you could do worse. She cleared her throat. "How…how do you keep from flinching when the clubs snap back?"

He went on for a few more rotations, and then as gracefully as he'd begun, caught all three clubs. "Practice. Like anything else. Do you know how to pass?"

She shook her head.

Smiling, Ralph grabbed a backpack and filled it with clubs and balls. "Then come with me."

* * *

Christina climbed into the front seat of Ralph's truck, an old Ford pickup that had seen better decades and smelled of motor oil and wet dog, while he secured the equipment in the back. The little park he drove them to off Soldier's Field Road wasn't the cleanest, but it had a nice view of the Charles. And after a long, sticky afternoon trying to keep a lid on Sal, the sunshine and fresh breeze on her skin felt like the ultimate in luxury and freedom.

Ralph handed her three balls and told her where to stand. He took three and positioned himself about four feet away. So close she could see flecks of gray in his dark blue eyes. "Feels weird," she said.

He shrugged. "Less tossing to worry about. And you need to get accustomed to having someone in your space. But first, we'll get you back into the standard rotation. Then we'll synchronize. Then we'll start work on the passing."

A lot to learn all at once, but damn it, she needed to earn his confidence. She sucked in a breath and hoped her palms weren't too sweaty to hold on to the balls. Ralph smelled good, not artificially scented but fresh, like he'd just taken a shower. She nixed those thoughts and tried to concentrate on what her father had taught her, at least to get back into the three-ball rotation. Two in her dominant hand. One in the other. *Toss. Keep tossing. Don't think.*

"Yeah!" Ralph said. "You got it! See, what'd I tell you?"

She was rusty, and she laughed as balls went wide, too high, too low, and she had to shift her weight and reach and bobble to keep the rotation going. She dropped a few and had to start over, but she was doing it, like falling in with an old dance partner. At times Ralph would stop her and set a hand on a shoulder or a hip, to remind her to stay relaxed. Sometimes the hand lingered. She let it. It felt nice. Steadying. Warm.

"Doing great, Teen." He patted her bare shoulder as he retook his original position and began a soft, low, three-ball pattern. "Okay, let's take this next part slow. Watch me. Pick up my rhythm. When we're in sync, I'll call 'pass.' That means I'll toss one toward you, nice and light. Just like when you're doing your own, don't think about the catching. That's a guarantee to screw it up. Think about throwing, not catching. And when you toss, toss it up, into my arc. At the same time, my ball will sail into your rotation." He laughed. "Easy, right?"

"Yeah," she snorted. "Thinking about throwing without thinking while we're throwing things at each other. Without thinking. Wicked easy."

* * *

They met twice more that week. There was tea, a frustratingly superficial introduction to his close-up illusions, and on to the park for juggling lessons. Her muscle memory was slow to lift its head; she had flashes of physical brilliance, even amazing herself at times that the balls did what she told them, before she inexplicably lost control.

The inconsistency vexed her.

"Okay, start it up," Ralph said. She began her rotation. He signaled the count, and she counted along with him. When he said "pass," she passed. But it was the wrong ball and it threw them both off. Everything went flying. While she swore and fumed, Ralph calmly retrieved the balls. As he pressed three into her palms, his hands closed over hers. They were hot from the exercise and stayed a few seconds too long. The low golden sun played up the highlights in his chestnut brown hair, and his warm, minty breath stroked the side of her face as he said, "You'll get this. You're quick. But you're overthinking it. Try again."

She tried again. It took a while, and the sun dipped lower, but she stopped thinking. And when she stopped thinking, it made all the difference. The ball floated out of her rotation; his floated in. It was glorious: the pattern, the rhythm, the sweet, cooling breeze, the seamless way they worked. She wasn't sure what broke it; maybe she'd started thinking how amazing it was that she wasn't thinking, but it all came cascading down, balls skipping away through the grass. And she burst out laughing.

So did he. He stepped toward her, curled a hand around her upper arm, smiling like she was the surprise in his box of Cracker Jack. "Don't tell the boss," he said with a wink. "But I think that sixty-forty split's looking damned good for you."

"Really." Still catching her breath, she edged closer. "You think he'll go for it?"

"He might. I happen to know the guy pretty well. Tell you a secret, he's kind of an easy touch when it comes to the talent."

"I'll bet he's an easy touch." Christina licked her bottom lip. "I'll bet he's…" As her gaze dropped from his expanding pupils to his softly parted mouth, he pulled her toward him and planted a kiss like an exclamation point, bringing her sentence to a halt. Words were overrated, anyway. She sank into him, letting his tongue find hers, letting his warm hands slide beneath her sweaty tank top to grip her waist and nearly lift her off the ground. Heat flooded her torso, urging her to press her belly against his hard muscle, to wrap her legs around him and climb him like a tree. Then he set her down and released her, almost pushing her away.

"No." He waved a hand across his face as if erasing the whole act. "This never happened."

She hated what he'd said, the gesture of canceling out what had indeed just happened, and was still happening in a very real way inside her body. The words, "Are you kidding, I thought you wanted…?" jumbled up in her throat, and all that came out was a kind of sob that made her feel thirteen years old. She swallowed, waiting for him to say something less hurtful.

"I think we should keep this professional."

That wasn't it. "After that? After kissing me like that?"

For a moment he looked confused, but then his broken eyebrow hooked up. "Should I have done it differently?"

She balled her hands into fists at her sides. "You shouldn't have done it at all, if you didn't want to…"

He stepped closer, eyes seeking hers, a hint of a smile in them. "Didn't want to…what?"

All of a sudden she was aware of the other people in the park. A mother pushing a stroller. A couple of teenage guys tossing a Frisbee. "Don't make me say it."

He sidled up even closer, inches from her face, and his voice fell a little deeper. "Don't make you say…what?"

Blood pounded into her cheeks, and other places. "You're evil."

He smirked and played with one of her curls. "You're the evil one. Right now it's taking all of my strength not to tumble you to the grass and lick every inch of your body."

Her breath caught, from the huskiness of his words. And that licking business. "Stop touching me."

"Stop looking so touchable."

"I don't look—"

"You do."

"So stop looking at me."

"I could just kiss you again instead. Although, as your employer, I should warn you of the ways it could complicate our working relationship. I'm not talking theoretical here, I've…well…"

She leaned into him, lips parted.

He took her by both shoulders, perhaps intending to stop her, but she pushed through his resistance and the hold softened into a caress, his fingers trailing along her bare skin. "Let the record reflect," he said close to her ear, "that I waged a strong protest before I let you have your way with me."

Yeah. She could feel his strong protest waging into her hip.

8

The life of a medical resident can be chaotic, the hours long, and the sleep in short supply, but there was a kind of order in it that Devon appreciated. Without the routine of work, his days bled one into the next. He didn't have the energy to impose a structure on his time off, and he was surprised when it was suddenly evening or when his roommates came home from their shifts. Thomas tried to coax him into being sociable, offering beer or an invitation to watch baseball or play video games, but mostly he wanted to be left alone. The Tank Engine didn't press, and neither did Gwen, Devon's sort-of girlfriend, who was doing her own residency at Newton-Wellesley Hospital, a short train ride from Boston. In fact, she hadn't as much as texted him in almost a week. Just as well. He didn't feel like talking about it, especially with her.

But every night at seven, he telephoned his nephew to wish him sweet dreams.

"Don't forget, Uncle Dev," Small Lee said. "Grandmimi says tomorrow you have to call Auntie Sook's number to say goodnight."

"Already?" Devon thought the sleepover party at the neighbors' was next weekend. It frightened him a little, this disorientation. He attempted to shake it off, wished his nephew a good time, closed his eyes for only a moment, and didn't wake until late the next morning.

The day stretched out dull and empty before him. Rejecting the prospects of lazing around in bed or drinking beer and yelling at the Red Sox with his roommates, he decided to visit his aunt and uncle. There might be a lecture about his plans for the future, but guilt from avoiding his family trumped everything. So he showered, put on a clean T-shirt and what Small Lee called "grown-up pants," and headed over to their condo on Rowes Wharf.

Uncle wasn't home, but Devon caught Auntie Mimi fluffing around the living room, picking up toys and putting cushions back on the sofas. She clasped him in a hug, and it didn't take twenty years of schooling to figure out why she held on tighter and longer than usual: Uncle had undoubtedly told her about the incident at the hospital. Perhaps she had made a few strong suggestions of her own—like go down to his apartment and make sure he was all right. Then she pulled back and, cupping a hand to his cheek, scrutinized his face with maternal concern. Her pin-straight hair, still mostly dark but seasoned with gray, straggled out of its elastic band; there were more lines around her eyes than Devon remembered, and he imagined the specific ones he and his brother had caused. And were still causing. In his mind he repeated one of the mnemonic devices he'd learned in medical school about the layers of skin: "Come, Let's Get Sun Burned." *Stratum corneum, stratum lucidum, stratum granulosum, stratum spinosum, stratum basale...*

"Are you hungry? I was about to make lunch. Well. Once I tidy up this tornado Lee Song created."

"Let me help you with that." Devon grabbed a cushion from the floor, undoubtedly one his nephew had used to construct the walls of a blanket fort, one of the boy's favorite activities. One that Devon had taught him. One that Devon had himself played with Small Lee's father when they were little.

As he straightened, he sensed Auntie's worry flowing over him. "We can find things for you to do. Keep your mind occupied. Surely better things than helping your old auntie with her housework."

"Really, it's no trouble. I'm happy to be useful. And fifty is hardly old." He bent to kiss her forehead. That seemed to mollify her, and they began putting the room back in order.

But a few moments later, she cleared her throat and said, "When I dropped Lee Song off, Mrs. Sook mentioned that her daughter could use a tutor. She's failing her summer classes."

"You, uh, know I'm seeing someone, right?"

"Yes, yes. I'm not suggesting marriage, Dae Soon. I just thought..."

That the prospect of a nice Korean girl would put his life in order? That bringing her elder nephew back into the family traditions would fix what the younger one had broken? What Devon's own mother had broken?

"...as I said, a way to keep your mind active and be useful at the same time."

"My mind is plenty active, thank you." Her nearly imperceptible flinch had him pulling back his tone. "But I appreciate the thought."

* * *

Soon after he returned to his apartment in Cambridge, Devon's phone trilled with a text from Gwen. Because of a complicated story that had to do with saving a fellow resident's ass, she had a few hours free for dinner, but only if he could come meet her.
And pick up the check.

He replied and scrambled to clean up and get to the Central Square T stop. When the trolley doors wheezed open in Newton, Devon heard her beat-up compact idling in the parking lot before he laid eyes on it. Her plan was to drive it into the ground and then lease something cool but unpretentious. So far she'd been sticking to the plan, although from the sputter of her engine, Devon predicted she might be car shopping sooner rather than later. He slid into the passenger seat, where he was met with a brief kiss and a long smirk.

"You look like shit, Park."

"Nice to see you, too."

She leaned back against her seat with a groan. "God, it's been so long."

Tell her. Tell her what happened at the hospital. But then she turned to him with a glint of mischief in her eyes and said, "So where are you taking me?"

He swallowed and would not allow his smile to falter. "Anywhere you'd like."

She wrestled the car into reverse. "My place it is."

* * *

His tattoo fascinated Gwen almost to the point of obsession. She must have seen it hundreds of times, in dorm rooms, in a series of shabby apartments. As they lay together, both of them spent for the moment, she traced the outline of the artwork from tail to snout. "Really, you never had to shoot anyone?"

Devon shook his head. She'd gleaned the significance long before he'd told her; any student affiliated with an urban hospital knew what a gang mark looked like. "It wasn't that kind of thing."

"Right," she said. "You just got together and traded baseball cards and scammed on girls."

"Well, kind of."

"Liar."

He'd only joined to protect Lee. And performed enough minor acts of misbehavior—shoplifting a few small items on dares, mostly—to keep the other guys from questioning his commitment. But in whatever romanticized broken-boy-makes-good past Gwen had imagined for him, these small crimes were never good enough for her. "What do you want me to tell you? That I was a dangerous thug?"

She laughed.

"I could be dangerous," he said, pouting.

"You?" She leaned over and kissed his cheek. "Please. Bambi is more dangerous than you."

"Yeah. Just what every guy wants to hear."

"Okay. You're frighteningly serious when you're mad. Better?"

"Not really."

She resumed her worship of Lee's legacy, stroking a finger up Devon's bicep and over his shoulder. The touch suddenly felt wrong, intrusive. Maybe his uncle had been right to suggest that he remove the tattoo. He considered telling her about the baby. But if she didn't understand why he'd left? How could he hold his head up beside her if she thought he couldn't take it?

Wanting comfort, not pity, he stilled her hand and turned to face her. He found the familiarity of her mouth and eased her soft heat against him, sliding a palm along her hip.

She shook her head, began to pull away. "Can't. I'm due back at ten and I need a shower."

He let his head fall against the pillow and blew out a breath as she stood and began tugging a brush through her unruly mud-brown hair.

To his apparent disappointment, she said, "You knew I only had a few hours." But then her gaze roamed his body, stopping to smile at the effect her naked hairbrushing was having on him, and with a coy lowering of her lashes, added, "Wash my back?"

9

During her short college career, Christina spent a summer she'd rather forget working for a theme restaurant that featured barely dressed waitresses as the daily special. The outfit Ralph selected for her didn't cover much more than her old uniform had. It looked like a mega-slutty version of what Madonna might have worn in the *Like a Virgin* years.

"It's only temporary," she muttered at her reflection in her bathroom mirror. Maybe after a couple of shows, he'd trust her enough to let her choose something less...*less*. But for now—

"I'm not sure I have this right," she said through the door as she pulled the bustier top higher and the insipid, flouncy bit of skirt lower. She didn't have a lot to work with in the breast department, but if the juggling routines got too aerobic, double-sided tape be damned, they could be looking at one heck of a wardrobe malfunction.

"Can I help?"

His playful edge spurred some interesting ideas, but Christina didn't want to make them late for their first street act. According to Ralph, if they didn't show up on time, they could be poached— another performer might claim their location. It wasn't the best of spots, he'd said, but it had the potential for decent traffic and seniority when a better one opened up.

Two raps sounded on the door. "Teen?"

"I think I have it." She gave the mirror one last glance, making sure everything was tucked and legal, checking for lipstick on her teeth before coming out for his inspection.

"Not bad. Not bad at all." He circled her, one hand rubbing at his jawline. Then he stopped, gaze falling briefly to her modest cleavage. "Heaven forbid we improve upon the nature of your, uh, nature, but would you object to a bit of embellishment in the balcony?"

He caught the look she shot him and held up his hands. "I'm just thinking of our income potential."

Her chin jutted out. No one had ever complained about her

income potential at the restaurant. "Forget it." Bad enough she'd given in and agreed to wear little more than two scraps of fabric and a smile without stuffing in—where, exactly?—a couple of fake boobs. But rather than rant on about how his request made her feel even more like a fluffy bit of window dressing, she decided to appeal to his professional side. "It'll throw off my juggling."

"You're right." He shrugged. "I don't know what I was thinking."

She knew exactly what he'd been thinking.

"Hey…" His voice held just the right level of softness and strength to cut through her anger. The hug and warm palm caressing her bare shoulder blades didn't hurt, either. Then slowly, he pulled back. "Come on, Teenster. We don't want to get poached. We can go over our set list on the way."

* * *

Each show went fifteen minutes. An ideal length, he told her as they drove downtown, to cram as much entertainment value and hat action into their two-hour slot as possible.

"Yep." He smacked the steering wheel. "Move 'em in, move 'em out, collect the dinero." He went over the finer points of building an audience, when to start each show, how to whip up the crowd for the next one. They even found a decent parking space in a nearby garage so she wouldn't have to walk too far in her heels.

At first she didn't understand why he refused to simply let her out, park, and meet her in the Marketplace. But when he grabbed their gear—three bags' worth—and delicately draped the cloth handle of the juggling bag over her shoulder as they began walking down State Street together, she got it. They were a team. They had to walk in looking like a team. She also felt less naked having him beside her, less alone, less nervous. It had been years since she'd pranced around in her silky, abbreviated uniform. Christina had gotten used to that, and she'd get used to this. She was even starting to feel confident and sexy as they strode along, his upper arm brushing hers. As if to bolster that confidence, he leaned close and murmured encouragement to her, especially as they passed men whose eyes eagerly claimed her.

So it was a bit out of the way; so the access to their small section of the courtyard was partially blocked by a building; so a few of the cobblestones were cracked. But it was a beautiful day for an outdoor performance, and she couldn't wait to get started. They'd already reviewed their patter, the little jokes they'd toss back and forth. Some they'd rehearsed, but he told her they should leave room for improvising in case they wanted to play with the audience or if something went wrong.

"Not that anything's gonna go wrong." Ralph knelt to the cobbles and unwrapped their folding table, a clever design that broke down small enough to fit into a manageable carrying case. He grinned up at her. "But I like to plan my spontaneity. You drop something, tell the folks it was a sudden gust of gravity and move on."

During his little speech, she'd tried to help him set up, mainly because passersby had begun slowing to gawk at them, jangling up her nerves, but he had other plans. "Grab some balls and work the crowd, Teen." He'd said it so close to her ear and so suddenly that she'd nearly dropped everything. Sucking in a deep breath for courage, she nipped three balls from his bag and, flashing a smile and hopefully nothing more, she began her rotation, pterodactyls flapping around her stomach as more and more people stopped to catch the next show.

It was the longest fifteen minutes of her life that had ever passed in a heartbeat. When the audience applauded and began crowding up to drop bills in Ralph's hat, she wanted to dance with joy.

10

The man at table three caught Christina's eye and raised his mug. She nodded, picked up the decaf and worked her way back, smiling as she topped him off. Then she realized she'd been smiling most of her shift, courtesy of Mr. Magnificent's handiwork over the weekend. On Saturday afternoon, they'd barely pushed through the door of his apartment before they were on each other, and they made love on and off into the evening. There hadn't been a ton of money in the hat from the shows, but those few hours of mutual appreciation were a damned fine bonus.

As she replaced the carafe on the burner, Desiree, her shift partner, shook her head, floating a wave of cloying perfume in Christina's direction. "Well, you don't have to flaunt it."

"Flaunt what?" Christina said.

"Seriously." Desiree rolled her eyes. "You can't see it? Swingin' around here like a cat in heat?"

"Sorry." She wasn't at all sorry for what she'd done with Ralph, but Desiree's boyfriend had just dumped her, and Christina didn't want to seem insensitive. "I'll try to keep my tail down."

"No, you got a guy worth shaving your legs for, enjoy it." She sighed, then gestured toward table three. "That's what, now, the dude's fourth refill?"

"I lost count."

"He better tip decent."

Christina shrugged. "He's all right." The man was a regular and had just lost his job, so they typically "forgot" to list a few things on his tab and didn't charge for refills. Rosa sometimes even told the waitresses to give hard-luck customers a free serving of whatever dessert wasn't moving.

Desiree made a noise of disapproval. "We're all gonna lose our jobs if we keep giving away the store."

True, business hadn't quite recovered from Rosa's absence, even though she was now feeling well enough to come in for a couple hours a day, but Christina willed a little magical thinking that their traffic would improve. After all, when it was slow, Rosa usually just kept on cooking and wrote it off to the weather or something equally changeable. Sal, however, had a different viewpoint. He blamed it on the corporations—the theme restaurants that were creeping into Boston like an opportunistic species of lichen.

That day, he'd learned of another restaurant that would soon be opening nearby and had been hunkered down in the back office making phone calls most of the afternoon. "Cheap food in a hurry," he muttered, when he came out and fixed himself an espresso. "People should want good food, comforting food like my Rosa makes, and they should take their time. The world would be a lot happier for it."

All you could do was agree with Sal. Even the busboys knew enough to agree, and most of them barely spoke English.

"Other countries, they don't have these monstrosities, where they pump the food full of chemicals and microwave it until it's dead. Have you seen these so-called restaurants?" He nodded to Desiree, who happened to be closest. "Huh? All of it comes in frozen. The avocados even, for the salad. A mortal sin, what they do to food."

Christina was better with customers than she was at managing Sal, so she busied herself filling ketchup bottles, but his rant had drawn Rosa from the kitchen.

"Avocados? You crazy man." She waved a wooden spoon at him. "I can't hear myself cook in here."

Her agitation immediately calmed him; so did the aroma rising off the spoon. "Is that chicken marsala?"

She shrugged. "It's Monday. Marsala."

"What's on the specials for dessert?"

"Cheesecake with tart cherry compote." She grinned at Christina. "If a certain young lady doesn't eat them all."

"Sorry, Rosa," Christina said over her shoulder. "But they're so good this season."

"I know, they're your favorite," Rosa said. "Must be what gives you that pretty hair."

Christina, blushing, touched a curl. If only Rosa knew the color came from a bottle, not the luscious fruit in her kitchen, and that the blush came from remembering how Ralph had played with her hair at one point during their evening, calling her his little cherry tart. From any other guy, it would have elicited an eye-roll or a groan, but coupled with what he'd been doing to her at the time, she could forgive him the occasional porn cliché.

Somewhat unruffled, Sal returned to the back room and Rosa to her cooking. Desiree brought a customer a check, and just as Christina had been summoned back to table three, a familiar face came through the door. Ralph. *Ralph?* The soft black T-shirt and jeans highlighted his athletic build, and her body began to hum. Apparently nobody else had as yet noticed his entrance. He shot Christina a wink and pressed a finger to his lips.

Hmm. What kind of game do we have here?

She went along with him and said nothing. He swung himself gracefully onto a counter stool. It was Desiree's station, but he couldn't have known that, and Christina sparked with jealousy when the waitress fired up some good old Southie charm and headed in Ralph's direction.

"What can I getcha, hon? Or would you like to see a menu?"

He lifted a brow. "I could go for a little cherry pie."

"We might have some of that." Desiree leaned closer. "Like something with it? Coffee, tea?"

"Coffee sounds great." Ralph drummed his fingers against the counter. Desiree filled his mug while he pulled a cheap set of Jumping Gems from his pocket.

"Those are pretty," she said.

Christina knew the smile. He had someone on the hook. "Oh, not just pretty, pretty lady. Watch carefully."

He waved the plastic rhinestone-studded sticks about, making it look as if one "gem" leaped from one wand to the other.

"Aw, serious! I wanna see that again."

Ralph obliged with an encore.

"Get outta town." At that moment, Rosa popped out of the kitchen, and Desiree called her over. "Mama Rosa, you gotta see this."

With a big smile and some effusive Italian, Rosa reached over the counter and greeted Ralph with a kiss on each cheek. Christina's jaw nearly fell to the floor when Ralph called her Rosabella and asked how she was feeling. The game was suddenly over.

"Fine, just fine, but Reynaldo, where have you been hiding?" She gave him a playful swat on the arm. "I know it's not at anyone else's restaurant, because you're getting too skinny."

"You…know him?" Christina had to force herself to move.

"He used to come in here all the time, do his magic."

"Matter of fact, I put a new show together. You and Sal should come out to Faneuil Hall some Saturday afternoon and check it out."

Blood rushed to Christina's face. *God, no. Don't invite them!* Rosa might say she looked adorable, but one gander at her costume and Sal would sit her down for one of his incredibly uncomfortable discussions about how young ladies are going to rack and ruin because they're giving the milk away for free. And when was Ralph here "all the time"? She'd been working at the restaurant for three years and didn't recall ever seeing him. Even if he'd come in during an off shift, she would have heard about him. All the waitresses gossiped about the hot customers.

"Hah." Rosa smirked as she served Ralph an extra-large piece of cherry pie. "Saturday. Like we'd have time. Although I would love to see your show." She turned to Desiree. "So talented."

"I know! Show her that trick again."

Feigning modesty, Ralph said, "Okay, but just one more time." He worked the illusion again, embellishing with a story about a sad princess charmed by a poor young man's ability to conjure precious jewels out of thin air. The patter was cornball stuff, not Christina's style, but Rosa's eyes glowed.

"See?" Desiree said. "Wha'd I tell ya? He oughta come in and entertain the customers. You know, when we get busy again." Once more she pushed toward Ralph, offering a glimpse of cleavage far less modest than Christina's, and lowered her voice. "I'm off Saturdays. When's your show?"

Enough. And get your boobs out of his face. "Starts at one and goes until three," Christina said, "with fifteen-minute shows on the twelve, twenty, and forty." Everyone turned to stare. She lifted her palms in resignation. "Okay, fine. I've…seen the show a few times."

Rosa passed her a sly look, which she then slid toward Ralph. "Somebody has a fan."

Ralph hitched an eyebrow and readied a forkful of pie. "Somebody's not just a fan. Somebody's my assistant."

Christina curtsied, holding out the edges of her sensible uniform skirt. "Ta-dah," she deadpanned.

Rosa whooped as if Christina had just announced her intentions to marry into the royal family and grabbed her into a hug that was like being smothered by a giant pillow smelling of marsala wine and talcum.

Sal clumped out from the back hallway. "What's all the nonsense out here?" His brow furrowed when he saw the source of his wife's enthusiasm.

"Salvatore," Ralph said with a cool nod and what looked like a forced smile.

"Well. No wonder my Rosa's in a tizzy."

"Nice to be back in your fine restaurant, sir."

"Sal." Rosa pulled on her husband's sleeve. "Reynaldo has a new act. And our little Christina is his assistant."

Sal didn't look thrilled about that. He leaned toward Christina. "Make sure he pays you in cash."

* * *

Christina stole glances at Ralph as he drove them back to his apartment for rehearsal. He didn't bite. When they reached the Citgo sign at Kenmore Square, she couldn't take it any longer and blurted out, "Okay. How do you know Rosa and Sal?"

"Like she said." He shrugged. "I used to be a regular."

She narrowed her eyes at him.

"A long time ago," he added.

Not good enough. He released a theatrically measured sigh. "Few years back, I hit a rough patch. I had a job around the corner from the restaurant. Paid like crap and it was boring as all hell, but I needed the money. When it was slow I'd sneak off there. Rosa was a real sweetheart. Gave her my hard-luck story, did a few tricks, and she'd slip me something on the house."

That explained part of it. Rosa was a marshmallow, and Sal couldn't have liked her comping anyone on a regular basis, especially an able-bodied man who could have been working to earn his keep and not scarfing food from his restaurant. But she sensed there was more to the story. It had to do with why Sal had spent the rest of her shift in the back office until she left with Ralph.

Christina kept staring as if she could boil the facts out of him.

He chanced a quick return before setting his eyes back on the road. His lips pressed together into a firm, bloodless line, and then he blew a few strands of hair off his forehead. Finally he spoke. "Well, you can hardly blame me. Can I help it if Sal has an eye for hiring cute waitresses? He thought I was working one of his girls—big misunderstanding," he added before she could reply or shoot him another glare. "There's only one waitress I want to work...I mean work with...I mean..." He flashed her an endearing grin. "Anyway. That's all in the past now. You, my lovely assistant, are my future."

She sensed that a healthy chunk of his story was bullshit. But for the moment, she was willing to give her magician the benefit of his misdirection.

* * *

Her breathing had barely returned to normal when she felt two firm pats on her rump. His too-small mattress sank and rebounded, like Ralph was springing out of bed. "Come on, Teen," he said. "Get dressed. I'll take you home."

Still foggy, half asleep and not sure if she'd heard him right, she rolled toward the sound of his voice. He already had his jeans zipped and was hunting for his T-shirt. "Um, you're kidding, right?"

He shook his head. "Have to keep up the discipline. That means practicing every morning without distraction." His gaze swept her body, half in and half out of the sheets. "And you are pretty damn distracting."

He was pretty damn distracting himself; at the moment, she couldn't help but admire the articulation of his impressive chest and arm muscles as he slipped the shirt over his head. "We could just stay at my place," she said. "My roommates are out of town. And my bed is a lot bigger."

The half-smile encouraged her to continue. "I have to get up early for yoga anyway, so you could get back to your discipline in the morning."

His eyes melted into hers as he sat on the edge of the bed and smoothed back her hair. "Christina?"

"Yeah?"

"Get dressed."

11

When she woke in the morning, the magician she'd fallen asleep with had changed into a note on the pillow.

Pick you up after your shift for rehearsal, Miss Distraction.

"Very amusing." Christina glowered into the empty space as she crumpled the scrap of paper and tossed it across the room. She was already awake and annoyed, so she threw on some clothes and left. Might as well walk to yoga and try to chill out. She slowed in front of the magic store and checked her watch; she had twenty minutes until class. Her cut from last Saturday had already gone toward paying the bills, so she couldn't even entertain the fantasy of a purchase that week, but she liked the place and the guy reminded her of her grandfather. When she padded up the stairs, she wasn't surprised to see him again at the counter, again with no customers.

As if he'd gleaned her thoughts, he said, "It's not always like this, you know. Magicians aren't exactly early birds. Except for a few. What can I help you with?"

She set her rolled mat on its end and leaned the heel of her palm against it, as if it were a cane. "Can I ask you something?"

"Shoot."

"Do you get any other women coming in here?"

He looked to be thinking. "Once in a blue moon. This one young lady came in, few weeks back, put up one holy mother of a fuss when I thought she wanted to be someone's assistant." The man answered her baleful stare with a lopsided grin. "You know, I don't think we've met properly." He stretched a hand across the counter. "Hello, I'm Herbert, the sometimes-boneheaded owner of this establishment."

She took his fingers and made a little bow. "Pleasure to meet you, Herbert. I'm Christina Davenport, waitressing to pay the bills and"—she sighed—"currently working as someone's assistant."

"So he found you." Herbert didn't sound happy about it.

She shrugged. "It's a place to learn. And…he's not so bad."

He gave her a careful study, and a flush ran up her cheeks. "Well," he finally said. "As long as you remember who you are, is all."

"I'll be fine."

"Sure you will be."

In the silence, her stomach pinched. She wondered if she'd done the right thing, signing on with Reynaldo the Magnificent, playing the assistant. It wasn't like she'd never traded on her looks to make a buck, never flirted with a customer to get a bigger tip. But that was just waitressing. It's what you did; everyone knew that. This cat-and-mouse game she'd started felt like a more serious breach. Maybe Ralph had been right when he'd made that lame attempt to push her away; maybe she should have listened and kept their relationship professional. Suddenly yoga no longer appealed to her, but needing a temporary reprieve from the claustrophobic crush of her thoughts, she offered to buy Herbert coffee. When she returned from the café next door, a cup in each hand, she was pleased to see that he had a customer. The guy didn't stay long, though, and after he left, Herbert pulled a stool up to the counter for her.

"So to what do I owe this attention?" he asked. "Class canceled?"

She rolled a cup between her palms. "I just like this place."

He lifted his eyebrows. "That and a few bucks will get you on the T."

"Okay." She exhaled in a rush and let her shoulders relax. "Do you think women really stand a chance in this business?"

Herbert tilted his head. "Practice your craft as good as the guys, and I don't see why not. One of Copperfield's assistants went out on her own. Damn fine magician she was, God rest her soul. And this one young lady in Los Angeles is doing pretty well for herself. She's about your age. But she started when she was a tyke. How long have you been at it?"

Christina was embarrassed to admit the last time she'd picked up a deck of cards or worked on her palming skills. "Not as long as I probably should have. Once in a while I mess around with a few tricks. I taught myself how to juggle. That was fine with my mother, because it was good exercise and kept me out of her hair. But magic wasn't exactly encouraged at home. My mom…well, let's just say the phrase 'something to fall back on' came up a lot." It was still coming up. Nearly every call ended with a not-so-subtle reminder about college degrees and income potential and the fact that she was twenty-five and still lacked a defined career path. To avoid another lecture, Christina had decided to hold off on telling Mom about her new job.

"Is *he* teaching you?" Herbert asked.

"We're working on the juggling routines, yeah. Says it makes me more valuable."

"But not the close-up."

"Not so much. He promises, but…"

His gaze dropped to her coffee cup. "I can't believe I didn't notice it before. Maybe because you were too busy getting mad at me."

Her whole body tensed. No. He wasn't one of the men who swapped stories in her father's basement. Before the divorce, before the accident, before Christina dispensed with her original hair color and the melancholy weight of the McNulty family name. She would have remembered Herbert's dignified bearing, his gentle voice; she would have—

But that wasn't a smile of recognition on his face. It was like he admired her, for some reason. "Don't take this the wrong way, Christina Davenport, but you have beautiful hands. And you damn well ought to be using them for something besides misdirecting his audience."

"I don't—" She cleared her throat. "I'm not sure where to even start again."

"I don't advertise this, but I've been known to give a lesson or two."

They spent the next hour going through a basic routine she could use to regain her skills. At first, like the juggling, she was clumsy as hell; her fingers felt huge and foreign. By the time she needed to leave for her shift at the restaurant, a few brain cells had kicked in. "How much do I owe you?" Christina reached for her purse. "For the gear and your time?"

He waved a hand. "Forget it. But it comes with strings attached."

What doesn't? She waited for the terms.

"Practice." He pointed at her. "Until you can do it without thinking. Then practice in front of a mirror. Lets you see if you're giving anything away. Come back, if you want, and we'll do this again."

"Herbert. You have a business to run, I can't—"

"Please. It's not like folks are busting the door down here."

* * *

Christina practiced. On breaks during her shift, she hid in the storeroom and practiced coin manipulation—false transfers to vanish a half-dollar, then rolling a quarter between her fingers to work on her dexterity. When Ralph dropped her off at the end of the night, she practiced palming sponge balls. Her hands were so sore she zoned out in the shower, letting the spray beat on her palms. Did the women Herbert told her about have these problems? Did people tell them they couldn't hack it?

"Girl magicians," she'd once overheard one of the men in her father's club say with a snort. "That's just a novelty act."

"Now, I'd have to take issue with you about that," Christina's father had replied.

"Come on, McNulty. Give me one name. And not that stripper you knew in Duluth."

Christina had squeezed her eyes shut, waiting for the laughter to stop. Waiting for her father to give her hope that it wasn't totally stupid for her to want to be a magician when she grew up, like the men and her mother seemed to think. Nothing. She sighed. The men started telling more dirty jokes about strippers and places they could make things disappear. The tiny bedroom in her father's new apartment felt even smaller than when he'd moved in. But it was on the first floor, so she tucked a tiny flashlight and her Jumping Gems into a pocket and slithered out the window. Nestled in a perfectly sized gap at the base of the hedges, she practiced the trick until the men went home.

"All clear, Chrissie," he called from inside. And as she wriggled back through the window, he said, "Sorry, some of the guys get really loud. It was easier when we were in the basement, huh?"

His eyes, green like hers, looked so sad. He got that way when he remembered how things used to be, before the divorce, and she longed to cheer him up. She pulled out the Jumping Gems. "Dad, look!"

"Maybe later." He came close to pat her cheek and she nearly gagged at the smell of alcohol on his breath. "Help me clean up first."

As she brought a picked-over plate of cheese and crackers to the kitchen, he watched her a moment, then said, "I'm filling in for one of the guys at a wicked huge talent show next weekend. You want to be my assistant?"

She smiled.

12

Christina had worked the breakfast and lunch shifts that Friday, and her feet were already aching. When Ralph picked her up and took her back to his place with the promise of teaching her a new juggling move, she refused to let herself wimp out and look unprofessional.

But because the move required more height than his apartment allowed, they needed to practice outside. The afternoon muffled Boston in a hot, sticky haze. Club handles slid through her damp palms; sometimes a spin disoriented her and she lost sight of a Dubé or two, either dropping them or getting clunked with one. When a club flew from her fingers and bonked her on the temple, she squelched the urge to throw herself to the grass and cry like a two-year-old.

"Okay!" She forced some moxie into her voice. "Break?" *Before I do?*

He nodded. "Yeah. You want to get a drink, sit down for a while?"

She was about to tell him it sounded like the best thing she'd heard all damn day. But then his hand landed on her forearm and she swallowed, pushing down the sudden rush of emotion, the catch in her throat from what seemed like such a simple act of compassion. She leaned her forehead into his shoulder and groaned. "I'm just… Oh, it's just so fucking frustrating. It looks so easy when you do it. Simple mechanics. Rhythm. I should be able to do this!"

"Hey, cut yourself some slack." He laughed, patting the back of her head. "I only taught it to you an hour ago."

"But I can get this! We can use it tomorrow. Maybe if I can get myself to stop thinking. You know. Like before. Just…stop thinking."

He pulled back and grinned at her. "And now you're thinking about not thinking."

Her shoulder sagged. "You're right."

He mussed her hair and started for his club bag. "So we'll use it next week. Or not. Whenever you're ready."

Pouting, she followed him. They grabbed sodas from the

convenience store down the block and sat on the picnic benches. He shared some juggling war stories and how many times he'd beaned himself with a club, a heavy stage ball, a ring. He pointed out the small scar that severed the tail end of his left eyebrow—the first and last time he'd worked with fire torches. At one point he reached over to stroke two fingers along her right temple where the Dubé had clocked her, examining her with the focus of a plastic surgeon. "Sorry if you were hoping for some kind of manly battle wound, but I don't think you'll even have much of a bruise."

A grin fluttered between them before he leaned close and planted a soft, brief kiss where the club had clubbed her. "So, what do you think?" he said. "Come back to my place, we'll rustle up some dinner? No more practice today if you don't want." He paused long enough for Christina to believe he was milking it for dramatic effect. "And if you want to stay over, I probably won't put up too much of a struggle."

"Oh, really?" She might have been reading too much into a lame attempt to lighten the mood, but it sounded like he'd finally realized how much she hated being dropped at her front door like a used plaything at the end of the evening. "Better be careful with talk like that, Mr. Magnificent," she said, "or you're gonna sweep me off my feet."

* * *

After a shower they dozed in his smaller-than-hers bed. Good thing she wasn't very big, and although he was broad across the shoulders, he wasn't that tall. She shifted to get closer and the move roused him. His arms circled her waist and he made love to her from behind, slow and lazy, and they found a rhythm like they did while passing clubs into each other's rotations.

"I get it," she said. Felt the pattern behind her eyes. The way her arms needed to move: the lift, the release, the catch. It was a kind of dance step. With the clubs, and him.

"Yeah, good," he murmured against her shoulder.

"No, I mean, I get it. The juggling."

His warm breath floated over her ear. "I knew you would."

* * *

She woke early, alone, her back in spasm like a too-tight belt around her kidneys. Maybe that was why he hadn't wanted her to stay over. Figuring he was probably ensconced in that early-morning practice to maintain his discipline, she worked on her own, trying a few gentle yoga stretches to ease the cramps from her muscles. With a combination of deep breathing and asanas, she was able to calm her insulted body somewhat, but what she really needed was to get up and move around. She slipped from the bed, her footfalls even quieter than usual as she padded around the back room. Stopping at the door, she extended her arms over her head, one and then the other, to work out the remaining kinks, feeling the stretch from her hips through her fingers.

She wanted a drink and his tap water sucked, but she didn't want to break his concentration by traipsing through the house to the refrigerator. So she tiptoed out, nearly tripping over Ralph in the process. He was sitting cross-legged on a pillow on the floor in the middle of the living room.

"What the…?" she muttered, before her brain registered that he was meditating. Eyes still closed, a corner of his mouth twitched for a second then relaxed. She let out a silent breath, pressing a hand to her belly. Okay, that would explain a few things, like his patience with her and his almost boundless reserves of energy.

She fetched a bottle of water and returned to the back bedroom and the adjoining bath, dawdling as she washed up to give him time to finish. When she heard movement from the front room, she came back out, and he greeted her with a relaxed grin and a kiss on the forehead. "Good morning, my flower of light."

When she tried to pull him tighter for a real kiss, he resisted, and she raised her eyes in question.

"It's show day," he said, as if this was an answer everyone should understand.

She didn't. "So it's bad luck or something?" It was intended as a joke, because she couldn't think of any other reason he'd deny her. But he wasn't laughing.

"More of a superstition," he said. "Trying to keep the energy for the performance."

Ah. That was why he could barely wait to get his hands on her afterward. She thought it had something to do with her little outfits. And the way he glared at men watching her prance around in them as she tossed assorted objects into the air.

His grin broadened as he took a step toward her. "But if you're in dire need..."

She put up her hands. "Nope. If you're keeping it for the show, so am I. All for one and one for all." She then decided to avert her desire by seeing what he had in the fridge for breakfast. It wasn't much—a few eggs, a bit of milk, some not-too-stale bread—but it would do. "I didn't know you meditated."

"Excuse me?"

She turned at the question. "Meditation. Pillow, om, all that jazz?"

"Oh, no." He reached around her for a carton of orange juice. "I was communing with the great one."

She stared at him while he filled his glass and took a sip. They'd never talked about religion before. It didn't have much of a place in her life, for a variety of reasons, but if he was a believer, it wasn't a deal-breaker, as long as he didn't insist on her involvement. "Well, as a wise man once said, to each his own invisible person in the sky."

"No, I meant the Great One." Reverence shaded his words. "Harry."

Christina blinked a couple of times. "Potter?"

"Houdini."

Right. She should have known. Her father had been obsessed with Harry Houdini; so had nearly every other magician she'd ever met, although actual theological-style worship was a new one for her. "Okay, not trying to be judgmental or anything, but you pray to him?"

"No." He curled his hand over hers, and its warmth made her tingle. "I commune with his spirit. It's part of my show prep. And"— he dropped his gaze for a moment, lifting the now-more-startling indigo eyes to meet hers—"part of my life. The one time I didn't commune with Harry before a show, it was awful. Like I'd been cursed. I dropped a club and nearly singed off an eyebrow." He pointed to the scar he'd shown her the day before. "It's probably bad luck to even talk about it. You know, you should probably commune with him, too. I'll introduce you."

She backed up a step. "Maybe next week."

He shrugged and downed the rest of his juice.

Christina eyed the ingredients she'd collected from the fridge. She'd intended to make breakfast as a nice gesture of reciprocity. Now it could be a sort of half-assed apology that she wouldn't be communing with the spirit of a dead magician. Ever.

"French toast?"

Ralph's eyes widened and he shook his head, as if she'd just offered him hemlock.

French toast was also bad luck? What, Harry didn't like it?

"No food before a show. It slows my reaction time. And I gotta have that lean and hungry look." As he moved by her, he patted her rump and landed a noisy kiss on her temple. "Makes for more money in the hat."

She selected a smaller bowl. "French toast for one, then."

He gave her a wary glance, which he slid to the clock over the sink.

"Unless we don't have time?" she said. "Or am I supposed to have that hungry look, too?"

"Sure, we have time. But there's something I have to do before we go."

Her stomach grumbled. "Maybe food slows your reaction time, but not eating might make me pass out. This thing you have to do, maybe you can do it while I'm getting breakfast?"

"Only if you take it with you."

* * *

Several minutes later, Christina threw on jeans and sneakers while the bread sizzled in the pan. Then she wrapped two steaming pieces of French toast in a paper towel and followed Ralph out. They walked three blocks to the quick-mart on the corner of Allston Street. He offered the clerk a nod and headed to the lottery counter at the side of the store.

When his intention registered, Christina had to suck in a breath to keep from laughing, nearly choking on her last mouthful of breakfast. "Lottery tickets?" She coughed. Why didn't he just take his money and throw it into the Charles? "That's what you rushed me out for?"

His brow furrowed. "I don't take show prep lightly. Neither should you. Harry won't like it."

She bit at the inside of her mouth and warned herself to try to be open-minded or at least respectful. He had agreed to take her on, an assistant with no experience that she'd admitted to except for the juggling, and they were a team. And she hadn't known a single magician who wasn't a little bit...quirky. "So for show prep, you meditate—"

"Commune."

"Okay. Sorry. Commune. No sex. No food. And now..."

With a flourish, he withdrew a chewed pen from his shirt pocket. "The magic implement. And Harry's numbers."

She mentally catalogued this new bit of information. "He tells you what numbers to play? During the communing?"

Ralph glanced up with a patronizing smile and shook his head. "Of course not." He propped an elbow on the counter and with a delicate touch that reminded Christina of other things he touched delicately, selected a blank Megabucks form. With the pen hovering over the card, he readied himself to fill in the circles. Then he slipped a glance to Christina—slow, seductive—and as her thoughts began to dissolve into memories of what they'd done the previous night and a sudden hatred of no-sex show prep, he leaned in close and gathered the collar of her T-shirt in one hand. In a quick, breathy whisper, he said, "He gave me the numbers five years ago on a full moon in October. 'Use them always,' he said, 'in the same place at the same time on the same day of the week, and you will have wealth beyond your wildest imagination.'"

And then he released her, casually returning to his card and pen. Sucking in a few quick breaths to silence her rattled hormones, Christina tried to shake off the utter weirdness of what had just happened. "So you've been playing them. Every week for the last five years?"

He nodded.

To her next, unasked question, he said, "Oh, I *will* win. *We* will. Because when you signed that agreement, our fates became intertwined. Now, are we done talking? Because this is also a ritual that must be done in silence."

The silence wasn't the problem. *Our fates became intertwined?* What the hell was in that agreement? It looked like a pretty standard nondisclosure to her.

Taking a deep breath, Ralph mumbled something and proceeded to fill in little circles. When he'd finished, Christina said, "And since I'm, um, intertwined with your fate, am I allowed to know what the numbers are?"

He cast a quick glance around the store. It was empty save for the cashier and a middle-aged woman perusing the candy rack. "As long as you obey the agreement and never share them, or the fact of them, with another soul."

She nodded with the reverence appropriate to the situation, and he slid the card in her direction. The six-number sequence looked pretty random to her, a mix of odds and evens. She couldn't resist a wicked grin, though. "What if one of Harry's rivals tries to torture it out of me?"

He was not amused. "This is serious shit, Teen. Get one part wrong and we might be out of work. And there goes our stage show."

"Okay." She made a gesture of surrender. "I'm sorry. Let's do this." But even though there was no one in line at the register, Ralph leaned an elbow against the lottery counter. "Don't we have to go pay?"

"Not until the stroke of ten."

It was nine fifty-six. "So we're going to stand here for four minutes?"

Ralph had been sizing up the woman, who'd selected a bag of M&M's, and then swiveled his head back to Christina. "Got a dollar?"

"You didn't even bring—?"

"Another part of the covenant," he said with a shrug. "It must be with other people's money bought." Ralph stuck out his palm.

She stared at it, her patience and desire thinning, and wrestled a crumpled bill from her jeans pocket. *This had better pay off.* "Where'd you get your lottery money before me?"

As he lifted his severed eyebrow, she decided she didn't want an answer.

* * *

Houdini-worship and other performance-day quirks aside, seeing the spiritual care Ralph put into his show prep had given Christina a hit of confidence in their act, at least. At the Marketplace that afternoon, though, something didn't feel right. The weather was fine, comfortable for late July. Setup had gone smoothly and they hadn't forgotten anything. On his signal, she'd grabbed three neon juggling balls and stepped out into the courtyard to entice passersby. She even gave it a little extra: a wink and a flirty smile to a knot of cute frat boys, a spin-and-catch for two girls who squealed and clapped their hands.

But when they started their first show, the sparkle wasn't there. A couple of Ralph's jokes fell flat, and he tried to cover with a nervous laugh and some corny lines. He even bobbled a club, something she'd never seen outside of rehearsal. She caught a quick creasing of his brow, a darkness in his eyes before he put his face back on and tried to make the error seem intentional. But as he fumbled for the misbehaving club, her mind blanked of all their studied excuses. Finally he came out with one—something about a sudden shift in the magnetic poles—and everything was fine again.

For a while. He was thinking too much, perhaps. Or he'd committed the performer's sin of letting a miscue get into his head.

Shake it off, she thought at him. But then he pulled the plug, giving her his secret signal to go into their finale so the crowd wouldn't know they'd bailed on that particular show. As she passed the hat and Ralph took his bows, she avoided meeting his eye, because every time she glanced his way he had that dark flash again, as if whatever happened had been her fault.

The next performance didn't go any better. She lured more people in, and she thought the bigger crowd would get him off her ass, but when she glanced at him, the evil look lasted longer.

Silence on the ride home filled the cab of his truck like the sour stench of flop sweat. *We had a bad day, so what, everyone has bad days.* But the warning on his face told her to keep her words to herself. Still, she began to speak and he cut her off. Twice. She turned toward the window. The breeze had picked up, ruffling the surface of the

Charles, just off Storrow Drive. Then she turned back. It was bullshit. She'd done her part, and she'd done it well. "So is that bad luck, too? Talking about it if something went wrong?"

He gripped the wheel tighter.

"I'll take that as a yes?"

Instead of heading up Storrow to Soldier's Field Road, he hooked toward Commonwealth and stopped the truck in front of her apartment building, where several of her Haitian neighbors were chatting on the stairs. Their language normally sounded like music, but at the moment its upbeat melody seemed to mock her.

"Almost forgot." He tugged a wad of bills from his vest pocket and dealt a silent count into her palm. Somehow she thought they'd earned more. "What?" he said. "That's your forty. If you'd like to recount our whole take, be my guest."

"No," she sighed. "It's fine."

Then, leaning back against his seat, Ralph crooked one arm up behind his head and waited for her to get out.

Fine. Let him sulk. "Okay, then."

She slipped out of the cab and gently closed the door behind her. But she couldn't let it go like that. When she turned back to stop him, to force him to talk this through, he was already pulling away.

* * *

"Ever seen one of these?" Herbert's eyes brightened as he pushed what looked like a standard Japanese teapot and cup across the counter.

Christina shook her head. She set down her yoga things and came closer.

He waved a hand over the top of it. "Allow me to demonstrate." He poured a glass of clear water into the pot, replaced the lid, waved a red silk over it, and poured red liquid into the cup.

"Sweet." Christina turned the pot around in her hands.

He flashed her a wink. "I'll let you have one wholesale. But only 'cause it's you." When she didn't play back, Herbert said, "Buy you a coffee? Since I just have tea here."

She grinned, feeling a little softer. His style was like her father's: sweet, gentlemanly. Old school. "We had a few lousy shows over the weekend," she sighed. "And he won't talk about it. Maybe he thinks it's bad luck to talk about bad luck. I know some magicians have their superstitions…"

"Heard 'em all," he said. "Most of them are bullshit, pardon my French. Superstitions are nothing but excuses bad magicians use."

Her eyebrows darted up.

"No offense, of course," he said.

He watched her for a long moment, his gaze falling to her left hand, curved around the white porcelain cup. Feeling suddenly self-conscious, she pulled it away. Herbert tapped an index finger against his lower lip. "Humor an old man for a second." He retrieved a pack of playing cards and snapped them onto the counter before her.

"Gin rummy or crazy eights?" she deadpanned.

"Just give those a shuffle for me, huh?"

She suppressed the urge to roll her eyes and did as he requested. *Chrissie, pick a card.*

"Fine. Now take the deck and deal it all out into four equal piles." She started. "Keep going." When she finished, she made a little flourish of her own. He grinned. "Thought so."

"Thought so what?"

"You've been practicing."

"Some."

"It shows. You want to end up a working magician and not some street hack like him, do more. Practice more. You'll be better."

From his inflection, it sounded like he meant *better than him.* Or at least that was the way she chose to take it.

13

Nothing more was said about luck of any variety. Ralph returned to his usual self, picking her up at the diner, teasing Rosa, rehearsing until they got too hungry or too tired to continue. In bed, though, he was distant, preoccupied. She called him on it and he apologized, re-upped his game, but then he'd drift away again. When she gave him the out of calling it a night, and in fact even suggested they put a hold on extracurricular activity until after Saturday's performances, his relief was palpable. Maybe he needed a reset button on his superstitions. Her claustrophobia was creeping in, too, so she liked the idea of some personal space.

The humidity over Boston, meanwhile, had been growing and settling thicker and hotter all week. By Friday afternoon, make-or-break time for adding new moves to the shows, the thermometer was pushing a hundred degrees. Thunder rumbled in the distance and the clouds built tall and swollen heading in from Framingham. The rapid drop in air pressure bristled Christina's nerve endings, screwed up her coordination, and had been making her cranky all day. But she'd be damned if she'd give up now. She knew she had the new move, saw it in her sleep, saw it in her dreams, and had already mastered it two out of three tries in rehearsal. They *were* doing it in the Marketplace, come hell or Christmas, and she didn't want to give him an excuse to cut it out of the act again. That would make two weeks in a row. Two cuts, two arguments. If she could increase his confidence in her ability to nail it cold, maybe it would up his game, too.

Set in their starting positions, Ralph nodded at her and began his toss. He said, "Step turn," the signal for the trick. Christina stepped, turned, and the belly of one of his clubs smacked her full across the left side of her jaw, rocketing pain all the way to her ear.

"What the hell?" He stomped toward her. "Why'd you move?"

She rubbed the injury. "Fuck you, why'd I move? You told me to."

"I didn't..." He tried to pry her hand away. "Let me see."

"No. I need to get this. Get back over there."

He raised his hands in surrender. "Fine. Whatever."

She snatched her clubs out of the grass, where the impact had shocked them out of her hands. Even bending down, the blood throbbed. "We're losing daylight."

"That's gonna leave one hell of a mark." He pointed a club at her.

"I'll ice it later. Let's just get this down."

She was throwing too hard—she knew it. Hell, he knew it, too. But he'd been loath to force her to stop. Maybe, knowing his own performance demons, he didn't think he had the right to stop hers from doing what they would. Lightning crackled over the Charles and he called it.

"No, dammit," she said. "We have to get this down."

"Teen—"

A growl of thunder shouted him down as fat drops began to fall. She knew when she was beaten; she could never get a clean grab on the necks of the clubs in the rain. "We're doing this tomorrow," she yelled, more to the clouds than to him, as they broke for the truck.

Ralph flung the door open and ushered her inside. "We'll talk about that later." His voice was a low grumble. "Let's just get some ice on that pretty face right now, okay?"

* * *

Against her protests—she wanted to continue their rehearsal in his living room, just keeping the throws in a lower arc—he sat her at the kitchen table with a firm hand on each shoulder. Heading for the freezer he said, "We wouldn't even be doing this if you hadn't—"

She wheeled around to face him; the sudden move made her wince. "You fucking told me to turn."

"Oh, for God's sake. Why the hell would I tell you to turn when I was about to wing a club at you? Do you think I want to stand up there for six shows tomorrow like an advertisement for a juggler who can't throw?"

"You wanted to say like an assistant who can't catch."

The ice pack landed in front of her on the table with a thud. She glowered at it. Everyone made mistakes, but she hated looking weak and needy, like some idiot who couldn't take direction. When he picked up the ice pack and tried to press it to her jaw, she nabbed it away and held it there herself. The cold stung, but it was a better sting than pain. It was a better sting than talking about why she couldn't manage a simple juggling routine or why he refused to talk about last week's show.

He flopped into the chair across from her. She glared, daring him to speak. "We're not doing it tomorrow," he said. "And that's final."

When the worst of the storm passed, she asked him to take her home, but sleep eluded her. Her jaw throbbed. She put more ice on it, but it didn't help. Each miscue played back at her as she tossed alone in her too-big bed. She almost called Ralph to cancel. But showing up damaged and inept wouldn't be as bad as not showing up at all. Damn it. She had to get this move right—no question. If she had to get seventeen more bruises, she was nailing this sucker cold. She owed it to her father. For all his faults, despite everything that had happened, at least he'd had faith in her. He'd stood up to her mother. When he'd called Mom about the talent show, Christina had slipped into the back room and eavesdropped on the extension.

"Ed, you can't be serious. She's only ten."

"She'll do great. Chrissie's a natural. Everything's gonna be fine. Can I at least tell you about the act before you dismiss it out of hand?"

Her mother sighed. "Fine. Tell me about the act."

"Just your average magic show. She'll stand there and look cute, hold my props, and it probably won't hurt too much when I shut her in a box and cut her in half."

Silence.

"It was a joke. You still remember jokes, right?"

"Yours? I'm trying to forget."

"Look. It'll be all right. It's about the simplest box trick there is. Easy as pie."

Christina shifted the ice pack on her face. She'd always wondered about that expression. Pie wasn't easy. The first and only one she'd made had been hideous—the crust was chewy and the filling exploded all over the oven. Maybe if she'd actually made more than one terrible attempt, or if there had been time to practice the "simple box trick," it would have been easy as pie.

14

"You don't have to be a doctor today, Uncle Dev?"

Devon bit the inside of his lip as—guarding against absentminded tourists, impatient locals, and hell-bent-for-leather cyclists—he shepherded his five-year-old nephew across Atlantic Avenue. He hadn't decided what to tell the boy about his employment status, and he hated the idea of lying to him. "It's Saturday," he said. "I'm not a doctor on Saturdays."

Small Lee tilted his head and scrunched his nose in a way that was so like his namesake it made Devon's breath catch. "Uncle Doctor says doctor is for all the time."

Devon swallowed and forced a smile. "Uncle is right." *Uncle is always right.* "Doctor is for—I mean, if you're a doctor, you're a doctor all the time. I guess I'm taking a vacation from being a doctor."

His hand wrapped firmly around his small nephew's as they approached the Marketplace and the enticing aromas of pizza and souvlaki that Devon swore they pumped out to draw people in.

"Do you think we'll see a fire-eater?"

Thank you for a five-year-old's attention span. "I don't know."

A knot of people loomed ahead in the square between two of the Quincy Market buildings. From the thrum of them, he heard a male voice, theatrical in its projection.

Small Lee, face brightening, tugged at his arm. *Grown-ups don't move fast enough*, he could almost hear the boy thinking.

Finally they reached the edge of the crowd. Small Lee nosed in, despite the firm hand on each shoulder. He turned back. "It's a magician!"

Devon fought a sneer. Fooling people was a sleazy way to make a living. He appreciated other types of performers, like musicians and singers, because those professions required real talent and skill. Mentally he slapped the side of his head when he realized those messages had been ones programmed by his family. But even at first glance, he didn't like this magician, who oozed studied charm with his too-bright smile and talk designed to be cunning and seductive.

Dismissing him, Devon focused on Small Lee's eager smile and his heart began to melt around the edges. If this was something his nephew liked, why not let him have it? He vowed not to do to the boy what his elders had done to him—stuff him into the Park family mold, bake until done.

He maneuvered Small Lee closer. Some understanding adults made room for him to see better. Then Devon glanced up, at first meaning only to watch his nephew's enjoyment. But a tumble of reddish-blond hair caught his eye, and the girl it belonged to turned his mouth to dust. Her delicate limbs and pale skin reminded him of a porcelain figurine. She was the magician's assistant, no doubt, her costume brief and sparkly, the colors complementing what he wore. Apparently her job was to smile and pass him his props. But it looked as if the smiling was causing her great pain. And when he said certain things, like making dirty jokes or egging the crowd on to ogle her, she winced. The heat of the day had spoiled her heavy application of makeup, which he didn't think she needed, and Devon frowned when he saw what appeared to be a fresh, extensive contusion from beneath the melting paint on the left side of her jaw.

She didn't speak at all. The magician, though, did the talking for her and then some. Devon had had his fill of jerks like that— desperate for attention. Lee had busted him about it when they were kids, accusing him of being jealous of anyone with a personality.

But something about the girl drew him in, beyond her pretty face, her fragility, her hair—had they met before? A moment later, it clicked in. It was at the hospital. She'd asked for directions. More than the physical state of being unable to find her way, in her glazed green eyes he'd sensed a person who'd been mentally or emotionally upended as well, flung around by a large force, perhaps, and still hadn't gotten her bearings. He'd wanted to fix that, too. He remembered buying her coffee, and if he hadn't been called back, he might have stayed, at least long enough to learn her name. The girl standing before him still had a bit of a lost, distracted appearance. His mind coupled that with the contusion on her jaw, and he wondered if it was the magician's doing, if he was hurting her. He'd seen abused women in the emergency room. The thought that she could be one of them tightened Devon's hands into fists.

"And for our finale..." the magician continued. Apparently he'd wanted to do something with fire, but his permit didn't allow it, much to the man's false-sounding irritation. So he nodded to the girl, and she handed him a set of long-bladed knives, like the kind from martial arts movies.

Devon surmised they were fake, but Small Lee was completely delighted, eyes round with wonder at how someone could juggle three knives and two grapefruits. The magician waggled his eyebrows. "Hey, little guy." He aimed a grin at Devon's nephew. "If you like this, just wait. Oh, lovely assistant?"

The girl stepped up on cue and curtsied.

"Ladies and gentlemen, right here and for the first time in Boston, a man will now juggle three knives, two grapefruits, a piano, and two balls."

A wave of *oohs* and *aahs* went through the crowd.

"Thank you. I need all the encouragement I can get. Heck, I don't even know if I can do this." But all pretense of humility vanished as he began the trick. With a nod to the girl, she tossed a tiny toy piano in an arc and he quickly worked it in with the other things. As he juggled the objects, he began hopping up and down. A snicker went through the crowd as they caught on to what he'd meant. After several rotations, the man stopped, grasped the handles of the knives, and bowed.

The audience applauded. A few people dropped bills and change into an upturned top hat on the cobblestones next to his magic stand. "Hope you'll come back next week," he said, as some began to walk away. "We'll be here every Saturday from one to three, and then any place they don't chase us out of for the rest of the afternoon."

Where is she?

"Can I go put the money in the hat?" The tiny voice pulled him back to reality.

"Go for it, *joka*." Devon ruffled his nephew's dark, silky hair and handed him a five-dollar bill. Not that the man deserved it, but Small Lee loved doling out what to him felt like a fortune. As the boy dashed forward, Devon worried that if the magician really was the type of man to abuse a woman, his assistant might not see a cent of that money. But he was also very aware of having charge of a young, excitable child in a crowd, so he kept his eyes trained on the small, sleek head.

"Hey, thank you, little dude," the man said, when he saw the denomination. "Where's your mommy, huh?"

Devon swooped in and, taking his nephew's hand, eased the boy behind him. "That's none of your business."

"Whoa." The magician stepped back. "I was just kidding around. I don't want any trouble here."

Devon didn't either. It was a beautiful Saturday, a perfect afternoon to spend with his nephew, his *joka*. He sighed, remembering his responsibilities and his manners. "Thank you for the performance."

"You're welcome, sir, and enjoy your day." The man handed him a card. It was crudely made, a sort of greeting-card-sized flyer with the time and date of the scheduled appearances of Reynaldo the Magnificent. Then, after a swipe of his hand through his elaborately styled hair, he strutted across their makeshift stage to a table and began packing up his things.

And there was the girl, only a few feet away, retrieving an errant juggling ball. As she rose to her feet, she flicked a glance up at Devon, brows lifting as if she recognized him, too. Her big green eyes momentarily diverted the function of a few brain cells, but her jaw looked so painful, he could not help staring. And wondering.

"Are you all right?" he asked, careful to keep his voice low.

Her mouth softened and her attention darted to the cobblestones. "Training accident," she murmured. Then she said she needed to help break down the set.

As Reynaldo cut a glare from Devon to the girl and back, the sunny performer's face grew dark. Devon knew he shouldn't be keeping her, but he swore a message had beckoned loud and clear from those troubled eyes: *help me.*

So while the magician focused on nestling the juggling swords into a foam container, Devon tore the card in half, careful to save the part with the times and dates.

Small Lee stared at him. "What are you doing, Uncle Dev?"

"Shh. It's a good-luck secret wish." Small Lee knew about those. It was unlucky to talk about them. Or so Aunt Mimi had said; she loved teaching them Korean customs from her girlhood.

Devon scribbled down his phone number. He extracted two twenties from his wallet, folded up the card, and tucked the bills inside. When the magician wasn't watching, Devon gave the card to the girl. Possibly seeing what he had done, she quickly stuck it down the front of her costume and mumbled something at him, again without meeting his gaze. He thought it sounded like "thank you."

15

While Ralph ignored her, mouth tight and glaring blue and steely into traffic, Christina mentally scrolled through that afternoon's shows, searching for anything she might have done to piss him off, but she kept coming up blank. Of what he'd allowed her to do—the club spin-turn was still off the set list, despite her last-minute pitch on the drive downtown—she'd been on her game. The crowds were growing. She'd caught every ball, every club, every cue, in heels and on cobblestones. The footwear needed to change, of course. One turned ankle and forget the club move—she could be out of commission for weeks.

Finally, as they rolled alongside Boston University, she said, "How much did we make?"

The eye she could see danced with the secret of it before he revealed that they'd pulled in almost two hundred dollars. Christina grinned. Eighty bucks to put in the bank, plus the forty that Park guy from the hospital had given her. In the ladies' room at Quincy Market, she'd extracted the note from her costume, gulping when she saw the cash, and shoved the money and folded paper into her purse. "Our best week yet," she said.

But the pleasure on his face quickly dissolved. For God's sake, did he still have a bug up his ass about that club move? Christina was about to plead her case again, but she was tired of arguing. The shows had gone well, and she wanted to enjoy that top-of-the-world feeling. Maybe when they hauled into Ralph's she could turn his mood around and get him to enjoy it with her. A few beats later, he said, "Who was that guy?"

"What guy?"

"He was staring at you."

"They're all staring at me." She shrugged. "I'm practically naked." *That's it. This costume has to change.* Maybe Ralph—and the crowd—would take her more seriously if she weren't strutting her goods, literally, in the public square.

"Do you know him?" Christina shook her head. "The Asian guy. With the kid who put five in the hat."

"No. I saw the boy. Cute kid." Dr. Park must have been his dad. But he looked too young to have a child. Too young, even, to be a doctor yet. *Oh, crap.* She slumped back into the motor-oil-and-dog-scented upholstery. He'd been staring at her bruise, then gave her money and his phone number, brow furrowing as he glanced toward Ralph. He must have thought the magician had hit her deliberately. Was there some kind of medical law that he had to report it? She reminded herself to put more arnica gel on her jaw when she got home. And maybe call the guy to explain. Part of her wanted to toss the bills back in his face. *Nah, that might make the situation worse.* "Anyway," she said. "I don't think you're supposed to say Asian anymore."

He rolled his eyes. "Chinese-Japanese-Laotian-Vietnamese-American. Whatever. He wanted you."

"Oh, please." So what if he did? She couldn't control other peoples' hormones. She hoped he wouldn't do anything stupid like contact the police. Then she decided it was unlikely. The guy was probably just some do-gooder swayed by a tight bustier and a little skirt. Not a bad-looking do-gooder, either. The T-shirt revealed more of his arm than the scrub top had; an intriguing tattoo peeked out of his sleeve.

Half a smile crooked up Ralph's face. "It's kind of hot," he said.

Christina flushed. "Get out."

Ralph grinned and slid a hand up her thigh, drawing patterns along her fishnets, tracing the squares of exposed skin.

"Hey." She shifted on the seat. "Eyes on the road, Mr. Magnificent." He withdrew with a chuckle, but at every red light, the hand returned. Lingered. Climbed the rungs on the fishnet ladder to the top. By the time Ralph pulled into the alley next to his building, she'd shoved off her heels, primed to race him into the apartment and out of their costumes. In her mind she already had him on his back, a slow tease flicking open the loops of his PT Barnum-era vest with her teeth. But at the front lock, he tugged her hand away from his precious vintage garment. Screw the vest; the pants were standard issue, but she'd only been able to undo the button of his fly before he denied her there, too.

"What's your problem?" she said, nearly stumbling behind him as he yanked her through the door and kicked it closed.

"Oh, no problem." His voice and hot breath fell thick against her neck as he pressed her to the nearest wall and slid down the zipper of her bustier, flinging it across the room. "No problem at all." His palms stilled her hips and their natural urge to rock against his, then began a slow journey up her nothing of a skirt to hook his fingers around the elastic of her tights. He pulled back enough to give her a flash of indigo and a growl.

"Wait." She tried to wrestle control of her fishnets from him, but he wasn't having it. "Let me—these were expensive."

The hunger in his eyes never wavered, and with one hocus-pocus move, he'd yanked them down. Before she could react, he tumbled her to the sofa and landed on top of her.

"This is what he wanted."

What? He...what? Christina opened her mouth to reply, but Ralph thrust deep inside her, making her gasp and grip him tighter. Heat flooded her body as he tantalized her with a slow-fast-slow rhythm. Soon she was nothing but pulse and pleasure, one fat, lust-swollen nerve taking its fill. She clung to his hard muscle, whimpering her need in a voice she didn't recognize.

"Who's that for, huh?" Ralph said into the hollow of her throat. "Him, is that for him?"

Christina's eyes shot open. "Him, what him?"

"You know *what him.*"

She didn't like this game anymore. "Shut up," she hissed, digging her hands into his back in a hope that it would spur him to keep doing what he'd been doing. "You're talking crazy, like some crazy jealous guy. Shut up and—"

But then he slowed. She glanced over in question. His lips worked, yet nothing came out.

"Don't stop, damn it." She arched up to find him, to search out that perfect pleasure again. But she couldn't. And his gaze was blank, miles away. She tensed in confusion at not knowing where he'd gone and what was happening and what she should do. *Get on with it,* her body decided for her, rocking against him. It wasn't enough. Finally in utter frustration, she rolled on top of him and grabbed the reins, squeezing her eyes shut as she found the sweet spot, the angle that hungry nerve demanded. When they were done she collapsed beside him, and after a few moments Ralph seemed to return to himself, stroking her hair and murmuring her name against her ear.

Her full name.

As silence overtook the sound of those three syllables, she chanced the inquiry. "What the hell was that about?"

His answer was a shrug, a twine of his fingers through her curls and, after she'd lain for a while with her head on his chest, an offer to drive her home.

* * *

Despite a long, hot shower and a cup of chamomile tea, Christina couldn't sleep. She lay awake in bed, studying street light patterns on her ceiling tiles, long past the time when the T stopped running. Her jaw throbbed, and she finally got up in search of ice, wrapped a cube in a paper towel and massaged it against her skin until the fire quenched. All the while she thought about what the hell was up with Ralph. The man who'd made love to her—no, that euphemism was far too tame for what they'd done—hadn't even felt like Ralph, in the beginning.

He'd felt like...Reynaldo.

Her shoulders twitched with a cold shiver, and she dropped the ice on the table. He'd used her—savaged her—as if he were trying to make a point, like he was jealous and out for revenge. Jealous of what? She barely knew the guy's name. It was so fucked up. Could she now expect Ralph to go all alpha-male-caveman when a random dude gave her the eye? But she'd practically exploded on his sofa. Was something wrong with her, something that Ralph or Reynaldo or whoever the hell that was had triggered? A therapist had once suggested that she had daddy issues, and Christina had gotten so pissed off that she'd stopped keeping her appointments. At the time, she'd taken offense at the pat pop-psychology diagnosis, the accusation that her father had been cruel to her or didn't love her. Yes, he'd done some things she wasn't thrilled with, and he drank too much, but he adored her; Christina knew that, although perhaps she'd been too hasty in dismissing the therapist's explanation.

Maybe that was why her last few relationships had landed in the dumper. She'd kept chasing the magic that had been missing from her life—and now, she was doing it quite literally.

A knot tightened her throat as she watched what remained of the ice cube soak through the paper towel and puddle on the tablecloth. And what about that club in the face? Had that truly been an accident or some kind of twisted attempt to dominate her? Like he had on the sofa, until she took charge, but then he'd shut down. After the disaster with her father, Christina vowed never again to let anyone put her in a position she could not control, yet she'd almost let Ralph steal her power right out from under her.

Sinking into misery, she sulked off to put more arnica gel on her face.

On the way to the bathroom, she spied her purse on the bookcase near the front door. She pulled out the twenties and Dr. Park's phone number, drew an index finger over the numerals as if her nerve endings could memorize them. Maybe, when he was staring at her jaw, he saw something beyond a bruise. Maybe he recognized her other scars, the emotional ones, her—

Oh, fuck this weak, needy bullshit, I have to practice. If, like Herbert said, she could be better than Ralph one day, then she had to work on her chops. She wrapped the paper around the bills and stuffed the bundle back into her bag.

After a while, though, the cards began blurring together. Herbert had warned her to stop and blink every so often. Let her eyes rest. That it was like throwing good money after bad to continue practicing when she was too tired to concentrate. But she had to stay awake, had to keep going. The movement usually calmed her, kept the memories at a safe distance. But that night she couldn't stop them from intruding. Her mind filled with an image of how handsome her father had looked in his tuxedo, like a movie star.

"Awfully quiet over there, Chrissie." He'd flashed her a grin before setting his gaze back on the road. "Are you nervous?"

"No." She worked her hands together, nearly crushing the map he'd given her to guide them to the giant outdoor theater where they were slated to perform. "A little."

He reached over to tug one of her dark brown braids. She'd redone them three times because her fingers kept shaking. "It'll be fine, honey. You'll see."

"What if—?" Her voice cracked. "What if I mess up?"

"You won't. But just in case, let's have a signal. If you don't remember what you're supposed to do next, tap your left index finger twice against your cheek. Then follow my lead. Whatever I do, just go with it."

It sounded like a good idea for most of the show, but—"How will you see that when I'm in the box?"

"Oh, that's easy. You'll be able to hear me through the air vent, and see a little bit, if you squiggle yourself around just right. At least that's what they tell me."

Christina swallowed.

"Look." He dropped his voice. "I'm sorry we didn't get to practice the box part. Leave it to your mother's keen sense of timing to be itching for a fight during our rehearsal time. But there's nothing to it. I put you in, I tell a story, I make you disappear, and when you hear our secret code word, you pull the metal lever inside and show everyone you've magically returned, completely unharmed."

Yeah, completely unharmed. She snorted a laugh as she fanned out her cards. *I'm sure a few therapists would beg to differ with you there, Dad.*

* * *

Ralph hustled them right into rehearsal the following afternoon. Fine by her. After working on palming coins and manipulating card decks far later than she should have the previous night, she'd grabbed a couple hours of sack time and sleepwalked through most of her day. At the moment, basking in the sun's warmth, all she wanted was to toss and catch until every last ounce of her energy was spent.

When they took a break at the picnic tables, gulping water and firming up that weekend's set list, she broached an idea that had come to her in the shower at three in the morning. Something that would kick her value up a notch.

"I know how we can make more money."

He took a drag on his bottle. "Talk to me."

"Juggling lessons."

"What, on the side?"

"Between shows, some after."

"Kids!" Ralph's eyes lit. "They'll eat it up! We'd only have to do a few minutes, the little suckers can barely pay attention longer than that."

"And what kid doesn't want to learn how to juggle?" she said. "Hell, I would have loved that, when I was little. It'd just be a start, maybe tossing a beanbag from hand to hand—"

"And they'll come back for more, bringing Mom and Dad and their wallets." He snapped his fingers at her. "Brilliant. Goddamned brilliant. I'm so glad I thought of it."

"*You* thought of it?"

"Okay, we thought of it. I'll throw you a bone. You get to do it. Kids like you."

She grinned. At least her three semesters studying elementary education hadn't been a complete waste.

"But I'm only giving it to you on a trial basis," Ralph added. "If this cuts too deep into our hat time and the parents aren't putting out, it's gone."

"Deal." She leaped up, ready to kick the ass out of that club move. And this time, she would fight like hell to keep it in the act—whether he liked it or not.

16

Weekends were easy to fill. Devon squired his young nephew around town, spelling Auntie so she could have lunch with her bridge club ladies and do other tasks that would have been hampered by the company of a five-year-old. There were also Red Sox games, beer-and-pizza nights with roommates and their friends. When her schedule allowed, he saw Gwen.

Weekdays, however, ate at his soul. He quickly realized that sleeping in tempted the desire not to get out of bed at all, and the despair in that frightened him. His uncle had been right in a few respects. Devon was lucky to have the life that had been taken from his brother, and to squander it would not only be a sin but an insult to Lee's memory.

So the first thing he needed to do was face his reality like a grown-up—at least among his Mass General colleagues. He applied for an official leave. But even with the task accomplished, Devon still felt the tyranny of those unscheduled hours weighing on him. He took long walks. He read. He did chores for his aunt. He went to Rowes Wharf every afternoon for lunch and hung out with Small Lee, building forts with the couch cushions or coloring or playing with toy cars. Video games and trips to get ice cream were not allowed during the week, and Devon respected that, but sometimes he and his nephew walked along the wharf and watched the yachts bob in the harbor before going to the science museum or visiting Edmond, their favorite sea turtle, at the New England Aquarium. Even though it was summer, Uncle and Auntie asked that Devon engage the boy in at least one educational pursuit each weekday.

"But we're still going to see the magician sometimes, right?" Small Lee asked one afternoon.

"Of course," Devon said. "And get ice cream."

"And see if the pretty juggling lady got her good-luck wish?"

Devon swallowed. He was curious about that, too.

* * *

At noon on Saturday, Devon bounded up the stairs to his uncle and aunt's condo, sat politely through lunch, and when excused, guided Small Lee through the crowded streets to the Marketplace. The courtyard was even more jammed than usual, and he listened for the magician's booming voice.

"Over there!" Small Lee said, and Devon gripped his hand tighter as he felt the boy start to run. But when Devon saw her, he nearly stumbled over his feet. The pair were juggling what appeared to be slim, multicolored bowling pins, although Devon had a hard time taking his eyes from her.

Ethereal. He didn't even fully grasp what that meant, but when the girl tossed a pin high in the air and twirled before catching it, that was the first word that floated into his mind, like cool water flowing over his skin. Her arms were sleek and limber, like a dancer's. Her hair streamed out behind her, glittering in the sun. This was not the fragile flower he remembered, the young woman who could barely meet his gaze, the lost girl in the hospital. This new version radiated confidence, her smile dazzling, her eyes sharp and calm, so sure of her body's ability to perform to her will. The change fascinated him and he tried to get closer, but the audience would not allow it, even with the excuse of letting Small Lee have a better view.

"Okay, now for all the marbles!" the magician called out, and their juggling grew more intense, both taking turns spinning and catching, to whistles and applause. After one last high toss and synchronized twirl, they finally grabbed their pins and bowed. A smile broke over Devon's face and he told his body to move, if nothing else so he could meet her properly and congratulate her on their performance. But as people streamed around them, laughing and jostling, almost fighting for the privilege of filling the man's top hat, Devon stood frozen to the cobblestones.

"Uncle Dev, Uncle Dev." Finally he shook enough sense back into his head to realize that Small Lee was asking for his hat money, and he gave his nephew a five-dollar bill then trained a careful eye on him as he dashed up to put it in the hat the girl was now holding. She grinned at his nephew. He watched her lips move, her green eyes sparkle. Moments later, Small Lee was back at his side, practically vibrating. "She said they're done and if we stay, I can get a juggling lesson, can we stay?"

He jogged his brain over to Responsible Uncle mode. Juggling looked safe, as did the beanbags the girl was setting on the table. His nephew was quick and athletic and this could be a fun physical activity for him. "Only for a little while," Devon said. "And I'll be right here."

While the girl gave lessons to a group of children, Small Lee, short for his age, danced from foot to foot on the edges trying to peer around heads for a better look. The magician took over the money collection. He thanked people for coming, bowing and waving his arm. When he lifted his eyes to Devon, they narrowed and lost their mirth. The blue in them darkened, and a corner of his mouth lifted in a sneer. In reflex, Devon stepped backward, but it wasn't far enough. The man advanced. In a low growl, he said, "Hey. Pretty boy. The lady's spoken for."

"I wasn't...I'm just here for the show."

"Yeah, yeah, tell me one I haven't heard before. Do us all a favor and take a hike."

Before Devon could respond, the magician was off, and with a big smile for the assembled children, said, "Sorry, kids. Show's over. We don't want to wear out my assistant before the warranty expires. But tell your mommies and daddies to come back next week, and we'll do this again! It'll be so much fun!"

And then, with a pointed glare in Devon's direction, he snaked an arm around the girl's waist.

* * *

After taking Small Lee home, Devon felt too restless to return to his apartment. He allowed Aunt Mimi to talk him into staying for dinner, but he was relieved when his nephew held court about the fun he'd had that afternoon.

"And she has really pretty curly hair and gives juggling lessons..."

And has a total asshole for a boyfriend. Devon poked at his broccoli.

"Well," Auntie said, "how nice of her to teach you how to juggle. I hope you thanked her like a polite young man."

"I did! She said you're not supposed to think about catching." Small Lee's face took on a solemn cast. "You're supposed to just think about throwing."

"Sounds very wise to me," Uncle Park said, and asked Aunt Mimi to pass the roast beef. "Good hand-eye coordination is a valuable thing. Right, Dae Soon?"

Devon winced at the sound of his Korean name, and the implication.

One thick eyebrow hitched higher. "What? I was only remarking that it's a good skill to develop. For life."

"For surgery, you mean," Devon said under his breath.

"You have something to say?"

For his nephew's sake, Devon let the subject drop. "No."

He stayed a while longer and made uncomfortable small talk with his uncle while Auntie gave the boy his bath and got him ready for bed. Uncle Devon was then called in for story time. After that, he kissed his nephew goodnight and headed back to Central Square.

He considered visiting the neighborhood pub; Thomas the Tank was bound to be there watching the Sox play the Yankees on the giant screen. Getting buzzed and cheering on his team was an appealing idea, but it required money he didn't want to spend, and he felt suddenly exhausted. So he continued the three blocks to his building and trudged up the two flights to the top floor. When his body hit the bed, he realized that he'd left his phone in the living room.

Screw it. His family was in for the night. Gwen was working. But as he was dozing off on a memory of holding Gwen's wet, soapy body against his, his ringtone cut through the hiss of his fantasy shower.

He groaned, but guilt propelled him toward the sound.

"You have to stop," a woman said. He knew her voice. She sounded rushed, as if she feared discovery. Before he could respond, her words pitched lower. "Please. I mean, thank you, that was very sweet of you, but no more money. Don't even come to the show. He might…"

Recognition dawned and his insides knotted. "Did he hurt you?"

"No!" The answer was quick and telling. "Look. I can handle him. But you seem like a nice guy, and I'm worried about you and your nephew. He is your nephew, right? I thought I heard him call you—"

A man's voice interrupted her, sing-songy and thick with need. "Whatcha doing, Teeny?"

The phone went dead.

17

If there had been a Nobel Prize for crappy afternoons, that day's would have won. Desiree called in sick. Christina dropped an order of spaghetti with marinara, got three tables mixed up, and spilled a Coke—extra ice—into a man's lap. The air conditioner was breathing its last; the squeaking belt set her teeth on edge. Rosa sulked in the kitchen. Sal clomped around, shooting death rays from his eyes. Clearly, they'd been arguing, and the negative energy made Christina want to burn sage to clear the air. The one thing she'd been looking forward to was Rosa's smile when Ralph plunked down at the counter to show her a magic trick. It would have gone a long way toward fixing this epic masterpiece of a lousy, lousy shift.

But the clock ticked up to four and he didn't show. As she slipped off her apron and punched out, Christina avoided Rosa. In case she'd missed a cue from Mr. Magnificent, she ducked into the break room and checked her messages. Nothing. He refused to own a cell phone, so she called his home number. Nothing there, either.

A shadow fell across the door. "So, we'll see you tomorrow?" Rosa said.

Christina nodded, unwilling to lift her gaze.

Her voice sounded tired, flat. "It's too hot to cook. You want leftovers, take home a little something for dinner?"

There was never any refusing, and ten minutes later, Christina was armed with at least six Tupperware containers of fresh pasta, lasagna, meatballs, and a large chunk of tiramisu, all tucked into a cloth shopping bag.

She hated taking the subway home, especially during rush hour on a steaming hot day. The elevator in her building was still out of order, and by the time she climbed to her floor, yoga bag pressing into one shoulder and the tote cutting into the other, she wanted to aim her rage square into the magician's sideshow grin.

She sighed as she grabbed for her keys, making a sloppy peace with herself that her only recourse was to wait him out. Fortunately, there was plenty to keep her occupied, starting with the plants that gave her the stink eye when she came through the door.

"First me, then you." After drinking about a gallon of water, saturating her roommates' greenery, and taking a shower, she sat in the window seat in her bedroom and attacked the cold lasagna with a spoon, just about the only utensil that was clean. That little bench, which fit little her so well, was her favorite feature of the apartment. It overlooked the big curve on Commonwealth, and she loved watching this part of the city pass her by.

Telling herself the break from Ralph was a good opportunity for some much-needed space, she did a few loads of laundry, and when the sun went down, she curled up in front of her little window and performed a few card tricks for the amusement of her reflection.

* * *

Two days dragged by before Ralph contacted her. Thursday afternoon, when she was on break, she checked her messages. There was a text from a number she didn't recognize: *Back by showtime, pick you up on the way, explain later.*

Whatever, she texted back. No response to the reply. She wondered where he'd gotten a phone. He'd probably borrowed someone else's; who that someone might have been, she didn't want to think about. As she was taking a long slug of her soda, Rosa drifted in, dabbing a towel to the back of her neck. With a whoosh of breath, she lowered her big, soft body to the chair opposite Christina's.

"It's like they tell you," Rosa said. "If it's too hot, get out of the kitchen." She nodded toward the phone on the table. "No trouble, I hope?"

She considered her response. Christina didn't believe in unburdening herself at work; it hadn't ended well at other jobs. But Rosa almost reached in and yanked the confessions out. She had one of those faces, so open and trusting.

"I don't know why I should be surprised," she said. "That a magician would know how to disappear."

Rosa broke eye contact just long enough to arouse Christina's suspicions. Did his absence have something to do with the waitress Sal thought Ralph had been working? If that story were even true.

"I'm sure he'll be okay," Rosa said, each word chosen like a perfectly ripened cherry.

"Oh, *he's* fine. He'll be back by Saturday." Christina winged the cell into her purse and plopped her elbows on the table, chin in her hands. In that opportunity he'd had to borrow a phone, why couldn't he have told her where he'd gone? "I'm just...we're partners in this thing. We need to rehearse. All the stuff's at his place."

"Maybe..." Rosa drew a fingertip across a droplet of condensation on the table. "Maybe he had an emergency, had to go out of town. You're a very fast learner and very good at remembering. I'm sure you won't forget all he's taught you in just a couple of days."

Christina shook her head. "That's not the point," she said. "Okay, it is, partially." What did it say about their other partnership if he could bail on their professional one so easily? That she was disposable all the way around? "He could have said something."

"I don't like when my girls are sad." Rosa patted a warm palm on Christina's cheek. "Especially you."

"Yeah," Christina grumbled. "Your little ray of sunshine."

A smile brightened Rosa's eyes. "Sunshine, I got plenty." She waved a hand toward the restaurant. "Desiree and other girls? Sweet, yes, but between you and me, they're dumb like the doorknob."

"Rosa!"

"It's the truth!" The Italian woman leaned closer. "Here's more truth. You're smart. I watch you. I watch how you work, how you connect with the customers. You're worth all the other waitresses combined."

"That's nice of you to say, but—"

"I mean it. And if all he sees is a pretty face, he's *un idiota*."

Christina groaned and dropped her head to the table. "That's exactly why I'd been taking a break from all this dating bull— nonsense. Too many idiotas in my life lately. I wasn't looking for a guy when I met him. It was a work thing, I wanted to learn from him, and it got...more. Now I just hate..."

"Yes, I know." Rosa let out a long breath. "Being taken for granted."

She lifted her head and stared at her boss. "But Sal worships the very air you breathe."

"Only because I taught him to."

"But you guys argue…"

Rosa shrugged. "Some days he forgets what he learned, and I have to keep teaching him. Crazy man. Look, every couple argues, right? You get over it, you have coffee, you move on."

Christina made an effort at a grin. "Yeah, I know something about that," she said. "My parents argued all the time." Mostly it was about magic, and why her father didn't use some real hocus-pocus to find a better-paying job. "I guess they didn't understand the getting over it and moving on part. Maybe that made me an idiota magnet, for some reason. Maybe it's not them, it's me."

"Honey, no." Rosa scraped her chair back and set a hand on Christina's shoulder. "Okay, look, maybe Reynaldo is good for bringing in business, with his tricks, and I give him a little extra smile sometimes. But you're my girl. Whatever happens, don't ever forget it."

With a final pat, Rosa returned to the kitchen. Christina hung back in the break room, wondering about this "whatever happens" business, until she started getting pissed off at Ralph again, and at herself for stewing on it. The hours dragged until the end of her shift, and by the time she finally clocked out, she knew that only one thing could salvage the day.

Well, two things.

When she reached her first destination, Herbert shot her a grin, eyebrows climbing north. "Well. Christina in the afternoon. To what do I owe the honor?"

She set a container of lasagna on the counter and nudged it toward him. "Rosabella's daily special for a favor?"

"You know the way to this old man's heart," he said. "Although all you had to do was ask."

"Thought I'd sweeten the pot. And it's more than I can eat." She nodded toward the juggling case. "Can you spot me some clubs until the weekend?"

He spread his arms wide. "Take your pick. But doesn't he have all this stuff?"

"Long story." She tested the heft of a few and selected a trio that felt right. "I'll have them back by Friday."

"You know what? Keep 'em."

"Herbert."

"Least I'll know where they are."

* * *

The afternoon heat soared, which gave Christina momentary pause about her second mission, but she refused to go home and sit around ruminating on what Ralph was up to. Plus, the ceilings in her apartment were far too low for decent club juggling. So she hopped the bus that took her closest to the park where she and Mr. Magnificent did their thing. As the vehicle rumbled through Allston, she dialed up a playlist that contained Pink and other girl-power anthems. One day when she had her own show, this would be her soundtrack. All she needed was the money. The connections. Luck. And more practice.

The green was fairly empty, so she commandeered the big maple for home base and made ready with the clubs. Counting to herself, she started the rotation, nodding the beats for when she'd do the toss-and-spin. Two. Three. Four. Damn. She grinned after she pulled off two pirouettes and still caught the club before it hit the ground.

"And the crowd goes wild!" She pumped her arms in the air. "Woo hoo!"

Screw Ralph. She had this *down*. But it was no excuse for complacency, so after a long swill of water, she tried it again, first with Herbert's clubs, then with the balls he'd also lent her. Then with three juggling scarves she purchased from him outright, because she had a little money now and couldn't stand that he was giving all his stuff away. Scarves were floaty, primary-colored fun; she could toss one up and do some fancy spins and dance moves before nabbing it out of midair. If only she'd brought a tripod so she could record some of this for later study. And to give Ralph a taste of how much more she could bring to their act, to show him that while he was off doing fuck-all, she was kicking ass and wanted this as badly as he did, if not more.

After blocking out the major choreography on a scarf routine she was certain she could convince Ralph to let her perform, a kind of visual palate-cleanser between magic tricks and more ballistic juggling, she flopped under the tree.

As she rested in the shade, sipping water and nibbling on trail mix, she admired the nice bits about the park—the Charles, mainly, and the sculls skating across the surface. It reminded her of being on crew in high school. Again, as in so many aspects of her life, she'd been called upon to play to type. Tiny girl gets put in her father's box. Tiny girl who can belt out orders is coxswain of the rowing team. Tiny girl gets plucked out of a yoga class to make another magician look good.

Movement in her periphery caught her attention. A round-shouldered woman approached, pushing a stroller. She looked friendly enough. "I'm sorry for interrupting," she said. "But I've seen you around, and I just love to watch you and Reynaldo practice. I'm Emily."

"Christina. Pull up a slice of grass, I don't bite."

Grinning a thank-you, Emily sat beside her. She took some strawberries out of her bag and offered them to Christina.

"I really admire your dedication," Emily said. "It must have been challenging, stepping in for his old assistant on such short notice."

A strawberry slipped from Christina's fingers and bounced against her thigh, but she grabbed it before it could hit the grass. "A little. But the show must go on, you know. I'm just glad we make such a good team." She popped the berry into her mouth, taking a moment to mentally regroup. "What was she like?"

A blush crept up the woman's cheeks. "Oh, God. I shouldn't have...it's really none of my business."

"It's okay, Emily." Christina gave her a shy grin and passed her bag of trail mix. "Reynaldo and I don't have any secrets. It's just that... I've never met the woman. I've heard *his* stories. It'll be really helpful to hear them from an objective source, you get me?"

"Well, I don't know."

"Hey, you want to learn how to juggle? Have fun, keep the kids busy?" She peered into the stroller. "When she's old enough, I mean. What a cutie-pie."

"Aw, thanks! That sounds great. Is it hard?"

"Piece of cake. All you have to do is think about the throw. The catch comes later. After that, it's just practice. So, this assistant. What was she like?"

"I didn't know her all that well. She looked a lot like you, though."

"That's…kind of creepy."

She shrugged. "Some men go for a type. She seemed decent, and like they were really into each other. One day I came out here and he was juggling by himself. I asked if she was sick or something. He just said she wasn't working out, and he had to let her go."

He fired his girlfriend? Christina struggled to keep her face a study in sympathy while she scrambled to catch up. Damn. That must have been rough, but it could account for his occasional dark moods, and why Ralph made that little speech during his lame attempt to hold Christina off. Unless that had been an act. Unless he tried to screw all his assistants, making it look like their idea. "Yeah," she said finally, letting out a sigh. "Hard to find good help these days, I guess."

18

Considering the clues Emily shared, Christina didn't blame Ralph for not telling her about his previous assistant. She blamed him for disappearing on Tuesday. She blamed him for his total radio silence—well, other than an eleven-word text. But now that he was standing at her door, she blamed him for looking so goddamned happy.

She spun away in search of the Keds she'd dyed to match her skin tone.

He followed, his footsteps fast and light. "Teen."

"No. We're already running late."

"Just let me explain."

Great, her sneakers were dry. They were perfect. His gaze dropped to them as she did up her laces; he scanned up her body, taking in the extra coverage she'd added to her costume. Blinking in confusion, he began to speak, but she stopped him. "I made a decision while you were AWOL," Christina said. "A little augmentation of my own design. And the heels and fishnets are history."

"O…kay. But I need to tell you—"

She grabbed her purse and shooed him out of her apartment. "Give me your sorry story when we get on the road."

Ralph didn't utter a word all the way down the stairs or while they got into the truck, but the second he blended into traffic he said, "I got a job."

"A job."

"Doing close-up at a bar on the Cape."

Well. That was about the last thing she'd expected him to say.

"Friend of mine tipped me off. I was filling in for some schmuck who broke his wrist waterskiing. Can you believe it? A magician. Waterskiing."

"And you couldn't have told me? I was waiting for you at the restaurant, we couldn't rehearse, you could have called."

He shrugged. "It was a last-minute thing. I figured you'd be psyched. It means money for the show. And contacts. *Union* contacts.

We'll need those."

Christina exhaled slowly and let her anger ebb. He made it sound so reasonable, something she should accept without being a total bitch.

"I would have asked you to come down, but, you know, Rosa…"

Right. She had to work.

"Hey, I got you something." He beamed an impish grin as he nodded toward the glove compartment.

She tripped the latch, half expecting spring-loaded snakes designed to lighten the mood. But inside sat a small black-velvet box with a red bow on top. *A guilt present? How…unlike him.*

"Go on, open it."

She lifted the lid. A gold chain winked at her. She didn't wear jewelry; she was allergic to almost everything. Surely he would have noticed.

"There was supposed to be a key on it. So you could, you know, after work, if I'm not around, come by and use the juggling stuff. But the key place wasn't open this morning."

The pieces came together in her head. "So this is going to be a regular gig?"

"For a while. If I'm lucky. Still mad at me?"

She let the chain dribble between her fingers. It was pretty. Maybe it wouldn't turn her neck into a giant blister. And the gift did show intention. But as Herbert would say, that and a few bucks would get her on the T. "I'm working on it."

"So what's with the sneakers?"

"Oh. An idea I had."

"With legs like yours? Damn shame."

Heat feathered up her cheeks, much to her annoyance. "I'm juggling on cobblestones. If I don't have to worry about breaking an ankle, I can put more into the show."

He gripped a hand over her knee. "You bring plenty to the show, Teen."

And soon I'll be able to bring plenty more. She dropped the chain into her purse with a triumphant flourish.

"It's only a few weeks."

"I'll manage."

"That's my girl. Believe me, when we're headlining in Vegas we're gonna look back on these days and cry."

"Just promise me you won't use that line in the act."

They did a quick set list rundown and a few minutes later he pulled onto State Street. Luck was on their side—they found a good parking spot in the garage and no one had poached their performing space. But when they were putting the table together, a sharp expletive from Ralph took her attention. He was examining one of his fingernails. "Teen, got a nail file?"

"No."

"Where's your bag? Did you check?"

When he reached for it, she pivoted smoothly out of his grasp and made the move look like she was adjusting her costume. His eyes lingered a beat on her purse before he turned away, as if he could see through the fabric to the secret compartment she'd sewn into the lining. "I gotta go fix this," Ralph said. "It'll snag on the silks otherwise." He waved a hand toward their props as he walked off. "Just...keep setting up."

* * *

Devon kept his aunt company in the kitchen while the coffee brewed. It was only the two of them that Saturday—Uncle had been called in for emergency surgery and Small Lee had left with a neighbor's family for an overnight camping trip. Devon added that to the list of things he wanted to do with his nephew one day. The "one day" list was piling up pretty high, and that distressed him.

"I'm so glad you were free this morning." Auntie Mimi pulled down two cups and saucers. "I just thought we could talk."

Suspicion had rattled through him from the start that this invitation was a setup, something to do with a nice Korean girl she wanted him to meet, and he leaned back against the counter, tapping his fingers against the edge of the marble slab. "All right."

"I'm worried about you."

He tugged in a breath. "Auntie..."

She shook off his protest and sagged next to him, arms across her chest. "Dae Soon, what will you do if you don't finish your residency?"

His Korean name on his aunt's lips was softer, pleading, and it made him itch with a different kind of guilt than when his uncle used it. "I haven't figured that out yet. It's only been a few weeks." He grabbed one of the empty cups, mainly for the security of having something to hold. It felt like he'd been working nonstop since his flight landed at Logan eight years ago. Undergrad, medical school, the start of his residency, whatever jobs he could get during semester breaks—he'd been working right up until the day he'd walked out of Mass General. At the moment he couldn't think about his future beyond what he wanted to do that afternoon, beyond his next outing with Small Lee. Crackling like static through the back of his mind was the dwindling balance in his bank account. He'd taken enough of his uncle's money to owe him for a lifetime, although Devon knew the man would never accept repayment. He had to do…something. "I don't know," he said. "For now, I'm happy to help with whatever you and Uncle need. And with Lee Song."

Auntie swung him a glare.

"He's my responsibility, too." Devon's grip tightened on the mug. "We're family." The boy would be starting kindergarten in less than a month. His brain was getting thirstier, his questions and needs more complex, and with Uncle's schedule, Devon was sometimes the closest Small Lee had to a father.

Aunt Mimi shoved a lock of hair out of her eyes. "Yes, okay. You come play blanket forts and mess up my living room, you come and have family time, but don't let him become your whole reason for existing. He'll grow up, like you, like…" Devon knew she'd been about to say "like your brother," and their eyes met with the memory of him. She continued, her voice softer. "Haven't you sacrificed enough of your own life?"

Devon opened his mouth to reply but could not summon any words.

She sniffed and turned away, busying herself with the precision of coffee implements, with spoons and sugar and cream. "I worry about you." Strength and a sharp edge built into her words as she spoke. "You're so generous with your time and care, and that's a wonderful quality in a man. Just like with your uncle, it's a good thing. But sometimes you can have too much of a good thing."

The corners of her mouth sagged and the small furrow between her brows deepened. Devon sensed she was worried about more than just him, and could only imagine the challenges of being married to a surgeon, especially one like his uncle. If Devon continued at Mass General, would he be committing his future wife to the same fate? At a loss for a way to comfort her, or himself, he eased the tray from her hands and set it on the table.

* * *

Two cups of coffee and some lighter conversation later, it was twelve thirty and Aunt Mimi needed to leave for a lunch date. The weather was perfect, and Devon considered hiking up to Fenway to score a bleacher ticket. He'd been strict with his money lately, walking instead of taking the T, buying beer at the market instead of drinking in bars, so why not a little splurge? He started toward Atlantic Avenue with the intention of cutting up through Government Center and along the Common to Beacon Street and Kenmore Square, but as he was crossing the cobblestones of the Faneuil Hall Marketplace, his attention was captured by some sparkly, colorful objects spinning in the air. He caught a flash of red curls and a slender arm. She was warming up for their shows, no doubt, because it was not yet one o'clock. A stone of regret sank into his stomach.

Devon knew he should have kept walking, shouldn't have even stopped, but he inched closer, joining a small crowd waiting for the show to start. He kept behind a tall man with a young child on his shoulders. The boy put up a fuss and the man stepped backward, nearly smack into him. He apologized and Devon waved him off, grinning at the toddler, who was doing his damnedest to kick away his shoes. Small Lee had gone through that phase, which was totally charming when it wasn't infuriating. He rescued a tiny sneaker that was about to go sailing to the ground, and when he slipped it back onto the child's foot, the father nodded his thanks. Devon then poked his head about, trying to catch a glimpse of her. He told himself that he just wanted to make sure she was all right, and then he'd be on his way. To his chagrin, he realized that he still didn't know her name.

He didn't see the magician anywhere. But he now saw the girl, who had caught her juggling equipment and was looking straight at him, and not in a good way.

She darted her eyes left, then right, and motioned him forward. He almost glanced behind to make sure she wasn't referring to someone else. But she waited, mouth tight, a fist pressed into one cocked hip. The costume had changed; she was wearing flesh-toned stockings now, and a light, filmy material covered her upper chest and shoulders. A matching length served as an overlay on her skirt, making it a couple inches longer. The overall effect was pretty and feminine, possibly designed to float while she juggled.

"My idea, but he hates it, in case you were wondering." The Boston accent shortened her vowels, but she still managed to make it sound sweet, musical. Either that or his ears were playing tricks on him. From a pile on the cobblestones, she grabbed a bunch of beanbags, the type she used for juggling lessons, and set them on the small table next to her. He picked a few up, thinking to help her, and she didn't stop him, although he might have been more helpful if he wasn't sneaking glances at her face.

The contusion on her jawline had faded, but she was wearing a lot of makeup and he caught the chemical scent of it when she shook her head. "Boy, you really are a doctor. Giving me the once-over like you're about to whip out a stethoscope."

"Oh." Blood pulsed up his cheeks and he took a step back. "I'm sorry."

"I'll take it as a compliment." She snatched more props from her bag. "But you really shouldn't be here."

Devon slid a glance over her shoulder. "Where is he?"

"Getting something from the drug store. There's one a couple blocks away and he just left. But he's a stealthy dude. He can sneak up on you like that, I swear."

Devon didn't want to make trouble for her. But a larger force kept him rooted to the spot. She was so delicate and small and he wanted to protect her. *No shit, Sherlock,* his brother would have said, with that little half-smirk of his. *She's one fine female, and you want to be her big hero.* Devon didn't dispute either fact, nor did the thrum of heat pulsing through his body, but it felt deeper than biology. Yes, she'd dodged his question about the bruise, and that raised a warning. Yes, the magician acted as if he owned her, and that wasn't right, either. But he couldn't help feel there was something more in that brief, silent conversation the day he first saw her in the Marketplace.

Her face softened, which turned her green eyes into a bottomless invitation that for the moment arrested his anger but not his curiosity. "Look," she said and sighed. "This—whatever it is you're thinking—is a monumentally bad idea. Please. Forget you saw me. Stop coming to the shows." She smacked the magician's top hat onto the table with more force than required. "And for God's sake, lose the phone number. I must have been having a weak moment when I called, but I'm fine now, really. White knights on horseback need not apply. Find some other damsel to rescue, Lancelot."

On the last few words, Devon's jaw clenched. "I wasn't trying to—"

"Yeah, yeah." Her shoulders stiffened all of a sudden, as if the man's approach would produce a change in air pressure only she could feel, and she made a get-lost motion with her hand. "Go."

"But I don't see—"

"Stealthy. Like I said."

"You think I'm afraid of him?"

"No, but you should be. Now scram."

"Scram."

"Do you need a definition?"

"I know what it means."

"So put it in motion."

"Fine," he said, staring down at her. "Motion happening."

Devon turned and stormed through the Marketplace. He was halfway to the Common before it registered that he was still holding her beanbags. That he still didn't know her name. And that right before he spun away, the tiniest of smiles had curved up one side of her mouth.

19

Following the afternoon's shows, Ralph's attention was also AWOL. No hand up her thigh on the ride home. No race to the door. He turned the key in the lock, wandered in, and when he set his bags down, he offered her tea.

Tea. "Seriously?"

He shrugged.

"You getting sick?" Or had he seen Dr. Lancelot talking to her? But then he'd be pissed off, not looking like his dog ran away.

She figured a distraction might revive his spirits—certainly hers—and cover a multitude of sins, so she took two steps toward him and trailed a finger up his many, many vest buttons, but with a small, apologetic smile, he said, "Just tired."

Tired. He was a lot of things, but he was never tired. Especially after performing.

"Guess last night is catching up with me. I drove straight through." He yawned and threw her a lazy wink. "Wouldn't say no to a nap, though."

Yeah. She knew that trick. It meant she'd do all the work and he'd pass out right after.

She wasn't in the mood.

"Teen. You're not still mad, are you? Hey, I said I'd get you a key. The place was closed, I swear."

She let out a long, even breath. "It's not that." Okay, it was sort of that. There'd been no time to deal with it before their slot, but when he picked her up and stood in her living room smiling at her like he'd done nothing wrong, for a second she felt like a piece of equipment. Put it down when something shinier comes along. Was that what happened to his former assistant? He got tired of her and gave her the boot? Was she next? No. No way. Nobody fired Christina Louise Davenport. Not until she was good and ready to be fired. Then she made the mistake of looking into his eyes. He was a study in contrition down to the tiniest of pouts.

Could be an act, could be sincere; she had a hard time parsing him sometimes. Either way, maybe she'd been going about this all wrong and needed to refine her approach to him. Keep the upper hand, of course, but soft-pedal it a bit. She shot Ralph a smile. "Hey, you know what? Why don't you sack out for a while? I'll make us something for dinner."

He grinned, like he'd be happier to have a good meal than a "nap." "You'd do that? Aw, that'd be great."

Score one for her instincts. She nipped a couple twenties from her afternoon haul and picked up some groceries, and while she was no match for Rosa, it didn't take long to construct a decent lasagna. He was still sleeping when she put it in the oven, so she set the timer and slipped into bed beside him.

Soon he wasn't sleeping.

She had Ralph and not Reynaldo this time, all the way through. When they were done, he pulled her to him and she rested her head against his shoulder. A few moments later, he said, "I'm really sorry. I know. I should have called you. I was just so jazzed and it came up so fast, such a sweet gig, and some deep pockets come to that place in the summer. I barely had time to park my gear before I had to start my set."

"Hey. It's okay. Over and done with. You had an opportunity."

"I know I can get us a backer. Our show is gonna be so amazing, Teen."

She forced a smile. "I know. I can hardly wait."

He yawned and traced two fingers along her upper arm to the tender skin at her throat. Damn how his touch made her shiver. She considered another round but before she lost him—

"Ralph?"

"Mmm?" He slid her hand south and she resisted.

"While you were gone, I met someone who knew your old assistant."

His body tensed. "Who?"

Crap. Overconfidence from having Ralph in bed, instead of Reynaldo, might have led her to miscalculate in her attempt to test him, and she reached for the handiest of lies to protect Emily from any repercussions. "A woman who comes into the restaurant sometimes. I don't even know her name."

"Sociopath," he spat.

A nervous laugh escaped before she could catch it. "The

woman?"

"The *assistant*." He said the word like it had an odor. "Caught her trying to steal from me. Nobody steals from me. Especially not some sneaky bitch who didn't tell me she was married—"

The oven timer blasted away the rest of his sentence. Grip tightening over her hand, he yanked her against him, his hardness asserting itself into the back of her thigh. "But you wouldn't lie to me, would you?" He spoke in a light, sing-songy way that chilled what remained of her desire. "You got some husband stashed away you haven't told me about?"

Her pulse thundered in her chest, and she fought for control of her emotions, instinct telling her that if she snapped back with the words that were threatening to leap off her tongue, the situation might turn ugly, and fast. "Of course not." He didn't respond. "Ralph." Nothing but the bleat of the timer. She tried to keep her voice soft, even. "Hey. Let me get that so we don't burn the place down, okay?"

Finally he released her. Her stomach quivering with relief, she nipped out of bed and rescued the pan. Legs still shaky, she grabbed a glass of water and steadied herself against the counter while considering her next move. Coax him into the kitchen for some food and reassurance? Plead a headache and take her ass home?

"Teeny, come back to bed." His voice cracked, and her eyes widened. Holy crap, why hadn't she seen that before? The assistant had broken him, humiliated this guy who was accustomed to being alpha dog; now that Christina knew, he was scrambling for cover.

She sighed. Dammit, she felt sorry for him. She couldn't leave him alone. Not yet. Christina returned to the back room, steeling herself for whatever version of Ralph might be waiting. But if Reynaldo showed up, she was taking her ass home and pronto.

* * *

Gwen was already waiting for Devon outside the restaurant. She smelled like antiseptic and her eyes shone, jazzed on whatever procedure she'd observed or scrubbed in on earlier that day. She landed a perfunctory kiss on him, her usual greeting, but the blood thrumming through his body on first contact after so long said *not so fast*, and he pulled her closer for more. Only a moment later, though, she eased away. "Whoa, Park. We've got all night. Let a girl get some food in her first, huh?"

Tamping down his disappointment, Devon guided her inside, and while they were being seated, he thought it puzzling that she didn't say things like, "I missed you." He might have liked to hear that occasionally, maybe even get a text that said she was thinking about him instead of mere announcements of her availability. Certainly he wouldn't expect a check-in every day; that would look needy and Gwen didn't do needy. It was actually one of the things he loved about her. That she was so driven, so independent, so…everything his mother wasn't. Uncle had once told him that marriage was like a boat; if both spouses tried to be captain, you'd only go around in circles. That might have been the old way on the Park side of his family, but that wasn't what Devon wanted for his own future. It seemed inherently unfair not to have an equal partner steering beside him.

During dinner, though, he was content to let Gwen do most of the talking, to feed on her excitement about what she'd been learning. She told stories about her colleagues, the weird cases she'd been seeing, how they handled the pace. Like Mass General, her hospital could go from zero to insanity in a nanosecond. At one point, while she was talking about a kidney transplant gone awry, he felt like he was watching the two of them at a remove. Did he truly miss this activity she chattered on about, or just the way it filled up his days?

When they finished eating, he invited her for a stroll along Newbury Street. They stopped for gelato at an outdoor café and made up stories about the people passing by. The game was so absorbing he'd almost forgotten about the thing he hadn't told her yet, the thing he'd intended to tell her that night.

"So what have you been working on lately?" she finally asked.

But he hadn't yet figured out how to tell her. Holding up a plastered-on smile to buy some time, he scrutinized her face.

"It's a secret?" Eyes locked into his, she licked strawberry gelato off her spoon in a slow, sexy glide that redirected the blood supply from his brain for a few moments.

Then he grabbed control and shook his head. "I'm taking some time off."

A brow lifted. She looked as if she were about to say something wiseass but stopped. "What happened?"

His world seized while memories of the infant and the multilingual lullabies flooded him. So little—so much blood. His eyes burned, and he squeezed his eyes shut as if warding off a blow. A hand closed over his, cool and strong. "Park. Talk to me."

"You'll think I'm a wuss."

She leveled her gaze at him. "Dude."

He leaned back in the hard wrought iron chair that felt altogether too dainty and frivolous for what he was about to tell her. "Baby," he huffed out. "Gangbangers."

Her eyes grew big and moist and watchful. Unable to bear the tenderness on her face or the feeling that he'd become less heroic to her, he turned away.

"Dev," she whispered.

Her palm lighted on his knee; the other—perhaps intentionally, perhaps not—touched the place where the serpent flicked its tail out of his T-shirt sleeve. It flashed an image of his brother's lopsided grin the day he'd left Boston to return to Seattle. They'd argued. Big brother Devon scolded, and Lee had tried to charm him out of it. Story of their lives.

"Can we walk?" Devon pushed a few bills at the waitress flying by.

"Yeah." Gwen still held her soft, stunned expression. "Sure."

* * *

The last time Devon had been at the Esplanade band shell, the day had been so bright the colors hurt his eyes. Small Lee had squeezed his hand, excited to be part of the crowd, eager to hear the music and eat the picnic feast Auntie had brought for their Fourth of July celebration. Even when day trickled into night, the boy fast asleep between them on their blanket, lights shone and the Boston Pops sparkled. Now the space was almost empty, save for a few late-night joggers and dog walkers. The air had cooled; the stone stairs felt colder through the seat of his jeans. Devon drew his knees up and leaned back.

"You would have stayed, wouldn't you?"

Gwen drummed her fingers against her thighs. "Hypotheticals."

"Right. Doctor Gwendolyn Siminski does not indulge in hypotheticals."

She grinned. "Shut up, Park." Then she grew more serious. "Given your background, the potential for self-preservation might have trumped everything else."

He was glad for the shadows and the chilled concrete that hid his shiver. "How do you handle it?"

"Just do." She shrugged. "Win some, lose some. You know the rules."

"I get it. But she never had a chance. Lee, he was strong. He made a choice to go back..." A sob swallowed the rest of it, and he couldn't stop the tears. "I'm sorry, I..."

A warm arm settled around him. "S'okay, Park."

"Not okay." He dragged the back of his hand across his eyes and glanced up, expecting to find her Chicago toughness, the hard edge that her cute button nose and freckles belied. But it looked like pity, and he hated it. Could one actually die from feeling so small and ashamed? He wanted to tell her to stop, to back off, but he also never wanted her to let go.

Maybe she felt his conflict, or could only sustain the empathy for so long, because she shuffled over to the edge of the stairs and tipped her face up to the sky. The faint orange glow of the city obliterated the stars.

Finally she broke the silence. "It happens to all of us, you know."

His brow furrowed. "Not that first one, for sure." She was the first of his peers to lose a patient, and the professional aplomb with which she'd handled it cemented her reputation as a kind of rock star in medical school. Time of death was called; she stripped off her gloves and went back to work. Devon kept waiting for her to crack. She didn't. In fact, she'd snapped at him for expecting her to be weak, to break down.

"It was later," Gwen said. "This patient. Eighty-seven, end-stage Alzheimer's, cops brought her in, no family. I was sitting with her. It just felt wrong, to have no one. I let her pretend I was her granddaughter. What's the harm, right?"

"Aw, Gwenny."

Her voice hardened. "Don't. Call me that."

"Sorry, I didn't mean…wow. Why didn't you ever tell me?"

"Why didn't you tell me about the baby?" As he was opening his mouth, she said, "Right. You're a Park." She'd snapped it out in the staccato manner he often did, like it was a curse. Often it felt like one. "If you leave medicine, what else? Can't exactly see you in a suit and tie."

He shrugged. "Don't know. Lately, I've been spending more time with my nephew."

"Oh, God." Her eyes shot wide. "They're not…tell me Uncle Doctor isn't already pushing him into the family business."

"Not if I have anything to say about it."

She smirked. "I'd love to be a fly on the wall during that convo."

"I'm subtle about it. I tell him being a doctor is good and helps people, but there are a lot of good things you can do with your life. That just because I went to medical school doesn't mean he has to. But maybe he's a little too young for that stuff, yet."

"He's what, five? He should be driving and doing your uncle's taxes by now. Slacker."

Devon grinned. She slid next to him and laid her head on his shoulder. It made him feel larger, more protective. "Let's go," she said. "Take me back to your disgusting apartment."

* * *

They walked in silence across the bridge and up Mass Avenue to his building. He was afraid to glance her way and see anything resembling the pity of before. Suddenly he regretted telling her about the baby. Maybe sharing the tragedies was the glue that bound surgeons-in-training, maybe it made it seem at least somewhat normal that occasionally, people died right in front of them for horrible, ridiculous reasons—babies from gunshots, Alzheimer's patients forgotten to death. But with the admission, something between them had irrevocably changed. And he wasn't sure yet if that something was good or bad.

"You're too damned quiet, Park. Tell me something. Regale me with stories from your mythical childhood."

Her sneakers padded up the stairs next to his. "I think you know them all."

"Quit being a dick and talk to me."

He stopped, shoulders slumping. "What do you want, Gwen?"

She looked confused. Her quick brown eyes not so quick, her mouth parted slightly. Kissable but warning him off. "I want…" Gwen sighed in frustration and resumed climbing. He followed. "God, just be my friend, okay? That was a pretty huge moment back there."

He knew that. But it felt too raw and tender to retread that ground. He cleared his throat. "Thank you for telling me…about your patient."

They'd reached his door and Devon pulled out his keys. She yanked them from his hand, jabbed them into the lock. "You know what? I don't want to talk anymore."

20

In the shadowed quiet of their blanket fort on a rainy Wednesday afternoon, Devon and his nephew built dinosaurs and boats and tall buildings with plastic bricks. "Uncle Dev," Small Lee asked, "what was my father like when he was five?"

Devon, as he always did when the boy had questions about his parents, weighed his words before speaking, considering the answer most appropriate for his age. "He was a lot like you, joka. He liked to play games and have fun. He was really smart and loved to tease our mother. But she didn't have a nice sense of humor about it like Grandmimi does."

"I wish I had a brother." His mouth settled into a thoughtful pout.

Devon's chest clenched, and he cleared his throat. "I could be a sort-of brother."

Small Lee's nose wrinkled. "What is sort-of brother?"

"Brother can mean more things besides guys who have the same parents. It can also mean guys who are friends. Like us. We play games and get ice cream and have adventures."

The boy looked up from his latest creation, half dinosaur, half truck, a mottled bluish cast from their woven roof falling across his face. "But you're Uncle Dev."

Gazing into that little face—his father's floppy cowlick and mischievous eyes, his mother's pointed chin and rosebud lips—Devon couldn't help a sad smile and a ruffle of the child's hair. When he'd finally regained his powers of speech after seeing his minutes-old nephew for the first time, he'd introduced himself as uncle. He could again feel that tiny squirming bundle in his arms, the first infant he'd ever held—in fact, Devon had been the first family member to ever hold Lee Song Park. The gravity of that stopped him for a moment.

"People can be"—Devon searched for answers in the stitching of the blanket—"more than one thing to each other. Like Uncle Doctor and Grandmimi are also like father and mother for you. I can be uncle and friend and sort-of brother." He paused, watching his nephew absorb the information. "Only if you want that, though."

"Can sort-of brothers have secrets?"

"Of course."

"Can I still call you Uncle Dev?"

"Sure."

"Can we still play Xbox at your house with Uncle Tank?"

"Yes, but that has to be a sometimes thing."

"Grandmimi's rules," the boy sighed, tossing in a dramatic eye roll.

Devon tried not to laugh. Yes, he was definitely his father's son.

* * *

Friday night, Devon broke one of his own rules and met his roommates in the pub after they'd finished their shifts. He only had two beers, but it was enough to play havoc with his system and cause him to oversleep, leading to a scramble out of the house and up to Uncle and Auntie's to be on time for lunch.

So he wasn't surprised that when he left with Small Lee for their Saturday afternoon adventures, he discovered he'd forgotten his wallet and his phone.

"Hey, joka?" Devon said as the boy bounded down to the wharf. "You mind if we stop at my place first? We'll take the subway." At least he had a T-pass clipped to his key chain and kids were free.

No protests from the nephew. He loved Devon's apartment and riding the subway.

When they arrived at his building and started climbing to the top floor, Small Lee said, "You have too many stairs."

"No," Devon said. "I have just enough stairs. If I had fewer, you'd have to jump higher to get from one to the other. If I had more, you'd have to take tiny baby steps and trip over your own feet."

He made sure his roommates were decent before letting the boy in.

"Can we play Xbox as our sometimes thing right now?" Small Lee said, momentarily transfixed by the giant TV in the living room.

"Don't you want juggling lessons?"

"Yes." Big brown eyes cast to the floor and back up. "But maybe after that we can play?"

It sounded like fun. And, as usual, fun warred with responsibility. Lee would have been the fun father. He would have said, as he often did, that Devon had a stick up his ass. "Tell you what? We can visit the juggling lady, and after that you can choose. Get ice cream, or come back here and play video games until Grandmimi wants us back for dinner. Does that sound like a good compromise to you?"

They had been working with him on the concept of compromise. He was being very good with it, most of the time understanding that he couldn't always do everything he wanted. They figured it was a good lesson to know before starting kindergarten.

Small Lee nodded.

"Okay, I see where I left my phone, but I think my wallet is somewhere in my bedroom. Maybe you can help me find it."

The boy dashed off to the room in the far corner. Devon searched his desk and the pair of jeans he'd worn to the pub. No luck. Small Lee launched himself into the unmade bed and rooted around in the covers. As Devon was double-checking his desk drawer, the boy let out a squeak. "Hey! Cool!"

"You found it, oh great." He turned, and Small Lee was holding up two of the three beanbags he'd sort-of stolen from the magician's assistant.

Devon, a flush rising up his cheeks, considered his response. His nephew might be mad that he'd gone to the show without him. But how to explain that he had her beanbags. He hated that the half-truths were already forming on his tongue.

"It looked like a lot of fun, learning to juggle," Devon said with a shrug. "So I borrowed a set of beanbags from the juggling lady so I could practice."

Small Lee's eyes widened. "She'd probably give you lessons, too. She's really, really nice." He tipped his head in a way Lee used to, often before making a joke. "But we might need extra hat money for grown-ups."

And suddenly Devon remembered what might have happened to his wallet. While he was flying around the room earlier that morning getting dressed, he'd checked to make sure he had cash for the hat, then tossed the billfold to the bed and meant to put it in his pocket after he zipped up his pants.

"Joka, I bet if you look behind the mattress, right there under the window, you'll find it."

He wiggled a little hand into the space, coming up with not only the wallet, but also the third beanbag.

* * *

The boy spun in maypole spirals around the subway car's vertical grab bar, something Devon only allowed when it was not too crowded. He grinned at the unselfconscious delight on his nephew's face, at his Spider-Man T-shirt and baggy cargo shorts, but Devon worried about him. Lee Song had been a small baby and was short for his age, but maybe it was no longer right for the family to call him Small Lee. His ears were disproportionately large and his hair stuck out in a funny way on top; the other children in kindergarten might tease him, like they'd teased Lee. But Lee Song did have some advantages over his father: two loving, parental-type figures, three if you counted Devon, and enough money not to want for anything. He worried about that, too. He'd grown up believing that hardship and desire built character. Of course, that was probably a defense mechanism, a rationalization for how he and Lee had been raised. Money was tight and the arguments plentiful, the strain stealing the beauty from his mother's face and lengthening his father's absences. Little wonder Lee found comfort in the band of neighborhood delinquents; they became a surrogate family for him. An escape.

Devon's body sagged with the shame of his failure, but in beautiful oblivion, Small Lee made motorboat noises as he trundled in circles around the pole. Devon grinned despite himself, taking a moment to vicariously enjoy his nephew's delight, until he noticed the approach of the next station and the people waiting on the platform.

"Joka, come over here and sit with me." It took two more revolutions before he slowed to a stop, and then he hopped into the seat, leaning his head against Devon's arm. His throat tightened with the sweetness of it, and he never wanted life to rob that innocence. He prayed for the strength to have the answers to his questions, especially as he grew older and they were bound to become more difficult. He felt more confident fielding questions about Lee. Questions about Darcy, he was not as sure about. Devon understood, most of the time, why Darcy had given up Small Lee and removed herself from their lives. Maybe in her situation, sixteen and newly bereaved, she considered that to have been the best choice. But Devon's stomach squeezed for the pain those answers might cause, and if delivered too young and in the wrong way, how his nephew might interpret a difficult act of kindness as abandonment. Lee Song Park was just—perfect. Small size, large ears, cowlicky hair, a tendency toward excitability and a too-loud voice in public, but he was perfect. And Devon longed for him to stay that way. He worked an arm around his narrow shoulders and thought about what Lee might do in this situation.

"If you promise not to tell Grandmimi," he said, "we'll get ice cream *and* play Xbox."

"We'll have a secret?" The boy brightened. "Like brother secrets?"

Devon smiled. "Yeah. Brother secrets. But we'll just have to be careful not to spoil our appetites or the jig will be up."

* * *

As they climbed the stairs out of Haymarket Station—the pervasive smell of old produce wrinkling Small Lee's brow—and walked toward the more appealing aromas of the Marketplace, the girl's pointed words played through Devon's mind. The damsel was not in distress and did not require a white knight. Beyond that, she said she had no interest in him. Fine. Message received, on both counts. He would keep his distance. But did that mean he had to deny his nephew something he had just begun to enjoy? And how would Devon tell Small Lee that no, you can't see the juggling lady because his uncle had embarrassed himself by riding in to rescue someone who didn't need or desire his help? Besides, if she wanted to be with some jerk, that was her business. She was a grown woman who seemed capable of looking after herself. Unless it was an act. Although if he ever saw another bruise—

He felt a tug on his hand, and Small Lee was navigating them through the crowd. Devon hung back a little, with a careful eye on the boy, because one of the shows had begun to break. Most of the adults were drifting away, but when the magician called out for "kiddies who want to run away and join the circus," a ripple of interest drew a few back.

"Yessir," the man called out, dandling his hat in front of him. "Ten bucks gets your knee-high-to-a-grasshopper child a ten-minute juggling lesson with our tiny dancer here! Hurry up, because we're starting now and can only take the first four kidlings. Five and under, folks, five and under. Old enough to teach, young enough to be gullible…oh, wait, was that my inside voice? Never mind! A bargain at any price, because my lovely assistant is some kind of talented!"

And with that, he threw an obvious wink to a knot of men in the audience. Asshole. Either Devon had missed the assistant's reaction or this was a rehearsed routine, because she was all light and sweetness, handing two beanbags to a little girl getting ready to start her lesson.

Small Lee yanked him forward. Devon had already planned five dollars for the magician's hat, and an extra ten might mean compromises in other areas, but he'd promised. "Okay, okay." He laughed as the child dug his heels into the cobblestones and pulled on his uncle's arm with all his strength. He raised his free hand to indicate another pupil who wanted to join in, so they wouldn't be shut out.

"And my good man over here is victim number three!" The magician indicated where Small Lee should stand, but cast cold, sharp eyes on Devon before flicking his attention away and working a different part of the crowd.

Christina knelt before Small Lee as gracefully as a Disney princess. "Hey, there's my buddy." The warm smile for his nephew dimmed when she glanced up and caught Devon. Her eyes scolded him. He made a gesture of helplessness, as if to say, *Kids. What can you do?*

Then she sighed and returned her attention to the three other children eagerly waiting their turns. She held a beanbag in each hand and made sure the students did the same. The magician looked on, riveted to the hatful of bills, when he wasn't eyeballing several pretty girls who walked by. Devon glared at him for this and the guy merely shrugged. Asshole.

Meanwhile, Small Lee danced from one high-top to the other on the cobblestones as he watched her with about as much focus as a five-year-old could muster. "You start with one beanbag in one hand," she said. "Put one down for now and we'll start." Each child placed one of his or her bags on the cobbles and the girl did the same.

"Now." She held her beanbag-laden palm up, fingers open, as if a bird perched upon it. "Very gently, and I mean really gently, toss it up and catch it in your other hand."

The kids had varying levels of hand-eye coordination. Small Lee, Devon noted with pride, did well. His toss was soft, made a nice arc, and landed with the perfect thump in his opposite palm. The boy searched out his uncle for approval and Devon grinned back.

"Nice job, joka."

The kids tossed a few more times; some dropped their beanbags on the stones, some of the projectiles flew into the crowd. The waiting adults gathered up the miscues and returned them to the children.

"Okay," the girl said. "Now I'll tell you about lesson two, and you can try it here and also do it at home. Ask your parents for something you can practice with, hopefully something soft that won't break stuff. Next we start with two beanbags. So here we go." She held one in each palm. "Don't do anything yet, because it's kind of tricky. Really, really softly, like before, you're going to toss one beanbag up. Not very far. When it's in the air, right at the top of the arc, you toss the other beanbag up." She wrinkled her nose. "Sounds kind of hard, huh? Well, just watch me first. I'll do it three times. Then it's your turn."

Devon was absolutely watching her. How could he not? Her arms were soft and agile, like her hands. Her smile and green eyes pulled him in like gravity.

Small Lee glanced backward, perhaps to see if Uncle Dev was still there, and Devon made a circular gesture with a finger that he should keep his eye on his teacher and learn his next lesson. She flicked one beanbag up and then the other, and—plop! plop!— caught them perfectly in the opposite palms. Then she repeated the maneuver twice more. It looked like an advanced move for a five-year-old and was probably why she'd had them merely observe to start with. His attending physicians had sometimes done the same with new procedures.

After the kids tried a few times, beanbags and laughter flying everywhere, the magician called time. He mugged a cringing expression and said, "All you parents out there, we sincerely apologize for what's gonna happen to your living rooms later tonight."

Devon stepped around a few people to collect up Small Lee. For a tiny, frantic second, he could not spot the boy. Then he saw his south end sticking out from beneath the table. Perhaps he'd dropped one of the juggling toys and had ducked down to grab it. The pouch of one of the lower cargo pockets of his pants sagged, revealing the outline of three round, smallish objects. No. He'd brought the beanbags from Devon's apartment?

At the moment Devon realized this, the magician's eyes riveted on his nephew. They narrowed and glared as he took a heavy step toward Small Lee. Devon's chest tightened and he launched himself forward to intervene.

"You," the man said. "Kid. What the hell?"

Small Lee pivoted backward, mouth rounding.

"You little… It was you. You're the one stealing my stuff."

Devon lunged for the magician's arm to stop its trajectory, but the man whipped his hand away. "Take your little Artful Dodger there and get lost. And I mean it this time."

"Hey!" the girl snapped. Neither man moved. Small Lee had scrambled out from under the table and quivered behind Devon's thigh, clinging to his jeans.

"Hey, Reynaldo. Give it up. Leave the kid alone."

The man's dark blue eyes shot daggers. Nostrils flared as if he might blow smoke. A primal rush surged through Devon like a volcano, and he reached behind his leg to secure Small Lee.

"*Ralph!*"

The glare shifted to the girl. A growl rumbled from his throat and through clenched teeth he said, "I told you never to call me that."

Her eyebrows pushed together, and she drew her neck up straight, as if trying to stare him into compliance. Devon recalculated the backbone of this girl as she jerked forward and dragged the magician away by his collar. But as Devon turned to console his nephew and shuffle him off to safety, he could still see those dark blue eyes burning.

They'd gotten clear of most of the crowd, but when anxiety cut too hard in Devon's chest to breathe, he dropped to his knees before his nephew. The cold, hard stone bit into his patellas. "Lee Song…" Words caught in his throat, and he could do no more than wrap the thin boy up in his arms. He'd made a promise. To himself, to his brother's memory, that he'd keep this child safe.

"I don't like him anymore." Small Lee's shaky, near-tears voice was barely above a whisper against the side of Devon's head. "I don't want to give him our hat money."

"You don't have to ever again." Devon stroked his hair and let his hand rest on a little shoulder a moment before pulling him back into a hug. "And I don't like him anymore, either."

A few seconds later, Small Lee said, "But the juggling lady tried to stop him from being mean. Can we still like *her*?"

Liking her was probably the source of this problem, and it was all Devon's fault. He eased back from Small Lee and sighed. "I think we'll have to talk about that."

"Do we have to tell Uncle Doctor and Grandmimi about the mean magician?"

Maybe we shouldn't have so many secrets. Some were good. Some were fine. Some were part of their bond. Brother-bond, Devon had called it, when he told his nephew a whitewashed version of why he had a snake tattooed on his arm. He'd known immediately that wasn't the best of ideas when Small Lee demanded a tattoo of his own—a concept nixed immediately and without explanation by the elder Dr. Park.

"Tell you what, Lee Song. Let's you and I get some ice cream, go back to my apartment, and talk about that, too."

"Special brother talk?"

"Yes." Devon's heart melted a little. "Special brother talk." And it was not until they were racing each other up the just-enough stairs to Devon's apartment that he realized the boy still had the beanbags in his pocket.

Apparently Lee Song had also become aware of them bouncing around, and stopped. "Do we have to give them back?"

Devon stuck out a hand. "Sorry, joka. I'm afraid we do. But we'll talk to Uncle and maybe he'll buy you your own. If he won't, I will. Because you've got some sick skills, dude."

He tilted his head as he handed over the goods. "What does that mean?"

"It means that once you learn, you'll probably be a very good juggler."

* * *

The day had knocked the starch out of Devon; he struggled to stay alert during dinner, and it took three stories to settle Small Lee at bedtime. He smothered a yawn as Auntie Mimi saw him out. "Must have been an exciting afternoon for my young men."

If she only knew.

During his trip home, he reviewed the conversation he'd had with his nephew over ice cream, hoping he'd said the right things. They both agreed that it was still okay to like the juggling girl, because she had good intentions, but perhaps it would be better to find something else to do on Saturday afternoons. At least for a while.

"What is intentions?" Small Lee asked.

Devon tapped a finger against his lower lip while he rattled up a good example. "Like when Uncle Doctor makes you eat your vegetables. It might feel like he's being a little mean, but he does it because he loves you and he wants you to be healthy and strong."

Small Lee's mouth pursed. "So the mean magician had good intentions?"

"Well. Probably not. I was talking about the juggling girl." Devon had to learn her name. It seemed only respectful. Plus she was definitely beyond girlhood. "She got mad and yelled, but she did it so the magician would stop being mean to you. That's good intentions."

He'd asked a ton more questions then, most of them starting with "why," and Devon did his best, but it quickly took what remained of his energy.

After he got off the T at Central Square, though, he caught enough of a second wind to succumb to a bit of guilt for thinking about the girl's lissome body and inviting eyes, the puzzle of why she seemed to be pulling him forward with one hand and pushing him away with the other, or if that was all in his imagination. He wondered what Gwen was up to, but when he hit her number he barely got two words in—she was rushing off to check on a patient who'd had an acoustic neuroma removed earlier that week.

"Get a life, Park," she said with her usual sarcastic edge before ending the call. Probably she'd just meant to bust his balls, but it cut a little deep. Combined with the events of the day and the silence of his apartment, both roommates still working, her comment had him sinking into the sofa with a Sam Adams, then two, then three.

Slumping onto his side and then his back, he cringed at the rank upholstery, and idly wondered if anything, even an Auntie Mimi-style power cleaning, could rid it of the smell of stale pizza, beer, and three twenty-something Mass General residents. He spied the beanbags he'd confiscated from his nephew, nabbed one, and tossed it up and caught it, over and over. Maybe he should learn to juggle. It might be fun. Then he could teach Lee Song. Also, if he decided to become a surgeon, it might be good to keep his hand-eye coordination sharp. He liked the sensation of the beanbag in his fingers, the casing butter-soft and smooth, and he wondered if the girl's skin would feel the same way.

"What are you waiting for?"

Lee. Devon squeezed his eyes shut. In his mind he could see his brother's lopsided grin. And not for the first time. *You're not real. You're a manifestation of…stress and grief and alcohol and…* Hell. He needed someone to talk to about this. "There's the boyfriend, for one. And Gwen."

"Another doctor. I bet that's sexy as all hell. *Ooh, touch my gluteus maximus…* Yeah." He snorted a laugh. "That's hot."

"Shut up." Maybe he should be talking to Thomas instead.

"She's cute, sure." He imagined Lee's shrug. "But not at all like a sweet little redhead you can bend into a pretzel."

"I'm not bending…holy shit, Lee. You're a total pig."

The laughter trailed off. "Call her," Lee-in-his-brain said. "Come on. Gwen's all right, but jeez. Why tie yourself to one woman for the rest of your life? Taste the rainbow, for Chrissakes. And what, I don't see her making all kinds of time for you, bro."

"She's training to be a neurosurgeon," Devon said. "It takes time and devotion and—"

"Yeah, yeah, yeah. So why do I see you one day like Auntie, making those brave excuses for why it's fine that she's alone so much?"

Devon's eyes pinged open. "She doesn't—" Crap. His throat thickened and he hugged a pillow tighter to his chest.

"You've seen it. Uncle doesn't. He's just happy to have his obedient little wife—"

"Don't finish that sentence—"

"—like Mom."

His stomach pinched. "Leave Mom out of this."

"You're just pissed because it's true."

He jacked up from the couch and stabbed a finger at where he imagined the spirit of his brother to be standing. "I'm pissed because you're ungrateful. You were always ungrateful. You did whatever pleased you, didn't care that you were hurting people who loved you, didn't care that it…that it…" His voice was too choked with tears to continue.

"I had a life, though," Lee said. "I had fun. I saw things. You? You sit inside a classroom, you sit in an emergency room. You wait for life to happen to you. That is no life."

"Again, ungrateful. You were gone and Auntie and Uncle were devastated. You left a child without a father."

Lee cursed in Korean. "That wasn't my intention."

"Yeah, yeah. Being the hero." He punched out a breath. "Being the hero got you killed."

"Again, older brother, not my intention."

He considered another beer. Maybe it would silence the voice in his head. Or make it worse.

"Call her," he wheedled. "Her number is in your phone."

"She told me to lose it."

"But you haven't deleted it, have you?"

With a defeated slump, he fell back to the sofa and stared at the ceiling. Then picked up the beanbag and turned it around in his fingers. What a brilliant thing, managing the art of gravity.

"Come on. You saw the way she was smiling at you. Flirting with you. Batting those big green eyes."

Devon exhaled a snort of derision. "I don't think so." He tossed the bag up, missed. It thudded to his shoulder. "And that magician. He's trouble."

"And if he hurts her, he's a douche asshole who deserves to have the living shit kicked out of him."

"You propose I do this? Fighting, that was your thing, not mine."

"At least sack up enough to find out her name. But you don't even want to try to do that, oh, no."

Devon flung himself to his side, facing the back of the couch. He knew what was coming.

"I mean, yeah, God forbid you wind up happy or something. No. We can't have that. Dae Soon Park is much too serious to be happy."

"I'm happy." His fingers tightened around the beanbag.

The laugh had him gritting his teeth. "Yeah. Happy. Ha-ha. Drinking beer alone in an empty apartment on a Saturday night and talking to your dead brother. Dude. You'd better slow down."

Devon squirmed around and threw the beanbag again. Wishing he could throw it through the window. Or at the memory of his brother's face.

"Make all the excuses you want," Lee said. "Maybe I was wrong. Maybe she's just not that into you."

"Funny, I don't remember you being this much of a pain in the ass when you were alive."

In his mind he saw how Lee's lips would twitch with a smirk. "Call the number."

21

Christina was scheduled for an early shift in the morning, and Ralph had a boatload of tasks to check off before he could head back to the Cape, so after rehearsal and dinner on Monday evening, he'd driven her home.

"Anything I can do while you're gone?" she asked.

He killed the ignition and leaned an elbow out the window of the truck's cab. "Pick up a few things from Herbert for next weekend. I could use more flash paper and—" He flicked a glance at her. "You writing this down, or is your superior waitressing memory enough?"

Christ, he'd been in a snit lately…well, for the last few days. "Fine, writing it down." Fumbling for her purse—it had slipped beneath the seat—her fingers closed around what felt like a slim metal cylinder. Air freshener, she noted. Unscented. No wonder the truck no longer reeked of wet dog and motor oil; in fact, it didn't smell much like anything.

"Stuff works pretty well," she said.

"Huh?"

She pointed to the can.

His hyphenated eyebrow hitched, ever so slightly, before his expression blanked. "Yeah. The club's full of smokers and I know you're allergic. Didn't want to make those pretty, pretty eyes all bloodshot."

She smirked at the cheesy compliment. He threw her a weak smile before turning away. Curious. They'd been together for almost two months, and he hadn't seemed to care about the effects of his truck cab's olfactory delights before. Well, whatever. She decided to let that one go; the juice wasn't worth the squeeze. "Okay." She found her bag and rustled out a pad and pen. "Flash paper and what else?"

"I'm thinking."

The T squealed around the big corner, sparks dancing from its overhead lines. A knot of Haitian women laughed on the stoop of her building. Christina had learned enough of the language to discern that the joke was about their husbands.

She keyed in on Ralph; his gaze was lost on something in the distance and she needed a hook to reel him in. "So, you've been talking to people about getting our show together?"

He snapped his head toward her, and his lip curled into a bit of a sneer. "Yeah, and when am I supposed to do that? I'm either working or driving or doing laundry."

"Jeez. Sorry I asked." No. She wasn't sorry. She was forty percent of this team, and her forty percent had a right to know. And as they said, bitchy mood or no, the show must go on.

His eyes darkened. "You think this is so easy? Just put on a show? No. It's a pain in the ass. You gotta suck up to the right people. You gotta prove you can put butts in the seats. Insurance, unions, sets, costumes…and you have to build the illusions. Don't forget that. I got a guy, but he ain't cheap."

She shifted around in the seat to face him. "But it doesn't have to all be on you! Ralph, I'm worried about you. It's not like you to yell at kids. We can't be doing that."

"He was stealing my—"

"Chrissakes, will you let that go? Going ballistic about three beanbags isn't worth getting a reputation as a magician who hates kids! I'm just saying…" Christina softened her tone, realizing that part of his obsession with the boy could have been linked to the assistant who'd ripped him off. And she didn't think going there would help her cause any, at least that night. "If this is stressing you out so much that you're popping off all over the place, I can help. I can make phone calls. I can chat people up, get the info, do the paperwork. Plus, I can rehearse the new juggling moves so we can hit the ground running on Saturday." She shrugged and offered up a smile. "And if I get bored, I could even take care of some of that laundry."

He looked dubious, but then, as if a light clicked on inside, he snapped his fingers. "Right. I'll get that key made and drop it off at Rosa's before I head out tomorrow. Though now I'm trying to get a mental picture of you doing laundry."

"What, you think the magic laundry fairies spirit my clothes clean?"

"No." He started the engine. "Just fantasizing about you bent over the dryer."

Groaning, she opened the passenger side door. "Why, Mr. Magnificent, you certainly know the way to a woman's heart."

His eyes brightened, and she could imagine him laughing all the way down Commonwealth.

* * *

"How'd those clubs work out?" Herbert took an experimental sip of a coffee fancier than the regular joe she normally brought. But he'd liked the aroma of the mochaccino she'd ordered last time, so she'd picked one up for him. He appeared to be enjoying the concoction, although he'd probably never admit to it. "They're from a new company. Dubé better watch their tails, 'cause I'm getting good initial reports."

"They're good, they fly nice," Christina said. "Sorry. I forgot to put them in my bag this morning."

He waved her off. "Keep 'em. You get spotted giving those a run in the Courtyard one Saturday, it'll be good for business. All the performers want the newest toys." His eyes narrowed. "So what's eating you?"

She pulled herself up tall. "Nothing. Fine and peachy, as usual."

Herbert quirked an eyebrow. Christina sighed. "I know—"

"Can't kid a kidder."

"I hate to even ask, if it's borderline illegal." She wrinkled her nose. "But do you know how a girl can get herself a set of lockpicks in this town?"

He gave her a long, hard stare. "That depends on whether the intent is criminal or for entertainment purposes only."

"Oh, I'm not planning a life of crime. Just..." She toyed with her coffee, dipping the skinny red stirrer into the foam. "Need to get into somewhere I've been given tacit permission to enter but not the means as yet."

"Miss Christina. You know what they say about a man's home being his castle."

Anger washed over her again that Ralph had blown her off. "He was supposed to give me a key! Look." She yanked the naked chain from beneath her yoga top. A rash was already blooming on her neck. "This was supposed to have a key on it. But he forgot. Twice, now." He'd also neglected to leave her any show-related tasks. "So I figure that gives me carte blanche. Oh, for God's sake. Don't look at me like that. I'm not planning to nest there or rearrange the furniture. I just want to be able to practice during the week with the same stuff we perform with. Keep the muscle memory fresh, you know? And how stupid would it be to have two full juggling kits when I can hop on a bus and use his while he's away?"

"Pretty stupid. And a damn fool waste of money." He patted his hand on the glass counter as if he'd made a decision. "Okay. Okay then." Herbert disappeared into the back for a moment and returned with a black case about the size of a skinny wallet. "One, you didn't get this from me. Two, don't go flashing it around. It's technically legal for your purposes, but there's a lot of misinformation out there. Three, do you know how to use it?"

Her father had a set; she'd seen him use it once or twice. A long time ago. She shook her head. "Is that mochaccino worth the price of a lesson from my favorite magician?"

He smirked. "You trying to sugar me up and blow smoke up my skirt?"

"That depends." She grinned. "Is it working?"

"Must be. Do me a favor. Hop downstairs, flip that closed sign and the deadbolt, and we'll practice."

She did as he asked, and an hour later, minus the itchy chain around her neck, Christina was off to the restaurant and practically an old pro at tripping locks—at least in theory. The act wasn't difficult, but it required patience and a keen sense of touch for the greatest chance at not damaging the tumblers. When she wasn't trying to remember who ordered the linguine and who had the gnocchi, she mentally rehearsed what Herbert had taught her, hoping that when she got down to a practical application, she wouldn't screw it up.

Luckily, by the time she got up to Ralph's neighborhood, traffic was still light. She had a passing acquaintance with the few people she did see, so there'd be no question that she belonged. Shielding the lock with her body so passersby would think she was perhaps wrestling with a sticky key instead of breaking in, she used the tension wrench and pick to trip the mechanism and allow entrance, letting out her breath when the tumblers finally aligned and released.

But damn, it was clean inside. A low whistle escaped her. There was a bit of clutter around, but she'd never seen his kitchen so sparkly or the living room that tidy. It even looked like it had been dusted and vacuumed. Another superstition, cleaning like mad before he left town? Well. She learned new things about Reynaldo the Magnificent every day. Careful not to upset anything, she found his bag of juggling props and headed out to the park.

* * *

The next day, Christina was returning an overcooked hamburger to the kitchen when in her peripheral vision she spied a dark-haired man waiting to be seated. Her stomach pinched as she recognized the tall, lean figure of Dr. Lancelot, pacing the length of their small lobby, head bowed, hands clasped behind his back. Sal waved him to the counter and he thanked her boss with a polite nod. The reminder of how mortified she'd been when Ralph yelled at his adorable little nephew made her wish magicians really could disappear. But what was he doing in her restaurant? She didn't remember telling him where she worked. Unless he'd tracked her down, planned on lodging a complaint or something with the Marketplace about how Ralph was endangering children. She swallowed. No. Dr. Park wouldn't do that. He liked her; he'd given her the money; he'd kept coming back, even when she tried to get rid of him. That felt kind of mean, especially the last time, but it was for the best. The last thing she needed was a guy with a crush hanging around, setting Ralph off. Maybe she'd pushed him away one too many times, though. She eyeballed the distance to the kitchen. He hadn't seen her yet, she hoped, so maybe she could go on break and slide out the back door before he noticed.

But then Sal brought him a menu and gestured toward Christina, telling him that his waitress would be by soon to take his order. Awesome. They were short-handed that afternoon, with Desiree taking yet another personal day and Rosa, at Sal's command, home resting. They were also slow, so Christina couldn't exactly beg off the station.

Suck it up, buttercup.

She tugged in a deep breath and swung behind the counter, unleashing her big-tip smile. "Welcome to Rosabella's. Our specials today include cold limoncello soup, bruschetta with fresh tomatoes, and bay scallops with garlic and fettuccine. Do you know what you want, or would you like a few more minutes?"

A softening of his mouth as she held eye contact confirmed that she hadn't burned all her bridges to his goodwill, and maybe a tiny footpath remained, but he quickly yanked that little tip of his hand back into a serious expression. Damn, he was cute, and after all the scruff she'd seen around Boston, it was refreshing to see a clean-shaven guy with hair that didn't look like he'd just rolled out of bed. But the grin her face seemed intent on shooting out dissolved when she thought about the boy.

"Is he okay?" she asked. "God, I'm so sorry."

Dr. Park straightened. "He's fine. Or he will be. One of the fortunate things about being five."

"I broke Reynaldo's legs after that, just so you know."

He said something under his breath that sounded like "A good start."

He then cleared his throat and gave up a brief smile that, at its onset, looked a hair forced. "Aren't you, um, well, I go to restaurants occasionally, so aren't you supposed to tell me your name? Like, 'I'm Suzie and I'll be your server.'"

She matched his smile and hitched hers up a few degrees. "Hi. I'm Christina, and I'll be your server today."

"Christina," he said, as if musing on the syllables. "Sorry. It's a device I learned in medical school. Repeating names makes them easier to remember."

"Sounds very helpful. Now, Doctor Park, what can I get you? Something to drink, for starters?"

"Just some water would be great, thank you. And please, call me Devon. How's your boss? I'm sorry, but I don't know her name, or I would have repeated it and remembered."

"It's Rosa."

He cast a glance to the sign on the wall and shook his head. "Right, of course. Rosabella's."

Ah. That was how he'd found her. She must have mentioned the name of the place in the hospital. Not much about Christina looked Italian, so he might have guessed that she was an employee. Clever. And kind of sweet. Even if he were wrong, at least he'd get a nice meal out of the trip.

"She's fine, by the way."

"Good."

Christina poked her head toward the kitchen, but Sal was nowhere in sight. "Tell you the truth, she'd be in here all the time if we let her, but her husband made her take the day off."

"Probably wise. I can imagine that being on her feet all day in a hot kitchen is a bit of a strain on her heart. She's getting good follow-up care?"

"And how. Sal would move her GP in with them if he could."

Another one of those half-grins momentarily brightened his face, warmed his deep brown eyes. Definitely cute. But so serious. Or maybe he was still angry about what Ralph had done. She wouldn't blame him. Christina didn't have Desiree's obvious charms, but she had her own ways of softening men. "So. Doctor Devon Park. Is that why you came up here, to check on my boss, or did you have a craving for Italian food?"

"Uh…both?"

"Tell you what." She pressed a hand to the counter. "Lunch is on me. I just feel so bad about what happened."

"No, I can't let you—"

"Please? After our little performance, I want to do something."

He reluctantly ordered the chicken parmesan sandwich special. She passed the ticket into the kitchen and returned with his water.

"Did your nephew like juggling, at least?"

"Oh, yeah." With an almost surgical precision, Devon pulled the paper off the top of the straw. "He's a natural athlete, very coordinated. I only wish I could help him more. Since…well, I'm sorry, and no offense meant to you, but we've decided to stop his lessons for now."

"Of course. I totally understand." She then sparked with an idea—a way to help the boy and clean up some of the mess Ralph had made. "Hey, are you busy this afternoon? Say, around four?"

His eyes darted up from a sip of his water, his brows pushing together as if picturing his schedule. "No special plans. I…it's my day off."

"Then meet me here. I'll give you a lesson. That way, you can teach him what you learn."

"Oh. I couldn't. Lunch, well, that's very nice of you, but this? I don't want to make trouble."

"He's out of town." She leaned against the counter. "And believe me, it's no trouble."

* * *

"Just one quick stop," Christina said, after they'd transferred from the train to a bus. "I need to pick up my gear."

Dr. Devon nodded. He looked more comfortable riding the T than she would have imagined, swiping his pass through the turnstiles like a seasoned commuter. But then again, a hospital resident probably didn't have money for a car, especially in a big city. When they got off the bus and a few blocks later stopped in front of Ralph's building, he turned on her with widening eyes. "You live here?"

"No." She rumbled around in her purse for her lockpicks. "*He* lives here."

"Is that legal?"

"The building or the lack of key?"

"Either."

"Depends who you ask. But generally, yes on both counts." By now, she could quickly spring the tumblers without fear of damaging the lock. "Just give me a sec."

She walked into the kitchen, the cleanliness still surprising her. Maybe it was more than a superstition. Maybe he was building a new habit for when she had her own key. Whatever, it was a nice change to see clean countertops and most of a table instead of piles of junk. She then grabbed the two bags from where she'd left them and locked the door behind her.

* * *

"I've never been up this way." Devon frowned with a hint of disapproval as their walk drew them closer to the Charles and the mossy scent of the water. "This is where you usually practice?"

"For now," she said. "It's nice, being near the river, and it's a lot less crowded than the Esplanade. Although I don't know what we're going to do when it gets colder. You can't get a nice high arc inside."

"Makes sense. You do throw awfully high during your shows."

She led them to the big old maple and set down the bag of props, grabbing out three of the beanbags she'd been using for the children. They were easiest for beginners. It also meant less chasing around for equipment: balls and rings rolled, clubs bounced, beanbags…just sat there. Dead drop.

He took them from her as if the feel were in his own muscle memory, as if they provided him comfort. "I should have brought them back."

"Beg pardon?"

"I still have yours. From my nephew," he added. "In the chaos, he ran off with them still in his pocket."

"Don't worry about it. They're easy for small hands, so he'll have his own set to practice with."

"Then I'll pay you for them." She began to protest, but he stopped her. "And your time. You earn money for this, I don't want to—"

"We have plenty of equipment; we won't miss them. And I need to practice during the week, so I'd be out here anyway. Now I just get to do it with company."

"I'm hoping that company isn't too unpleasant for you." The shy smile made her heart thump a little faster. Then he lowered his gaze to the beanbags in his hands. "So, uh, how do we start?"

Right. We should start. She wished she'd brought some water. Or could muster the ability to stop thinking about his warm, kind-looking eyes. "Okay, let's get on with it," she said, more for her own benefit than his. "I think you're a bit beyond the skill level of my usual clientele, so let's start you out with two." She reached for the third beanbag at the same time he handed it to her, and it rolled off the edges of her fingertips and into the grass.

"I'm sorry," he said.

"Occupational hazard." She plucked it up. "There's your first lesson. Gravity."

"Got it."

"See? You're already smarter than the average five-year-old. Now. Let's take it from the top."

Firmly setting one beanbag in each of his hands, and taking two for herself, she showed him the over-under method. As she figured, he caught on quickly.

"Nice coordination," she said. "You must cut people open for a living or something."

"Learning to, at least."

She let him go on a while longer, wanting to lock the two-ball exchange into his memory and raise his confidence before making the pattern more complicated. But adding the third proved his undoing. Oh, how she struggled not to smile at the seriousness with which he made his many attempts, as he plucked beanbags out of the grass and began again, over and over. As she watched him bend for the umpteenth time to snag her juggling gear from the ground, she shook her head. She could imagine that he'd been the perfect student, with all that determination and focus. How rare in a guy that young.

Or maybe only his outsides were young.

Finally, wiping the sweat off his brow with the back of a hand, he said, "This is really hard. It must have taken you a long time to learn."

"Practice, like anything else. But maybe that's enough for one day. I don't want to make you too sore to take care of your patients."

Ever the gentleman, he helped her gather her gear, walked her back to Ralph's house, and held her juggling bags while she performed another break-in. "Come on in, grab something to drink?" she said over her shoulder.

He protested that she'd already been too generous with her time, and she countered with the fact that while she appreciated the acknowledgment, the time was hers to give. After a last dig that it would be rude of him to refuse her hospitality—even though it wasn't her home and it was dirty pool to press the politeness button on a polite young man—they were seated at Ralph's almost clean kitchen table, sipping glasses of iced tea.

"I'd hardly have imagined from the outside that this place would be habitable," he said.

"My initial sentiments exactly. I'd pictured a warehouse with throw pillows and folding chairs. But it's actually kind of cozy." She gestured across the main room. "There's a little suite back there. Bedroom, bath, closets…pretty clever use of the space. I'd be happy to show you."

"No, that's okay, in fact I should be going—"

As she turned toward him, their elbows knocked together, the impact jarring the glass from her hand. Iced tea spilled onto the table, rivers of it racing toward Ralph's things.

"Oh, I'm so sorry." Devon jumped up, scanning the kitchen for the means to mop the spill.

"Under the sink." She grabbed the glass. In the sweep of her arm, several smaller pieces of paper blew off the table and onto the floor.

Hyperconscious of leaving everything the way she'd found it, she scooted underneath the table and plucked up the bits and pieces. Flyers, mail...

Devon's lean, blue-jeaned legs darted back, the motion of his arm indicating that he'd found a cloth.

...and then she saw the paper.

It was a note, in Ralph's familiar scrawl, addressed to "Sweet Cheeks."

Still apologizing, Devon dashed back to the sink, rinsed out the cloth, and returned to the table.

Make yourself at home and I'll wake you up in the morning just the way you like.

Christina froze, the paper crinkling in her fist.

"I'm sorry," Devon said. "Was that ruined? Was that important? I—"

"Stop it!" Christina snapped. "Stop fucking apologizing! Everyone's gonna live, okay?"

Silence. She got to her feet and scrubbed a hand across the back of her neck. "I'm sorry. I think I'm just...must be low blood sugar or something. Come on. I'll show you how to get back to the T stop."

* * *

Maybe the note had pre-dated Christina and had found its way to the floor a long time ago. He'd certainly never called her "sweet cheeks." Or maybe it was new. She steeled her spine as she jabbed her own key into her own lock, grateful for the absence of roommates in her apartment. She let out a healthy scream and kicked a wall, then threw herself facedown on the sofa.

How could she have missed the signs? The clean apartment, promises of a key that had never materialized. And remembering the air freshener in the truck just made her feel stupid. Like hell that had been for her benefit, or it would have happened a lot sooner. *That's it. I'm done.* But they were committed to two more weeks at Faneuil Hall. She needed the money. She needed the experience. She needed their stage show to happen.

It damn well better happen. He owed her that. And if he'd been screwing around on her, he owed her big time.

After a while, she considered that lying there moping in her sweaty workout gear wasn't going to accomplish squat, so she stripped off and took a shower. The phone rang as she was toweling down. For his sake, she hoped it wasn't Ralph. She didn't know if she could keep her emotions in check—if she confronted him too directly, he'd probably lie, then scramble to cover his ass.

But the number on the ID made her smile. A house call might be exactly what she needed. "Well, Doctor Devon," she said. "Shouldn't you be in bed by now on a work night?"

"Perhaps. I just wanted to make sure you were all right. Low blood sugar can be very serious."

Why'd he have to be so nice, when she'd been such a bitch? She opened her mouth to tell him she was fine, just peachy, but her throat tightened on the words. Her eyes burned and she swore, but that didn't stop the tears. She grabbed the tissues and, still wrapped in her towel, flopped down at the kitchen table.

"Christina?" His voice was so soft it could have killed her.

"I'm okay, I'm—" Dammit, she hated crying. It was probably good for her to let that shit go every once in a while, but she hated how it left her feeling so weak and squishy.

"I don't want to make you uncomfortable."

"No!" She didn't want him to hang up. "You're…I kind of like talking to you. You're not unpleasant company."

She heard the smile in his voice. "That's very nice of you to say. I also meant to tell you that you're a really good teacher. I only hope I remember all the things you showed me so I can show my nephew."

They chatted a while longer, which helped her reel herself back in, and she passed along some of her tips for teaching children. Like keeping the instructions simple and direct, and the sessions short. During their conversation, she shuffled the phone from hand to hand, exchanging her towel for an oversized T-shirt, poured herself a glass of wine, and got comfortable in the window seat in her bedroom. Christina wondered where he might have been sitting. She imagined an apartment, probably with roommates. A television droned in the background.

"Where do you live?"

"Central Square in Cambridge. Just stand at the corner of Mass Ave and Hancock and follow the aroma of three guys sharing an apartment."

"That's charming."

"How about you?" His voice cracked a bit. "Where do you live?"

"When I'm not at Mr. Magnificent's, me, a couple of roomies, and a bunch of roaches are living the dream on Commonwealth just west of BU."

"You're a student?"

"Nah. Kinda had to drop out for a while." She ran the smooth rim of the now-empty glass against her lower lip. He'd probably gone to a bunch of fancy schools.

"You're young, you have plenty of time if you want to go back. What are you, twenty?"

"Twenty-five. God, you're cute." She imagined him blushing. *Nice-looking, smart, modest, sweet, loves kids. Jeez. And he's a doctor. How often does that come along? One day, some girl's gonna think she hit the jackpot.*

22

An elbow to the ribs jolted her from a dream about performing with Cirque du Soleil. "Hey, Teen. Give a guy a little space."

"What the—?" Crap. She knew staying over at Ralph's had been a bad idea. It was a slow night at the club so he'd left early. He'd insisted that show day logistics would be easier if he picked her up on the way back from the Cape. Remembering the note, she'd almost told him to take a flying leap. But she didn't want to arouse his suspicions. In fact, she didn't have much desire to arouse anything, and to her surprise, he was okay with that. Since it was already after midnight, it was technically show day: hands off the goods. But his bed was so goddamned small.

She moved to the sofa but she'd barely slept.

He hadn't, either, and in the morning he blamed her for it.

"So get a bigger bed," she snapped at him. "It's almost as if you don't want anyone sticking around." An argument ensued that had to be tabled because of time constraints. He had to buy his lottery ticket. She volunteered to fetch it, just to get away from him for a while, but he insisted on doing it and towing her along. What was his problem about leaving her alone with his stuff? Because of his last assistant, did he think Christina would steal from him, too? Photograph his secrets and send them to other magicians? Or were there more notes tucked away for Sweet Cheeks? Or maybe for someone else?

She swallowed down her annoyance, for now, shoved her feet into sneakers, and followed him.

It had been cool overnight, but the humidity remained over the city like a rude houseguest. She didn't look forward to putting on her costume later, abbreviated as it was, and standing out in the heat for most of the afternoon. Juggling was sweaty work. So was helping Ralph haul the equipment from the parking garage to the courtyard. As they walked to the market on the corner, she tried to think Zen thoughts about the day ahead, imagining the applause and the money in the hat and the smiles on the kids' faces. She was bummed that Devon's cute little nephew wouldn't be among them. Just as she was wondering if she'd done enough by the doctor to set things right, a familiar voice called her name.

"Oh. Hi, Emily!" Christina said.

"Going to be another scorcher, isn't it? Hey, what time's your show? I have family visiting and we want to do something different."

"We start at one and go until three, shows every twenty minutes or so," Christina replied. Then Ralph forced a smile for the woman, tapped his watch and gestured that Christina should come into the store with him.

"Have you met Emily?" she asked Ralph. "She lives in the neighborhood."

"Nice to meet you, officially," Emily said. "I've seen you guys practicing. You're so good together."

It was as if someone had flicked a switch from the grouch who'd been arguing with her into a suave gentleman. He let his eyes warm and bent low to kiss Emily's hand. "Pleased to meet such a lovely neighbor. And bring your guests, of course. Now, I hope you'll excuse me, because Teen—*Christina*—and I have a mission to perform."

"The Megabucks ticket?" Emily said. "I just bought mine. Ten million dollars. Can you imagine what you could do with that money?"

Ralph pulsed with annoyance, and he slid a fast, nasty look in Christina's direction before lavishing it, more softly, on Emily. "I have a few ideas."

After she'd gone, Ralph grabbed Christina's elbow and yanked her inside.

"Hey." She shook out of his grip. "What the hell?"

"We'll talk about her later," he said through clenched teeth, then put out his palm. "Pen."

She patted her pockets. "I don't have it."

His eyes shot wide. "You don't have the pen."

"Oh, for God's sake, it was like a fire drill, you rushed me out so fast. Use a pencil. I won't tell Harry. If you've been betting the same numbers in the same place at the same time, what does it really matter if—?"

"You know why it matters. Did you tell *Emily* about this? You swore...you signed the agreement! It was proprietary information."

He checked his watch again. "If I run I can make it home and back. Wait here."

Before she could say anything, he'd taken off. When she turned back, everyone in the store—well, at least a young couple and the cashier—was staring. She shrugged. "It's his time of the month, I guess."

They didn't buy the ticket until two minutes after the designated deadline, and Ralph blamed her all the way back to his place. He blamed her for everything that went wrong the rest of the afternoon. When her pantyhose shredded on his truck door and she had to buy a replacement and change in the cab in the parking lot. When a misunderstanding with another performer bumped them to a less well-maintained section of the cobblestones and she nearly turned an ankle from the heels he'd badgered and cajoled and nearly blackmailed her into wearing until she'd given in just to shut him up. He'd also blamed her when she dropped a ball in the first show because Ralph had thrown it to her at the wrong time in the rotation.

And during the final performance, when her hands were sweaty and one of the clubs got away from her, he laughed and said to the crowd, "Sorry, folks. Guess Teeny's drinking again. Oh, how we tried to get her off the sauce, but you know how it is. Just can't get good help these days."

Fuck you. She glared at him, but he even played that for the audience, pretending he was in trouble with the "little woman" and joking with the guys that he "wasn't gonna be getting any of *that* later." For the second time that day, she'd been sorely tempted to drop everything and quit. But she held on. She was a goddamned professional, after all.

It had felt like the longest two hours of her life. Finally, the gear was packed, Ralph pocketed the cash, to be divvied up later, and Christina switched from heels to a pair of ballet flats she'd slipped into one of the juggling bags. Then he started in on her again. The day's haul was crap and that was her fault, too, for messing up so many times and making him cover for her.

"Cover...cover for me? Fuck you, you were covering for me. You threw that ball out of my rotation on purpose. And it's four fucking hundred degrees. What are you, some kind of alien that you don't sweat out here?"

"No." The calm in his voice made her want to pop him one. "I'm a professional. And when you're willing to be a professional, and stand out here and do your job, you'll know where to find me."

She stabbed a fist into her hip. "No! I won't know where to find you, because I never know where you *are*! You won't even give me a key to your apartment so I can at least come by and practice with the equipment so I can be even more of a professional and learn how to cover for your fucking mistakes."

And then she spun around and fled, putting as much distance as she could between them. Her eyes stung from the sun's glare, sweat running makeup into them, and from a supreme effort to hold in the waterworks. She was still fuming and not even sure where to go except *away*, when she heard a thin, clear voice call out.

"It's the juggling lady!"

God, no.

"Uncle Dev, Uncle Dev, it's the juggling lady!"

Just kill me now and get it over with. She didn't think it possible, but her heart banged even harder against the plastic underpinnings of her bustier. She sucked in a few quick deep breaths, dabbed at her sweat-errant makeup and a couple of tears she hadn't been able to stop, and turned, willing herself happy and charming. The little floppy-haired boy running up to her made it so much easier.

"Joka, wait for me." Dr. Park, all long limbs and tension, emerged from the crowd. Relief softened his face as he set a firm hand on the boy's shoulder, but when he noticed her, and only her, his mouth worked to the side and his eyes narrowed as if evaluating her condition. She couldn't bear his scrutiny and dropped her gaze. It fell to where his gold-colored T slid into well-cut jeans, and the arms of a light, long-sleeved shirt tied around his hips. He started to say something, a few soft words, but his nephew interrupted.

"We just saw a puppet show. We're getting ice cream. Can you come have ice cream with us?" Devon cleared his throat and patted the boy's arm. "I'm sorry, Uncle Dev. Is it okay to ask if she can have ice cream with us?"

In spite of everything, Christina laughed. That kid, so sweet with his wacky hair and huge brown eyes and adorable manners, five-year-old exuberance vibrating under his skin. "It would be my pleasure," she told him. "I can't think of anything I'd rather do. Although I feel a little weird, walking around in my costume."

"We can fix that." Devon untied the sleeves and draped what turned out to be a soft cotton shirt around her shoulders. The fabric whispered comfort against her skin and had a light scent of aftershave that she didn't find annoying in the slightest.

With the boy between them, holding a grown-up's hand in each of his, they crossed Atlantic Avenue and headed toward the place where her father used to take her when she was small. She'd almost forgotten it existed. The little café wasn't all shiny and flashy with neon and brand names, so few tourists knew about it. But the moment she walked in, she realized that her purse was in Ralph's truck. With her wallet, her phone, the key to her apartment. And even her lockpicks.

"You look pale," Devon said. "Of course, you've been out in the heat all afternoon. Sit, let me get you some water."

"No, it's…"

A question dawned in his eyes and he said to the boy, "Lee Song, would you please be a nice gentleman and find us a table?" He pointed toward an empty booth in easy viewing distance. "That one looks clean." The boy nodded and took off.

The young doctor turned back to Christina. "We had an argument after the last show," she said under her breath. "I left. And my purse is in his truck. With…everything in it. I don't even know if he's still here. With the mood he's in today, I wouldn't put it past him to have left without me."

"Where are you parked?" he asked. "If you stay here with Lee Song, I'll try to find him."

"No," she said quickly. "I should go." She pulled Devon's shirt closer to her body. "It's not far." She'd almost said, "It's not fair."

He shoved his hands into his pockets, and he lowered a glance as if checking that she was sufficiently covered. Actually, his shirt ended only a few inches above her knees. "You're sure?"

No. "Yeah."

"Okay. But if he's gone, come back here. I promised ice cream, and I hate not keeping my word. After that, we'll take my nephew home, and I'll drive you wherever you need to go."

* * *

From halfway across the second floor of the parking garage, the lack of brown truck told Christina that Ralph had already taken off. This fact didn't stop her from walking the distance, from standing in the empty space while rage boiled out of her, calling him names that would make half the guys in the Red Sox clubhouse blush. Leaving her stranded downtown with no T fare and no alternative to her tiny costume—was that supposed be some sort of punishment? Force her to beg for change, get on the subway, walk from the Allston bus stop to his place? And what if he wasn't even home? There was no super in her apartment complex, only a number that either went straight to voice mail or told her to call back during normal business hours.

Bastard. She hugged her fury tighter, like an extra layer of clothing. Besides, staying pissed at Ralph was easier than allowing the other emotions out to play. Wanting to shove a fist through a wall, she let out a loud groan and stomped back to the ice cream shop. But when she walked in and caught sight of the Park men—before they saw her—she smiled. They were laughing. Lee Song was trying to make a spoon stick to his nose. A second after Christina hoped Devon wouldn't scold him for playing with utensils at the table, the doctor tried the same trick, and it was damned near impossible to hold back a snort of amusement. But he saw her and, flushing up to his temples, set the spoon down and folded his hands on the table.

"You two make quite a team," she said, sliding in beside the boy.

"No luck?" A faint blush still colored the doctor's cheeks.

She turned up empty hands. "Guess I'll have to pay someone back for my ice cream."

"Did someone take your hat money, Miss Christina?" She didn't remember introducing herself to the boy using that name. Devon must have coached him. It was sweet, but inwardly she cringed, because it made her sound like a dominatrix, especially considering what she was wearing under the doctor's shirt.

Christina tried to think of a way to explain her predicament to a five-year-old. "The magician took our hat money home to put it in the bank and keep it safe." She pouted. "But he forgot to leave me enough for ice cream."

"That's not nice," Lee Song said.

"No," Devon said, "it's not. It's not nice at all. But luckily for us, we brought extra."

* * *

"My aunt and uncle are just at Rowes Wharf," Devon explained as he held the shop door open for her. "I can call for a cab, if you'd like."

She shook her head. "Walking's fine. Since I'm not wearing my heels of death."

"What's a heels of death?" Lee Song asked.

"Shoes like Auntie Sook wears."

The boy made a face. "Those are *so* loud. And she's not my real Auntie. She's Grandmimi's friend."

"But we still call her Auntie, and why do we do that?"

"For respect," Lee Song said with a groan and stuck out his tongue, making Christina laugh.

"Well, I think it's very gentlemanly," she said.

They turned right onto the wharf. The windows of the adjoining townhomes glittered in the sun, and the bay lapped gently against the dock.

"It must be nice to live on the waterfront," Christina said. And probably honking expensive, too. If Devon came from money, he didn't show it.

"Would you like to come in?"

"Seriously?" Christina gestured to her getup. Devon's shirt, now buttoned all the way up against the breeze coming off the water, covered the bustier and the mini, but still made her look like she was wearing nothing underneath. The slutty stage makeup probably wouldn't help the impression.

"Ah. You have a point. My aunt and uncle are kind of old-fashioned. But I don't want to just leave you here. Come up, wait in the hall for a second. I'll explain. Maybe Auntie can loan you something to wear."

She followed as he and Lee Song climbed a short set of stairs and keyed open a door. Her mouth fell open. The "hallway" was pretty chichi. Her shoes didn't make a sound against the plush salmon-colored carpet. The walls were lined with art and illuminated by posh track lighting. Devon stopped in front of a door and rapped his knuckles against it.

A woman's voice said something that sounded like "Day Soon?"

"My Korean name," Devon said. "Like I said. Old-fashioned. Yes, Auntie Mimi."

"Did you lose your key? Come on in, then. I'm cooking."

Devon glanced at Christina over his shoulder. "Just give me a second." The two disappeared inside. As the door closed, Lee Song yelled, "Grandmimi, Grandmimi, we had ice cream with the juggling lady!"

So much for making a subtle entrance.

* * *

After kissing the top of Small Lee's head and sending him off to wash his hands, Auntie frowned at Devon and asked about the juggling lady.

Devon stalled a moment, thinking of a good way to explain without prompting a lecture or, God forbid, getting Uncle involved. Fortunately, he appeared to be napping in his study, noise-canceling headphones firmly over his ears. "A friend." Then he realized this admission could lead to questions about how well he knew this half-naked friend whom he'd apparently introduced to the impressionable child, so he held up a hand and quickly explained Christina's predicament.

"Actually, she's just out in the hall. Because of…well, like I said, she's a little embarrassed about coming in."

Auntie's eyebrows climbed a couple notches higher. "And you leave her in the hall in this state? Dae Soon, you know better than that. Bring her in here, please."

Stupid. Should have just done that in the first place. Mumbling an apology, Devon peered out the door and hoped she hadn't bolted. But she was sitting in a chair, her slender legs tucked gracefully beneath her, eyes closed. Her chest lifted and sank with long, deliberate breaths, as if doing some sort of calming exercise. A tumble of gold-red hair curtained her pale cheek. He was struck by the dichotomy between her brave talk and tough exterior, and how vulnerable she looked curled into the overstuffed chair like a study for a painting. Adding to his pleasant confusion was how he ached to smooth the hair from her face and scoop her into his arms.

Instead, though, he cleared his throat to get her attention and motioned her inside.

Auntie's expression melted when she saw her and murmured something in Korean. It translated roughly into "poor small animal," but he was never quite sure what all the words meant when she spoke.

"Auntie Mimi." Devon swallowed. "This is Christina. Christina, I'd like you to meet my aunt, Mimi Park."

"It's nice to meet you, um, Mrs. Park?"

"Call me Mimi, please. I would introduce you to my husband, but it's his nap time. Come. We'll find you something to wear. Dae Soon, move that pan to the back burner, please. And wash the broccoli?"

Before disappearing into the master bedroom with his aunt, Christina smiled at him and mouthed a "thank-you." The Sahara Desert had made a sudden landing in his throat. Damn. A woman in his shirt. *Christina* in his shirt. Probably the hottest thing he'd ever seen. He'd never be able to wear it again without thinking of her. A pulse of heat rose from his chest and prompted a return grin that lingered long after they'd closed the door.

The groan of Uncle's recliner snapped Devon back to reality, and he hustled to do what his aunt had requested. He also fixed a glass of ice water, because that was what Uncle liked upon waking. And, finally, the man came out, looking relaxed and in what could almost be described as a good mood. "Ah. You had an enjoyable afternoon with our joka?"

"We always have fun."

He patted Devon's arm and picked up the water glass for a long sip, then gestured to the closed bedroom door. "I thought I heard voices. Your aunt has a visitor? One of her church friends?"

As Devon was about to explain, the door opened. Christina came out, wearing one of his aunt's silky tops over a pair of gray trousers. She'd also washed off her makeup. He was right; she was so much prettier without it.

Christina stopped his thoughts with a quirk of a grin. "Yeah. Don't recognize me with my clothes on. I get that a lot."

Before anyone could react, she walked over to Uncle and stuck out her hand. "You must be Devon's uncle. Doctor Park, it's so nice to meet you. You and your wife have a beautiful home, and she was really gracious to help me."

Uncle blinked in apparent befuddlement. "Thank you," he said. "Er..."

"Christina Davenport."

"Whom I'll be escorting home now," Devon added.

"You're not going to invite this young lady to stay for dinner?" Uncle said. "We have plenty."

Christina's cheeks colored. Something Devon had never seen. Or Uncle, attempting to be charming. "Oh. That's...really nice of you, you've all been so great, but there's something I need to take care of. It's a little hard to explain."

"Maybe another time," Auntie said. She nodded toward Devon. "Take my car."

* * *

As she'd suspected, Ralph wasn't home. Christina dropped her head against the rest and tried not to panic. She squeezed her eyes shut and tried a few yoga breaths, because one of her instructors once told her it was impossible to breathe and panic at the same time.

"Is there...at your apartment building, maybe a landlord, a roommate?" Over the purr of Mimi Park's plush sedan, idling at the curb, Devon's voice was soft and a little tentative, as if she were a spooked and maybe dangerous creature that needed soothing. It pissed her off that she found the treatment irritating. What the hell was wrong with her? He was only trying to be nice. It was just a crappy situation. She pulled in another slow inhale and let it out to a count of eight.

"No, and no," she said. But it was worth a try. "Can I borrow your phone?"

To her shock, someone answered. To her further shock, it was someone who was in the area and, after answering a few security questions that satisfied him that she indeed lived there, agreed to meet her and let her in. She grinned, thanked Devon for the use of his cell, and told him the address. Maybe there was something to all those lottery tickets, all those pre-show superstitions. Maybe Houdini had decided to shine a little luck her way that night.

She directed Devon to her apartment building and showed him

where he could park along the access road. The manager met them at the door and—*thank you, Harry Houdini*—one of her vacationing roommates had left her keys behind. While she hadn't expressly committed them into Christina's care, who would mind if she borrowed them for a while?

Devon tagged behind her, saying little. She was suddenly mortified at the state of her digs. With roomies away on a summer backpacking trip across Europe, she hadn't been as diligent with her share of the cleaning chores. "Just try not to look at the mess."

"It's still nicer than mine," Devon said.

She turned, thinking perhaps that he'd want to get going. But he lingered, checking out the books and CDs on the shelves in the living room.

"I don't want to keep you. Whatever your aunt's making smelled really good."

"I can eat later. Oh. Right. It's been a long day for you. I should let you relax."

True, she ached for a glass of wine and a shower and a voodoo doll shaped like Ralph, but Devon looked reluctant to leave her alone, which was kind of sweet.

"I'll be fine," she said. "Really, Doctor Lancelot."

A hint of a smile played on his lips. "Tell me where you sit."

"Huh?"

He cocked his head, reminding her of his nephew. "When we talk on the phone. Where do you sit?" In response to her skeptical eyebrow, he added, "I'm just trying to get a picture."

"In my room. In the window."

"May I see?" He peered toward the three bedrooms.

Christina couldn't figure out if he was flirting with her or trying to take her mind off her horrible afternoon—maybe a little of both. What the hell, she'd let him have this one. She tapped a finger against her lower lip. "Only if you can guess which one's mine."

He quickly scanned the open doorways and pointed to hers.

"Too easy," she said. "You must have caught that from the unmade bed and the general air of 'I don't give a crap.'"

"Actually, from the window seat. And this is only an assumption, but the extra keys you found tell me that at least one of your roommates is away for an extended period of time. In my experience, most people tidy up a little before going on a vacation. They might not leave the, um, garments hanging over the chair."

She snatched the pink bra and panties and tossed them into the closet. "Sorry, I…left in a hurry."

"Hey"—Devon lifted his palms—"I wouldn't have even let you into my apartment, so no judgment here."

"You sure I'm not holding you up?"

"No. Not at all. As long as I'm back in time for Small Lee's bedtime story."

"That's sweet." Christina grinned, loving the mental image of the so-serious Dr. Devon Park reading *Green Eggs and Ham* or whatnot to a little boy in footie pajamas. "I've been wondering, why do you guys call him that?"

The gentle pleasure in his face faded as his gaze slid from hers. "He's named for my brother."

Her breath caught as she recognized the pain behind those words. "Oh, I'm sorry, I didn't mean to…"

He shook his head and gradually some light came back into his expression.

"Anyway, thank you." She gestured to her outfit. "For this…and for everything."

Devon sighed and made an attempt at a smile. "I'm just glad we were there."

23

Devon set his book facedown on his chest then stretched an arm behind his head and closed his eyes. The sun warmed his skin as the breeze off the river cooled it. The grass cushioned his back; the birds twittered; the leaves overhead whispered their secrets. He couldn't remember a time when he'd felt so balanced, so in harmony with the world around him.

"You don't add up, Doctor Devon."

He turned his head toward the voice and opened his eyes to Christina, sitting cross-legged on a sunny patch of ground a few feet away. The afternoon heat had also been making him drowsy, so maybe he hadn't understood. Was she mocking him?

"Such a polite and serious young man. Sorry for everything, holding doors open, and you would slay dragons and leap tall buildings to protect your family and rescue maidens in distress." She shook her head. "But that…whatever that is on your arm tells me a different story."

He'd almost forgotten about the tattoo, and that distressed him, because it was like he was forgetting Lee. Something must have shown on his face that amused her. She smiled, pushed herself up, and grabbed three brightly colored scarves out of the mound of juggling gear he'd helped her carry to the park. The neighborhood was dodgy and with the magician still gone, he'd offered to accompany her to her practice session. He was only surprised that she'd accepted. And that she'd procured another lock-picking device, seemingly out of thin air.

The scarves fluttered in the breeze, sparking his curiosity. With the fluidity of a harem dancer, she tossed them up one after another, and began slinking around them as they floated down. He wasn't aware that you could juggle with scarves, but as she continued, he realized it made perfect sense. The movement entranced him, as did the sunlight painting her hair and the slender contours of her body, and he sat up so he could see better. The story of Scheherazade came to mind. As well as the dance of the seven veils and men seduced to their doom. He imagined his toes tucked up to the edge of doom, teetering on the precipice, and his heart beat faster, waiting for what she'd do next.

"It tells me you had another life." When again he couldn't find the words to answer, she added, "It's okay. I had one, too." She bade him rise and enter her circle of floating silk. He got to his feet and stepped forward. The colors swirled as she danced, a shiver racing through him when the silky fabric brushed his skin. Then she nodded toward his arm. "Show me?"

Blood thundered in his ears as he rolled up his T-shirt sleeve; she caught her scarves and his voice cracked a bit as he said, "It keeps going, up over my shoulder."

"That's kinda hot. Were you trying to impress a girl?" Silence and the dip of his Adam's apple lifted her eyebrows. "A boy?"

"No." Although that wasn't exactly right. "Well. Sort of." He longed for her to resume her practice, but he felt beholden to explain. To hide his past would mean deceiving her. "Can we sit?"

"Sure." She curled down next to him, beneath the tree, and offered him a bottle of water from her bag.

He picked at the label, not knowing where to start his own Scheherazade tale, so he told her he'd been born in Seattle, to a Korean mother who cleaned office buildings and an American father whose job required so much travel he was rarely home.

"Because we often had to fend for ourselves, I tried to be a good influence on my younger brother." He swallowed hard but in that moment didn't feel strong enough to say Lee's name aloud. "And then he got the bright idea to join a neighborhood gang. I went along to look out for him. Two for one, right?"

Christina drew a finger along the mark, making his insides quiver. Her touch was slow, gentle, oddly innocent in its curiosity, and so different from Gwen's. "Artistic for a gang tat."

He couldn't help a sad smile as he remembered how Lee, at all of eleven, had refused the tattoo, arguing with the tenacity of a pit bull that he was their true brother in his heart and therefore didn't need some cheap brand to tell the world he belonged. Devon, sixteen then, needed the identification. He needed it to help him protect Lee.

"Sorry. I distracted you," Christina said.

You have no idea. He caught the comfort of her scent, an intriguing mixture of rainy day breezes and Rosabella's kitchen, before letting the years out. Never had he felt so old and so young at the same time. "I was almost eighteen when my father died in a car crash."

A small sound eased from her throat, half whimper, half sigh, and she pressed a hand to his arm. He hadn't intended the admission to earn her pity, but he appreciated the gesture and was glad she didn't feel the need to rush in with the usual things people said.

He steeled himself to continue. "Destroyed is too tame a word to describe what happened to us, and my mother, after that. She'd become a ghost, unaware of her surroundings, unaware of us. And my brother…he was skipping school, getting into trouble, each time worse. My aunt and uncle took us in, but that didn't help his behavior. For him, life was about the here and now and his loyal band of brothers." He paused. "And a girl."

"Ah," Christina said. "There's always a girl. Was she in the gang, too?"

"No." Devon evaluated which veil to remove next, but the pretext, the juggling of versions of the truth, became too difficult to manage, and he gave up trying.

He told her all of it—about the pregnancy, about chasing his brother to Seattle. And the shooting that ended his life. "I wonder sometimes if I'd worked harder to convince him not to go back…" A scull skimmed by on the Charles, the unified articulation of the rowers' arms always a minor marvel to him. "Well, it's useless to think such things now. He's gone and the girl gave the baby up for adoption and my aunt and uncle are raising their child."

He'd never said it like that before, so big and bold. It scared the crap out of him, yet it was liberating in a way, like he'd shed a yoke holding him to the ground.

"So young." Her voice was barely above a whisper. "That sweet little boy."

Christina drew herself up straighter and turned to face him as if performing her own examination. Finally, she said, "So I guess medicine was the obvious career choice."

"Yeah, right?" Relief washed through him that she understood, at least that part, but his smile felt weak and shaky. "Like on some level I thought if I could save other people, I could bring a bit of him back. But it's also why I'm considering leaving." He dropped his gaze. "Christina, I haven't been honest with you."

She was silent for a beat.

"I'm actually—" He glanced up and the empathy in her hypnotic green eyes made his train of thought skip off the tracks for a second. "I'm actually on leave from my residency."

"Explains all the days off. I was starting to wonder."

"I needed a break."

She shrugged. "Don't blame you one bit. That place must be nuts."

The beginnings of a headache pulsed behind his eyes, and he didn't want to talk about himself anymore. "Your turn."

"Are you going back?"

"I don't know yet."

"Because…" She twirled a finger around a few blades of grass. "Well, maybe in a less completely insane environment, I think you'd make an awesome doctor."

"You think?"

"You remembered Rosa."

"She was pretty memorable."

"You were in the ER, but you remembered that she'd been in Cardiac Care."

"I wanted to make sure she was okay."

"You were in a rush and you helped me find the cafeteria when I was losing my mind."

"You looked stressed, and I was going there anyway."

"You bought me coffee even though the cafeteria lady told me you never do that."

He blushed. "It felt like a nice thing to do for someone."

She gave him a slow grin. "Doctor Devon's a *playa*! Shame on you, taking advantage of poor sad girls visiting their sick loved ones."

"I wasn't! I wouldn't…"

Christina laughed.

And they sat for a while, watching the sculls on the river, the birds swoop and dive. The tension thrumming through his head ebbed, and the sun dappled through the tree and sparkled on her hair. He would have liked to stay there all afternoon—hell, he could have stayed there all week, caught in her web of silk and her magical scent—but eventually she said she had to go and so did he, really.

When the trolley stopped near her building and he said goodbye, he realized as he watched her walk—floating, almost—across Commonwealth that she hadn't told him what had happened to her. What previous life she'd survived.

It made him sad to think that a girl so beautiful should have had to suffer anything. But maybe she'd held back her end of the bargain, her seven veils, on purpose. Maybe, like forgetting a small token at someone's house after a visit, it meant she wanted to return.

24

Colliding storm fronts slapped New England with a forecast full of lousy weather, and Christina had never been more grateful. She needed a break. Yes, it was the height of gallantry that Dr. Devon had offered to tag along and carry her things earlier that week, all six-foot-something of Boy Scouty goodness. And he was pleasant enough company. But almost every time she'd looked at him, she damned near started crying. For his family, of course. But it was more than that. This thing with Ralph pushed everything up to the surface—every emotion, every battered nerve ending, every argument she had with herself for sticking with him versus bolting. Not only was he still MIA, but to keep up with her practice she had to go to his place, break in with a new set of lockpicks she'd charmed out of Herbert, get his stuff…it was like ripping open the wound all over again.

She called Devon on the landline in her apartment—fortunately she'd memorized the phone number—and told him what he'd probably guessed already, that she couldn't juggle outside in wind-driven rain. He agreed, and they chatted for a bit, but when he asked her how she was doing, it was all she could manage to keep from dissolving into tears. She hustled him off the phone before she totally lost it. Because she knew he'd be nice and sympathetic and maybe even offer to come over. Christina couldn't have that. She refused to become someone else's responsibility. Especially not his. Life had dealt him a crappy enough hand without pressing her cards on him, too.

It rained for a second day, and a third. The sun came out around noon on the fourth day, but she figured the grass would be too spongy and she was too damned tired after a tough shift to go through all that rigmarole, so after Rosa piled her up with leftovers, she went home. A quick session of stretching revived her enough to think about doing laundry, and as she was gathering up a load, the phone rang.

"You're late for rehearsal, Teen."

She wished he could see the hate beams she was sending him.

"Seriously. Is that all you have to say to me?"

He didn't even hesitate. "Are you coming over, pretty please, my beautiful assistant, without whom my days are mere shadows?"

She snorted and winged a pair of yoga pants into the basket. "Ha! What book did you steal that from?"

"Made it up myself, God's honest truth."

"Do you have any idea what I've been through?"

"Missing me? Must have been horrible."

Maybe he'd been clunked on the head one time too often. She'd love to give him another. "How's this? Last Saturday? When you took off without me and left me stranded in the middle of Faneuil Hall, in costume, *with my purse in your truck*?"

"That was *your* purse?"

She dropped a few expletives and then he said, "Yeah. That. Okay. My fault. Totally my fault. I flew off the handle. Seemed like you wanted time to cool off and I had to go back to the Cape, and I guess I thought you had your purse and some of the day's take—"

"Not a red fucking farthing. Or my phone. Or my keys."

Silence, then: "Can I make it up to you?"

"How? Turn back time and *not* strand me in the middle of downtown Boston wearing barely enough fabric to make a bathing suit?"

"I said I was sorry. Look, just come over so we can talk about this."

"No." She wasn't ready to stop being angry. And she was starting to think about the note again. Sweet cheeks. Maybe it was old and maybe it wasn't, but the idea of it still pissed her off.

"How did..." He swallowed. "How did you get home?"

"Like you care."

"I do. I was having a bad day. A really bad day. I know, I overreacted, and I shouldn't have taken it out on you. I'm horrible. I'm a horrible person."

Cripes.

Before she could reply, he spoke again. "Can you please come over? I promise you won't regret it. I have something to show you."

She rolled her eyes. "And that's not going to make it go away, either."

"I didn't mean that...well, I did. Sort of. But, Teeny, we have to practice. How long are you going to stay mad at me?"

"As long as I fucking feel like it."

"We can use that," he said.

"What?"

"Oh, it'll be great! I saw Harry Anderson do it. Hysterical routine. You can play my angry assistant and you're trying to take it out on me."

"Awesome. I'm already in character."

"Perfect. Stay right there. I'll pick you up."

"Don't you dare come over here!"

"Ha! Love it. See you in a few."

With a loud groan, she hung up.

* * *

When she opened the door, Ralph was standing in the hall, clutching the handles of her purse in his mouth like a puppy. Cute wasn't working. Then he set her purse on the coffee table and attempted to sweep her, Hollywood-style, into his arms. Christina backed away, glowering.

"Still in character, huh?"

"Do you have something to say to me?"

He stretched out his hands in surrender. "I'm sorry. Again. You have a blackboard? I'll write it a hundred times." He stroked a finger through the air as if scrawling. "Reynaldo the Magnificent is sometimes not as magnificent as he thinks he is."

She cocked an eyebrow. "Really, sweet cheeks?"

The hesitation spelled his doom, the recovery not fast enough. He swallowed, his smile dissolving. "She told you?"

Although Christina's chest ached from the effort not to scream and her fists tensed with a desire to clock him, she mustered all her reserves to stay cool. She leaned close enough to smell his extra-minty toothpaste. "Yeah. She told me everything."

He looked to be divining exactly what she knew. Which was nothing more than the fact of a lascivious note of newer-than-she'd-hoped age in his kitchen and the confirmation that the third party was female, but she felt no compunction to let him off her hook. Then he rubbed the back of his neck. *Getting a little warm under that collar?* "But we have a show," he said.

"Yeah, that sounds like so much fun. Prancing around in the courtyard of Quincy Market making you look good when you've been—"

"It's over," he said. "With her. Because—"

"None of my business." She shoved out a palm. "You know, maybe you were right. We should have kept this professional."

He winced as if she'd socked him in the gut. "Teeny…Christina. It's over because, well, I felt like a total shit. Because I kind of have…*feelings* for you."

"Feelings?" She fumbled back a step. "Oh, my God. Don't you even—"

"I kind of…think I…sort of…love you."

Christina wheeled around and glared. *Fuck you. Fuck you for saying that now. Like I'm the fucking back-up plan? Sweet cheeks kicked your ass and I'm on deck to make you feel better?* "So…what? You say that and I'm supposed to fall at your feet?"

This new blow seemed to have fallen decidedly lower on his anatomy. A wobbly smile started yet failed. "Well…yes."

She stabbed a finger toward the door. "Out."

He hesitated, and she swore she saw the gears spinning around in his head, still calculating a way to make her forgive him. He, apparently, had nothing. But Mr. Magnificent stopped, one hand on the knob. "We do have a show, by the way."

"Forget it. Like I said. No way I'm standing up there with you tomorrow, two hours of smiling until my face hurts when all I want to do is—"

"I can't do the street act without you. You know that. But you don't get it—"

"What? Tell me what I don't get." *And why the hell is he grinning like that?*

"Okay, forget tomorrow." He paused to examine a fingernail and exhaled a measured sigh. "Just as well. You'll probably be off your game, anyway."

Damn him for playing that card. "You still owe me from last week."

"Check the purse."

She did. A wad of bills sat in the center pouch.

"Teen—"

"Shut up, I'm counting." All there.

"Teen, will you just listen for a second?" His voice fell, and in her peripheral vision, she saw an arm reaching toward her.

"Don't. Don't even try apologizing anymore. Yeah, all right, I'll do the Marketplace tomorrow, only because I don't want to disappoint the kids who want juggling lessons. But I'm one wrong move from walking away from this whole deal, so you'd better choose your next words extremely well."

"We have a show. A real show."

She blinked in confusion.

"Yeah," he said. "It took some doing, but I made it happen. Just like you wanted."

"An actual show. On an actual stage, where actual people will pay more than a few bucks in your hat to actually watch us perform?" It still meant she would have to work with him, but knowing they had a goal, a direction, that influential people might take notice—

"Well, it's a showcase," he added, "in a lineup of other acts. But it's a firm date. A contract. A venue. With stage illusions. I got my guy building one right now, should be at my place in a few days. I wanted to show you a copy of the blueprint. It's a spin on the standard Houdini's Metamorphosis. There's this box, see, and you get inside…"

She froze. *Oh, crap.* Getting it together to work with Ralph was one thing, but could she really do this? Images flew into her head and she couldn't push them away fast enough—the heat, the darkness, the cigarette smoke. The blood on her fingers from tearing at the metal latch she couldn't open in time. Her father's hand, shaking in the strain to reach for her, before going still.

"…and when we get to the final reveal, it's gonna be so amazing. Hey. Teeny. Are you getting this?"

Christina tugged herself back to the present, but she still saw her father's open, unseeing eyes. She gulped hard.

Ralph reached for her arm and, perhaps thinking better of it, withdrew. "This is it. What we've been working for. And if we get the right people there, it'll be everything I promised you. This is gonna be huge."

She forced a smile. *Huge. Yeah. Can't wait.*

25

When Christina stepped into Ralph's living room and saw the wooden box, about as big as an old-fashioned packing crate, cold sweat broke on the nape of her neck. A bead slithered down the back of her leotard and she swallowed.

Ralph grinned, indigo eyes twinkling. "Gorgeous, isn't she?"

She pulled in a deep breath. *Mind over matter, right?*

"Get in and I'll show you how it works." When she didn't move, he sank a fist into one hip and said, "I'm not gonna stick swords into you or anything. At least not yet. I need to see how you fit."

She eyed the illusion. A rather grand name for what it really was: at its essence, a latch-lidded box, constructed from planks and two-by-fours. "Uh, all right." She circled it as one might a tiger in a flimsy cage. "And the lid comes off how, exactly?"

He crooked a finger, drawing her closer. "Voila." With one swift move, he lifted the cover and spoke with the intonation of a carnival barker. "And there you have it, one not-quite-standard Houdini's Metamorphosis." He dropped to his regular voice. "Now get in the box."

Avoiding the rough spots in the wood and a couple of screws that poked through from the other side, she lifted one shaky leg over the edge. "Your guy sands these down, right?"

"Of course," he said, much too quickly. "This is just a prototype he let me borrow so we could check it out. Ours is being finished as we speak. It should be all smooth and pretty by tomorrow."

"Okay." She hoisted the other leg over, telling her heart to stop flailing around in her ribcage. "I'm in."

He gave her a patient smile and gestured with an index finger that she should get down. She knew she was supposed to do that but couldn't make her body cooperate.

Ralph cleared his throat. "While I still have my original parts?"

Christina sank to her knees. At his direction, she lay on her right side, her back pressed up against one of the walls, her head upon her elbow. Her tiny body had little padding, and it didn't like where wood met bone.

"I guess I fit." She peered up at him. "Are we done?"

Chuckling, he shook his head. "You crack me up. 'Are we done?' Hardly. You are just the right size. But the bigger barrier is the one between your ears." He pointed to his head and began to pace slow circles around the box, his hands clasped behind his back. "That's what we need to train. So I'm going to simulate the approximate amount of time you'll be stowed away before the transfer."

"How long do you usually—?"

"Ah. No more questions." He rested a palm on the corner of the lid. "Stage simulation starting...now."

The cover came down with a bang. She let out a squeak and a curse as she started, knocking an elbow against the wood.

"Bruising is an occupational hazard," came the muffled voice. "But you know that already."

Dark. So dark. So small. So...silent. Christina's heart thudded in her ears. She squeezed her eyes shut. *Is he gone? Is he just going to...leave me here?* Her breathing came out in short bursts that echoed in the small space. The cold sweat started again. On the back of her neck, behind her knees.

Then pages rustled, while slow, measured footsteps circled her. "Once upon a time, a princess lived in an enchanted kingdom..."

From the depth of her panic attack, she felt her eyebrows scrunch together.

Fairy tales?

I'm fucking dying in here and he's reading fairy tales? Dude's got a wicked strange way of marking time. How long do I have to stay in here, how long—?

Then the images invaded, no matter how hard she tried to slap them away. She saw her father's smile as he joked around with the audience, right before he put her inside the box. So tiny. Smelled like cigarette smoke. Ten-year-old Christina gasped for air, the weight of all his expectations, all his dreams for her, crushing down on her small chest.

Couldn't find the latch.

Couldn't save him.

"But an evil wizard wanted the kingdom for his own..."

Christina pressed a palm between her breasts as if it could keep her heart from flying out, as if it could soothe her lungs into pulling in more than a few shallow gulps.

Shit, I'm gonna have to do this. On stage. How the hell am I going to do this?

Calm, she said to herself on a shallow inhale. *Cool,* she thought as she let it out.

Repeat.

After a few rounds, the meditation started working. But the ebb of her panic allowed physical sensations to rush in. The initial meeting of bone on wood was now discomfort. A few sentences later, pain. The tip of a screw pressed into the meat of her right calf. As he talked about a castle and a spell placed upon the princess, she focused on the metal spur, letting it loom as huge as a spire, and reclaimed her yoga breathing, timing it with the cadence of his voice. First her shoulders relaxed, and then her upper back, sending the flow of relaxation down to her toes. The pain faded. Only when he said, "And they lived happily ever after, the end," did the ache return, along with an itchy tingle that ran down the outside of her left leg. When the lid opened, she eagerly grasped the hand he offered to help her out.

* * *

He'd been right about the bruising, and a week into rehearsals, Christina had not gotten over the alarm of peeling off her clothes and seeing the topography of discolored blotches on her pale skin. Yoga outfits and a respectable waitressing uniform covered a multitude of sins, as her grandmother would have said.

A small price, she told herself in front of the mirror each night, for the knowledge she was quickly gaining, for the payout her amended contract promised. Positioning her body correctly and enduring the dark, close sub-trunk weren't even the biggest challenges. Most of the hard work—and most of the damage—came in the transfer: the quick, terrifying moment when coordination and reaction time meant everything. He'd be standing atop the box. At his prompt, she'd release the trapdoor from inside. He'd drop down as she swam up, effectively making it look to the audience as if they'd magically changed places. They'd clunked elbows, knees, foreheads. Since the sweet cheeks episode, Christina had nixed any physical contact with him that went beyond these unavoidable mishaps during practice, but some days it was damned hard to ignore how good he smelled, and to quash the temptation to skim her hands along his hard muscle as his body brushed hers.

At one point, he grabbed a length of black silk and some aluminum rods and hopped onto the lid of the box, straddling the open trapdoor. While he set up a contraption that looked like a circular shower curtain, he explained. "This is just for practice. We'll have a slicker setup on stage. It'll be weird at first, basically doing a blind transfer, and we'll end up kind of swimming over each other like salmon. It can get confusing. I drop down and try not to land on you. You're the salmon going upstream."

"Salmon," she repeated.

"Yeah." He grinned at her. "And since I'll have to supply a little manual assist, I'm issuing a blanket apology right now for hands landing in bathing suit areas. We are professionals, after all, and these things happen." He raised an eyebrow and added under his breath, "Although lately, not often enough."

* * *

Christina knew something was wrong, because Sal met her in the break room right before her shift. He never came into the break room. He'd also never offered to pull her an espresso, and he was doing that, too. Her shoulders stiffened. "Rosa. Is Rosa okay?"

"Fine, she's fine. Just out getting her hair done." He waved a hand, but the set of his brow spelled trouble. "Can't I get a little coffee for my second-favorite girl once in a while?"

Second favorite? "Uh, I guess. Except you never do."

"I can start. Sit, sit." Sal lifted a weak smile and rounded the doorway into the back corridor, and within seconds, the espresso machine began gurgling and spitting.

She was still trying to figure out what the hell was going on when Sal returned, balancing a tiny cup on a tiny saucer and setting it before her so daintily you'd think he was serving Sophia Loren.

He'd even put a little orange twist in it. Was she being fired? She lifted her gaze from the garnish to Sal's face and back again.

He shrugged, and wouldn't meet her eye.

"Sal. What's up?"

His big, rough fingers drummed on the table. "Maybe you noticed…one of the other waitresses taking a lot of time off lately?"

Holy shit. "Desiree. Sal. Is she all right? Is she sick? Is there anything we can—?"

"We had to let her go."

That shut her up. The pieces started flying together in her head: how slow they'd been since Rosa's heart attack, Desiree's fretting about comping orders, Sal's rants about competition. She cleared her throat and took a deep breath. "Tell me straight. Are we closing?"

"Not if I have anything to say about it."

"I know we've been slow, but she's a good waitress, the customers love her—"

His mouth pursed. "A little too much, the customers love her."

She cringed and hid her face in her palm. "Oh, jeez, don't tell me." Christina owed her job in part to a waitress who'd been caught servicing a customer in the restroom and was summarily fired. That didn't sound like Desiree's style, though. She wouldn't even clean the restrooms, let alone—

"It was the busboy—"

"Desiree was with the busboy?"

Sal shook his head. A sheen of sweat had formed on his neck. "The busboy saw them leaving together."

"Leaving the restroom?"

"No. In his vehicle. Doing things that should be saved for the moonlight."

"Hell. That's hardly a crime. If you fire every waitress that lets a customer, uh, pick her up, nobody in America is getting fed."

He didn't respond.

"Wait. I'm *involved* with a customer. Is this a wholesale policy change? Should I be worried?"

Sal's jaw tightened. So did his fist on the table. "I won't have this, this…conflict in my establishment." He slashed a hand through the air between them. "When she confessed to it, I had no choice. I didn't see a way to set the schedule so you'd never work at the same time. That meant it was you or her. And you're practically family."

A different set of puzzle pieces began coming together in her mind, and color raced up her cheeks as she crowned herself the world's biggest sucker. All that sick time just happening to fall on days Ralph was out of town? After Ralph discovered air freshener and cleaning his apartment, probably to cover up the smell of her gross perfume? *Sweet cheeks* had been her friend, her shift partner, sticking her cleavage right in her face! *And Ralph's, apparently.* She rose, blood rushing to her feet, gripping the edge of the table for support. "I should get to work, I guess. Especially now that we're down one waitress."

"Christina." He stood, reaching for her. All the muscles in her body tightened as she stepped back from him. Nothing would be more humiliating in this moment than a pity hug from Sal. "Rosa and I will always be here for you. Rosa said, especially if you want to talk..."

Rosa knew? Doubly humiliating.

"...and I know it's a lot to ask, but we'll need your help to train the new girl. She starts tomorrow."

She sucked down the espresso like a shot of tequila, wishing like hell it were, smacked the cup back to the table, and flashed him her big-tip smile. "Sure, Sal. Anything you want."

"You're...okay?"

"Peachy keen. Never better." She grabbed her apron from the rack and tied it so tight one of the strings ripped.

"I could get one of the other girls to come in, if you want to take the day, we'd understand."

"Enough. Please." She reined in her suddenly too loud voice because it was Sal, for one, and for two, she was getting a raging headache. This was going to be the longest shift in the history of time. And Ralph? He was in Cape Cod, working off the last of his commitment to the job, which made him the luckiest man on the face of the earth.

Because, for now, he got to keep his manhood intact.

But she wasn't making any promises what would happen upon his return.

* * *

Ralph's latest trip to the Cape was proving to be a hat trick of blessings in disguise, for the health of his reproductive organs and her sanity. Prior to her little meeting with Sal, Christina had been struggling with how to get past his betrayals and stay professional during all those transfers in the dark. Learning about Ralph and Desiree just made that task a hell of a lot easier: nothing motivated her to succeed as well as pure, unadulterated anger.

Meanwhile, she tried not to think about either of them.

The sun baked her hair and the air lay dense over the city, but getting outside felt like she was breathing with new lungs, touching the world with new fingertips. She dialed up Pink on her iPod and juggled her scarves, a sensation as close to pure joy as she'd experienced lately, while Devon leaned against the tree, reading *Anna Karenina*, occasionally sneaking less-than-subtle glances at her until he finally set the book in his lap.

"Interesting choice," Christina said. "I'd have pegged you for avant-garde poetry."

"I like the classics."

She nabbed all three scarves out of the air and waggled them toward Devon. "Wanna try?"

"They look easier than the beanbags." He got up and brushed dirt from the seat of his jeans.

"They are. I'll show you." After a while, though, she began overheating from the exercise. "Wait a sec. But don't freak out."

She pulled off her long-sleeved T-shirt, revealing the tank underneath and a mess of bruises on her arms. His eyes narrowed.

"Apparently you missed the memo about the not freaking out part."

He said something that sounded like a mixture of Korean and English.

"It's from the box." To his still-alarmed expression, she added, "We're doing a show. A real show. With stage illusions. You know, like David Copperfield?"

"And getting hurt is part of it?"

"Well, it's not the goal, but accidents happen. Hopefully fewer the more I learn. It's going to be a decent show. There are some other acts, too. You should come, bring Lee Song. I can get you tickets." His gaze dropped to the grass before his feet, then back up to her face. "There will be more for him to watch than just the mean magician."

The mean magician who'd been screwing around right under her nose. Before Christina could stop it, her lower lip began to quiver.

"Hey…" Devon pressed a hand on her arm, obviously trying to avoid the larger bruises.

"I can't…"

He folded her into him, and she laid her head against his chest. "Christina." His voice floated between them.

"God, stop it." She pushed back, brushing the tears from her eyes. "Stop being so nice to me. You don't know me, I—"

"You're right. I don't know you. But I'd like to. If you'll let me."

"I'm a fucking broken mess." She attempted a smile. "There. That's fact one on Christina Davenport, formerly McNulty." Feeling suddenly too exposed, she grabbed for her T-shirt and tugged it over her head. "Fact two. The guy who claims he loves me has been sleeping with one of the other waitresses from the restaurant."

He opened his mouth but before he could say some kind, sympathetic thing that would probably make her cry again, Christina said, "Sal let her go. I don't know how the hell I'm going to keep waitressing there. It was totally mortifying."

Devon surprised her by staying quiet. Her pulse thumped in her ears and her palms were sweaty and she grabbed three stage balls just to have something to do. He said her name again, which made her feel soft and weak, and she cursed under her breath. The balls fell to the grass, and she pressed her hands to her face. She expected arms around her again, the heat of him closing in, and it would be such a guy thing to do, such a Devon thing to do. Maybe she would have liked that, latched onto him like a life raft in a storm. She heard his breathing, the sound of several attempts to communicate, the whisper of his approaching footsteps in the grass. Finally, he said, "And yet you keep working with him."

The words punched a dagger through her heart. Lately, whenever Ralph set a hand on her or made one of his corny jokes, she wanted to pound the smile from his face. And the act required a lot of corny jokes and a lot of touching. There wasn't much room to maneuver through the drop hatch in the box. Now, no matter which way she spun the Desiree situation, playing Mr. Magnificent's assistant would only get harder. "I don't expect you to understand, and I really don't want to explain, but I have to see this through. It's not just about the money. I have to prove something to myself."

"No." He shook his head. "I do understand."

"Right." He'd lost his parents, he was helping to raise his dead brother's child, and there was a gang tattoo on his shoulder. "You would."

The soft fingers along her jawline took her by surprise. No one had touched her so tenderly and gazed at her like that since—well, maybe ever. *God, don't fuck this up by kissing me. Please don't.* But he just said, "I would. And I won't make you talk about it. But at some point, maybe you will. Because you promised me a story, Scheherazade."

Everything about him in that moment made her smile. "Are you flirting with me, Doctor Park?"

His blush curled her toes into the soles of her sneakers. "Um. A little, maybe? I'm sorry."

"I'll attempt to forgive you." She handed him the scarves. "Now, let's get to work on that hand-eye coordination."

* * *

Ralph's heel had landed square in her gut on the last transfer attempt, and she was still rubbing the pain out.

"The costume." He glared as he waved a hand. "It's not working. It's too slippery."

She groaned. "I thought that was the point! So there's nothing to hang us up when we switch places."

"It's working too well. I gotta have *some* friction."

She bit back a comment about the waitress he'd been having friction with. Two weeks. Two weeks and she could kiss this dickhead goodbye.

"Maybe we need a break." Christina wondered if arnica was good for internal injuries as well as the bruises all over her skin.

"No time," he said. "Let's rack it up again."

She shoved out her wrists, waiting for the cuffs. Of course he'd insisted on the classic Houdini style. Her, handcuffed, tied in a sack, locked in the box. He'd jump on top, presto chango, then she'd be out and he'd be inside, cuffed and bagged, to the delight of the astounded audience.

But all they'd been getting so far were more bumps and bruises and hands landing in bathing suit areas—mostly his hands.

"This is all in your head, Teeny." He slapped the cuffs on, not being as careful with her as he used to be.

"My head? My head? I'm not the hundred-and-seventy-pound guy who keeps landing on his assistant's stomach. Maybe you'd better work on your aim instead of worrying about my head."

"No. My aim is fine. You're not getting out of the way. I'm starting to think you're doing this on purpose. That you're trying to sabotage us."

"You're delusional. I'm as out of the way as I can get, and I barely take up any space. It's your big-ass foot that can't get out of the way."

"Okay, time out. Yeah. Okay. I made a mistake. It's over. Yell at me all you want after the show. But right now we have a job to do and that's not to look like amateurs in front of an audience of important people who could hire us for major work. Now, I need for my assistant to honor the contract she signed and not act like a total bitch."

Fuck you. Fuck you fuck you fuck you. She wished for the superhero ability to kill people with her eyes.

He rubbed at his temples. "Look. I'm sorry. Let's just try it again." After a long moment, he said, "Idea. I'll go in the box, you get on top. Maybe a different perspective will help."

"But I don't know how to get into the stuff. We've never—"

"Don't worry about that part yet. Let's switch it up and see."

Whatever. Maybe he was right. She slipped out of the cuffs. He stepped into the box and she clamped the hardware on his wrists, then pulled up the bag and cinched it over his head. His voice was muffled by the burlap. "When I get down, put the cover over me."

She did. And as she climbed atop the box, he called out the sequencing cues. She counted down the seconds he'd need to free himself.

"Almost ready, Teen." He chuckled. "Kinda like the idea of this. Angels raining from heaven."

"Shut up. I'm trying to concentrate."

"Maybe there's something else you need. It's always helped you concentrate before."

"Okay, seriously. Seriously, you just said that to me."

"You know, maybe the Desiree thing happened because she was nice. Maybe it was a pleasant change from someone who always acted like I was some kind of asshole."

If the clown shoe fits…

"Okay, flipping the hatch in three…two…one…"

Maybe she was distracted. Or maybe it was intentional. Because when the wooden hatch dropped, both of Christina's feet landed squarely on Reynaldo the Magnificent's groin.

* * *

"Why so glum, chum?" Herbert gestured to the stool across the counter. Christina set down their coffees and collapsed in an ungraceful heap.

She recounted last night's rehearsal with Ralph, including the arguments, the miscues, the injuries—the accidental ones as well as the blows she gave him sort-of-on-purpose—while leaving out the sleeping with Desiree part. She scrubbed a hand across the back of her neck. "You've gotta be able to trust someone whose job is basically to keep your skull from hitting the floor, right?"

Alarm passed over his face. "Theoretically, yes. Did something happen?"

No. She couldn't tell him. But clearly he had a clue that something was wrong. "Every other minute I think about quitting. Just telling him to shove his stupid act and his stupid jokes and his stupid face."

"Maybe you should."

She straightened up, tossing a questioning glance across the counter.

"Yeah." He pressed a fist to the glass. "Bail out. Give up." He let a dramatic pause fall. "Let him win."

Her jaw tightened. Herbert smiled and snagged a deck of cards from beneath the counter. Shuffling them up, doing rudimentary things. "When's the show?"

"Two weeks."

"Big cut?"

She shrugged. "Not a ton. Backers are gonna be in the house, though. Could be a great opportunity, if we pull this off."

"If *you* pull this off, you mean."

"Right. Can't kid a kidder."

"Pick a card," he said.

Pick a card, Chrissie.

She snagged one, and for a few moments she watched his hands, his light touch, and her mind reached back to the days of spying on her father and his friends as they tried to impress each other with their tricks. *What the hell*, she thought. *Why not just ask him and have this over with?* "Herbert, did you know a magician named McNulty?"

His hands stilled. "Rings a bell. Old-school type. Decent guy…" Herbert's eyes sharpened into hers and then softened. "Well, I'll be dipped. You're Ed McNulty's girl."

He said that part as if learning she had a terminal disease. Words wouldn't come out of her mouth.

Herbert hitched an eyebrow up ever so slightly. "Davenport—?"

"My mother's maiden name."

He nodded. "That hair color. It suits you better. Flashy, but not too. Nice on stage, no doubt."

She reached up, smoothed a hand through her curls.

Cards fluttered again in Herbert's skilled fingers as he dealt out three piles. "Picking up the close-up again, I'd understand. That gets in your blood. But I don't know how the hell you got back in the box after…"

"Please. We always called it 'the incident' in my house. When we talked about it at all. I thought changing my hair and my name would be enough to help other people forget. Maybe I convinced myself it would help me forget, too."

"God, I'm sorry." He shook his head and gave her a sad smile. "But you got some kind of moxie."

"More like some kind of desperation," she said. "I got stuck, Herbert. My life was going nowhere. I realized that the day I auditioned for him. If we get some work from the showcase maybe I can eventually parlay that into my own act. I'm getting the chops. I'm learning the big illusions now." Her shoulders sagged. "Who knows, maybe I did this all wrong. Maybe what I really need is a fresh start. A place where I'm not Ed McNulty's girl."

After giving her a long appraisal, he tapped his temple but said nothing.

"Yeah. I know. Wherever I go, there it is. My own personal horror movie." Christina watched him work the cards while their coffees went untouched. "I mean, don't get me wrong," she added. "I wanted to be Ed McNulty's girl. I loved him like crazy. But I don't want to keep letting one horrible night own my ass for the rest of my life. I can do this. Keep working with him, do this trick. You can do anything for just two weeks, right?"

"Mind over matter," Herbert said. "Just smile and pretend it don't matter. That's misdirection at its essence, really." He flourished a queen of hearts. "Is this your card?"

"Of course it is." She considered a sip of coffee but suddenly the aroma repelled her.

"You do realize that if Reynaldo the Ridiculous hurts you, he'll never work in this town again. Plus I'll get my hombres together and beat him with a sack of oranges."

"Thank you."

He drummed his fingers on the counter and tilted his head. "Tell me, Christina Davenport. How do you feel about New York?"

"As a general concept, or in a more specific fashion?"

"I got some friends there. Not that I can afford to lose a customer, but if you're serious about that change of scene, I could make a few calls."

26

Two faces turned when Devon came through the door of the condo on Rowes Wharf. "You look very handsome, joka."

Auntie shot Devon a grateful smile, and instantly he knew the struggle it must have taken to get the boy from cargo shorts and T-shirts into clothing more suitable for his first day of kindergarten.

"It itches." Lee Song pouted and pulled at the collar of his starched white shirt.

"And your hair looks good, too." Devon turned to Aunt Mimi. "How'd you get the cowlick to stay down?"

"She sprayed gunky stuff on it." Another thing his nephew apparently didn't like.

"I think it might be time to start going to Uncle's barber," Devon said.

Auntie knelt before the young man and smoothed down the still-smooth hair. "You're probably right. Lee Song, how about this weekend we go to Uncle Doctor's barber, get you a real grown-up haircut?"

The boy gave an obedient nod. "But I want it to look like Uncle Dev's. He has way cooler hair. Uncle Doctor's is too short."

Devon shrugged at his aunt. She shook her head in reply and muttered a Korean phrase that meant "troublemaker," then straightened and reached for her small charge's hand. "Come. Time to go. We don't want to be late."

It was a day Devon had been dreading all summer. He'd been dropping subtle hints about school into their conversations, about all the children he'd meet and the teachers who deserved his respect. But lately Devon wondered if the advice had been for his own benefit as well, to prepare himself for losing a piece of his nephew to the world. Without speaking, the three headed down Rowes Wharf and up Atlantic Avenue, a few blocks into the North End. The closer they came to the school, the heavier Devon's legs felt. His mind, too, was weighed down by how the leave-taking would occur. Would there be tears? How would he handle that? Auntie's eyes were already reddened, and the splash of cold water she'd probably given them earlier hadn't helped much. He slipped an arm around her shoulders, and she squeezed him back, then ruffled his hair, nodding toward Lee Song, who was skipping a couple of steps in front of them.

"You were that small once," she said, close to his ear.

"Hard to believe."

"I have pictures to prove it." Her voice broke. "Of both of you."

He remembered the pictures. Even then, Devon was the good boy and Kwang Lee was the troublemaker. An instant ago, and a lifetime. Funny how Auntie Mimi had just called Devon the troublemaker. He smiled at that, as if he held another piece of his brother along with the mark on his shoulder and the memories.

They'd arrived at the school. "You have your lunch?" Auntie asked.

Lee Song nodded, his attention drifting toward a few other children filing into the building, welcomed by friendly-looking grown-ups.

"And our telephone number?" Nod. "A clean handkerchief?" Nod.

"May I go in now, please?"

Auntie, eyes moist, caught a quick glance from Devon before turning back to the boy and saying, "Of course you may."

And he ran. Without a look back, he ran to those children, those smiling teachers. Devon's chest tightened. His nephew hadn't even waved. It had seemed so simple for him to run off toward a future that would include them less and less. But part of Devon reveled in that. Lee Song Park was ready, and eager, and would probably do wonderful things with his life.

He heard a soft snuffling to his left, and wrapping an arm around his aunt, he walked her home. He stayed through two cups of coffee and a stroll into his past. Auntie took out Small Lee's baby pictures and continued expressing her disbelief about how quickly the years had sped forward. Occasionally she excused herself to the bathroom and cried. He was surprised that he didn't feel so much sadness, although his thoughts did reach out in kindness and empathy toward his aunt. And Uncle Doctor, even though he was busy with work, had expressed his wistfulness about this day. During one of her crying jags, Devon's phone buzzed with a text. It was Gwen. She wanted to get dinner that night.

Can't, he wrote back. *Family.*
Blow them off.
First day of kindergarten.
Right. Forgot. Rain check.
And she was gone.

As he tucked the phone away, he wondered how she could have forgotten. Then he realized that it was perhaps the first time he hadn't apologized to her for being unavailable.

* * *

During the walk back to his apartment that evening, Devon decided it was unreasonable of him to be angry with Gwen for not remembering the significance of the day. Her training required supreme dedication and sacrifice. And the fact of that filled him with a sudden sense of loss, of disconnection from the world. Gwen had her residency. So did his roommates. Small Lee was now in kindergarten. Auntie and Uncle were now guardians of a school-aged child and soon would be diving into the activities that required. Christina had her magic show and would probably be very successful, because of her hard work and skill.

And he was on pause.

He wondered again what it was that he missed about his former life. Certainly he lacked a feeling of usefulness at times. But he might have missed that had he walked off a job as a plumber, a teacher, or a surgeon-in-training. He hadn't been fond of the pace of the ER, the paperwork, the sudden craziness. Working with people, though—he missed that. He remembered one child who'd come in earlier that year with a broken arm. It was a difficult set, and the child, a bright little boy a few years older than his nephew, had been allergic to nearly all painkillers. While the ortho on call tended to him, Devon distracted the young man with a series of Small Lee's favorite elephant jokes. The parents had been so grateful they made a massive contribution to the hospital. The money went toward desperately needed improvements to the pediatric center, but Devon was interested in more intrinsic rewards. He'd brightened what could have been a very traumatic experience in a young life and provided a family with comfort.

Then he wondered if this disconnection had more to do with his personal situation or the fact that it was September. From kindergarten through medical school, September had meant the start of a new year of learning. Yes, even though his first year of residency had begun in July, fall still brought the same enthusiasm, the same sense of possibility.

Now he just had…a new month.

He climbed the two flights to his apartment and let himself in. Thomas the Tank was half asleep in front of a televised soccer game. "Evening, mate." Eyes drooping, he nodded toward Devon's bedroom. "Visitor."

Gwen didn't want to wait for a rain check? He smoothed his hair and reached for the doorknob. First he saw the strawberry blond curls—then the bruise on her cheekbone.

27

"Did you get that checked out?"

Christina shook her head and winced as he gingerly palpated the bone. It didn't feel broken. But it looked plenty painful. His belly tightened at the prospect of causing her any more discomfort. "I'll get some ice."

He began scrambling out, but she said, "Wait." He did. "It's not what you think."

An automatic response came to him, that it was none of his business. But was it? They might not have known each other for long, but surely they'd crossed that threshold to the point where what happened to her mattered to him. As a fellow human being, as someone who wanted to be her friend, as a man who could not abide the idea of some cowardly jerk hurting a woman. And if she didn't want his help, why was she in his apartment? He wasn't even aware she knew the address.

"I *think* you look like you need ice." *And a new partner.* He sucked in a breath before saying the next part. "And you realize that in my profession, if in my judgment I consider you the victim of domestic abuse, I'm sworn to direct you to services that can provide help."

Her eyes flashed, and even that seemed to hurt. "For one, I'm nobody's fucking *victim*. Two, you're on leave."

He sighed and sat next to her on the bed. "Can you tell me what happened?" In response to her hesitation, he put up his hands. "It doesn't leave this room."

The illusion was brilliant. Devon had grown well aware of her strength and tenacity, yet in that moment, to him she appeared as fragile as a dragonfly's wing. Whether it was something she projected or something he inferred, he didn't know.

She bit at her lower lip. "I'm...claustrophobic."

Before his mind got much beyond thinking that the condition wasn't such a big deal, she continued. "Like freak out, panic attack, hyperventilating think-I'm-gonna-die claustrophobic. For someone who wants to do stage illusions, this kind of sucks the big one."

"There's therapy for that—"

"Yeah. Been there, done that, got the T-shirt. Didn't help."

"Is that how you got hurt? A panic attack when you were rehearsing?"

"Do you know Houdini's Metamorphosis?" He shook his head, and she explained the box. "That's what we're doing at the showcase. We couldn't get it right, he was being a total ass, I couldn't stop thinking about him and the waitress and—well, I kind of landed extra hard on a sensitive part of his anatomy. Yesterday, I swear it was an accident. Today, it was kind of accidentally on purpose."

Devon did his damnedest not to wince.

"Okay, I felt bad about that. Not one of my finest moments. But then…" She gulped. Even in the dim light of his room, he saw the color drain from her face. "He locked me in."

* * *

Christina's throat tightened, and she knew she'd need some long, slow breaths before she could speak again. Devon encouraged her to take her time. He nipped out and returned with an ice pack, which he held so gently against her cheek she could barely feel the pressure. The television in the living room murmured the play-by-play of the soccer game; his roommate snored on the couch; street noise filtered in from outside. The concern in Devon's eyes damn near made her burst into tears, so she turned away and curled into herself. The ice shifted to accommodate her movement; his arm wrapped around her from the back, and he even smelled safe—a mixture of baby shampoo and his aunt's cooking.

Then she remembered. "First day of kindergarten. Did Mimi cry?"

"Like Niagara Falls."

"And Uncle Devon?"

"Not as much as you'd think."

She began to laugh, but the pain made her wince. "Did he have fun?"

"Fun, yes. Today my nephew discovered a whole new world to charm. We may never see him again."

"He adores you. I don't think you'll be free of him that easily."

"One can only hope."

Finally Christina said, "So…yeah. I'm a cautionary tale in Boston's magic scene, did you know that?"

"No."

She told him about her father's club. How she'd loved to learn new tricks and practiced everything he taught her.

"I'd had my heart set on being a magician in my own right. But after the divorce, I would have done anything to cheer him up. He needed an assistant for a talent show. It was at a really big outdoor venue. Started out okay, then…" She sucked in her lower lip again to keep it from quivering. "I was in the box, and I felt…vibrations through the panels. Like the stage was moving. I found out later some of the crew was setting up for a big act behind us. One of the spotlights wasn't secured well enough to the scaffold. I heard metal creaking and then…I couldn't help him." She attempted to swallow the lump from her throat. "I was stuck in a box illusion, couldn't pull the latch, couldn't get out. The spotlight landed on him and the tent caught fire and he—died. Right on stage. I was only two feet away."

Devon's voice cracked as he said her name, and she couldn't stomach the silence that followed.

"Hence the claustrophobia," she said. "The nightmares. The therapy. And a whole lot of other fun and exciting things."

The ice slipped from her cheek and, with a finger on her chin, Devon prompted her to turn toward him, and he examined her bruise. His eyes, steady and soft, roamed it as he said, "Well, you did promise me a story."

"Not quite *A Thousand and One Arabian Nights*, is it? Anyway, after I, uh, expressed my disapproval with my partner, Ralph came roaring back, leaped out of the trunk, and shoved me inside. I must have gotten the bruises then."

"There are more?"

"Probably." She'd blocked some of it out in the stress of the moment, apparently, but now she was starting to remember the sequence of events. He swore at her when she landed on him. Sensing his impending explosion, she tried to leap out the hatch. He grabbed her legs and yanked. She hit her face on the way down. He pinned her beneath him, his voice a low rasp in her ear.

"If you ever pull a stunt like that again…"

Nearly smothered by his weight, fear had rocketed through her.

"Get off me!" She rammed an elbow backward, connecting with his jaw.

"You little bitch." He rolled off, grabbed the cuffs, and snapped them around her wrists. They were stage cuffs, so she would have been out of them easily enough, but it gave him enough time to jump out and lock the cover down. And the hatch. "And you can stay in there until you cool off."

* * *

The way Christina described the impact to her face made Devon concerned about a possible concussion, so he begged her indulgence long enough to let him turn on the light and run through a few basic neurological tests. Her memory, vision, hearing, balance, reflexes, and coordination seemed normal. She didn't have a headache, wasn't dizzy or nauseated, and didn't remember passing out. All in all, a trip to the trauma center wasn't indicated—as if she would have gone—but he did think it wise to observe her for a few hours, just to make sure.

He made her a cup of tea because according to Auntie it fixed everything, then he grabbed a fresh ice pack and went back to his room.

Thomas the Tank was still snoring.

When he sat on the bed, she lowered her gaze, hugging one of Devon's pillows to her chest as if it could keep her from drowning. He held the ice to her cheek until his fingertips grew numb.

Christina's pulse thrummed through the pale skin of her throat. Then it began to race.

"I think he knew," she said. "I think somehow he found out I was the girl in my father's act. And thought that would give him a way to control me." The pillow dropped to her lap and she turned to him so quickly he pulled the ice away. "Holy shit, what if that's true? And he uses it as some kind of bargaining chip to get me to stay? He could spread the word that I freak out on stage. No one would hire me!"

Her breaths came in hitches and gulps. "Hey," he said. "Hey, slow down. Breathe. Yeah. Like that." He matched his breathing to hers, keeping it long and slow, hoping she'd stay with his pattern.

Inhale for seven, hold for four, exhale for eight. After a while, she seemed to relax.

He weighed his next words carefully. "Christina. It's okay to leave. If it's too painful for you, nobody in the world would hold it against you for not staying with him, for not continuing to work with him."

Her voice was so faint he barely heard. "*I* would." And then, a little stronger, "I hate being such a damn weakling, but do you mind if I stay here tonight?"

"I was going to suggest that, to make sure you're okay after that injury. But there's nothing weak about not wanting to be alone."

"I don't mind alone," she said. "I'm just not ready to deal with him yet. And he can't find me here."

Since Thomas looked comfortable on the sofa, Devon thought about putting her in the big man's room, but it smelled like old pizza and gym shorts, so he spread his winter quilt on the floor and gave Christina his bed, along with a couple of ibuprofen.

Sleep claimed her quickly, and he was glad for that. He watched her chest rise and fall, the faint illumination from the streetlamps outlining her sharp, small features, leaving her bruised cheek in shadow. Something fierce and hot burned inside him to hurt the man who'd done this to her. But physical violence went against everything he stood for, everything he'd hated about the world Lee had fallen into. Uncle had been right. He'd tried to get them both out. He'd given Devon an opportunity, taught him to value life. God knows what might have happened to him if he'd stayed in Seattle in the first place, or what could have occurred if Devon was walking alongside Lee and Billy that night. They might both have been lost. Maybe in the end he could have done nothing to save his brother. But as he watched Christina's slender form curled in his bed, he pledged to do what he could to protect her.

The ferocious heat of anger changed in that moment, made him want to pull his whole family to his chest and keep them safe. He grabbed his phone off the desk and tapped out a text to Auntie: *Please hug Lee Song for me tomorrow before school.* He paused a moment, staring at the screen, blinking the blur of tears from his eyes, then added: *Love you guys. I don't know where I'd be if not for you and Uncle. And I know I don't say this enough, but thank you.*

Devon hit send and set the phone down, thinking she'd get the message in the morning. But seconds later, the small chirp alerted him that she'd replied: *The pleasure, my dear Dae Soon, is all ours.*

28

Ralph.

Christina woke with a jolt, gasping for breath, heart pounding like a jackhammer. She groaned in relief when she realized the crush against her back and growl in her ear was just a memory. But the left side of her face throbbed like a mother, and that was all too real. Then she remembered running to the subway. She'd huddled in a corner of the car, searching for Dr. Devon Park's address on her phone. Cambridge, he'd said. Central Square. Mass Ave and Hancock...

She glanced over the edge of the bed. Devon slept on his back atop a puffy quilt, no blanket, wearing only a pair of sweats, one arm crooked over his forehead. He'd told her he was twenty-six, but damn, he looked so much younger, too young to carry that ink. The black snake crawled up his bicep and over his shoulder, the forked tongue licking at the notch between his collarbone and his neck. It was kind of hot, and she could look at worse things in the morning than a cute doctor with his shirt off, but she wondered if he ever thought about having the tattoo removed. It had to have been horrible to bear a permanent reminder of the way his brother died. Maybe it had become invisible to him, like anything else. She didn't think about her various battle scars every day. She wouldn't be able to function otherwise, if she were constantly bombarded with every crappy thing that had ever happened to her. Perhaps it was the same for him. How could he have worked in the emergency room and helped save lives if every waking moment he thought about the ones he couldn't save? The baby dying in his arms, that must have broken him wide open, torn down the walls of everything he'd been trying to contain. No wonder he was having doubts. It sucked, because he was exactly the kind of person who should be a doctor. She couldn't imagine having that much responsibility in her small hands.

She recognized the peep of her phone and fumbled around the nightstand for it. The message was from Ralph, wanting to know where she was. Dammit, he was like some kind of spy. Where was he getting these phones? Unless he'd had one all along. She couldn't discount anything about him at the moment.

Glad she'd turned the tracking off, she replied, *Yeah, I'm ok, thanks for asking.*

Sorry I had to do that.

You locked me in a fucking crate, you fucking Machiavellian cretin!

Big words from a little girl. So unprofessional.

Bile burned in her throat. He thought that was funny? She stabbed at the buttons. *Again. Locked. In. Fucking. Crate.*

Again. Sorry. I let you out, didn't I? Can we move on, please? Where are you? I'll pick you up, we need to work on the act.

Not today. She peered over at Devon and admired his mussed, silky hair and the slope of his abdomen, then added: *I have plans.*

What? You're not on at Rosa's today. What is more important than this?

Christina crinkled her brow at the screen. How did he know she'd begged off sick? She'd only texted Sal a few hours ago. Was he checking up on her?

Before she could answer, another message popped in from him: *You have a contract.*

Which I will honor, because I'm a fucking professional. I'll see you tomorrow. But today, plans.

And after she hit send, she turned off her phone.

The force field radiating off her must have disturbed Devon, because he shifted in her direction and opened his eyes, blinking so softly it punched her in the gut.

Oh, God. Don't you dare fall in love with me, Devon Park. Bad, bad idea. How did he come out so good after everything he'd been through? Was it some kind of trick of positive thinking her therapists had failed to teach her? Or was that just his nature?

"Did you sleep well?" he asked.

"Mostly." She didn't want to talk about the nightmares. Smothered in the dark.

"Pain?"

She touched her face—not her best idea. "I've had worse. Kind of stiff, though." She stretched a leg out straight and rotated an ankle.

"From the impact, probably. Everything tenses up. You see a lot of that in car accidents, falls. It'll peak tomorrow, most likely."

"Awesome," she said. "Can't wait."

He got to his feet, grabbed for a T-shirt that had been slung over the back of his desk chair. "Drink lots of water, that helps. Moist heat. Our shower is decent, and not too disgusting, considering three guys use it. And some gentle movement to expel the waste products from the muscles. Maybe we could go for a walk up to Harvard Square, get lunch?" He dropped his gaze. "Unless you have stuff to do. I'm sorry. That was kind of presumptuous of me."

She shook her head. "I've given myself the day off."

"Okay." He rubbed the back of his neck and shot her a little crooked grin. "Probably a good idea to rest up, anyway. Coffee?"

"That depends, Doctor Devon. Will the caffeine help or hinder the healing process?"

He studied her cheek, a corner of his mouth falling. "Data conflicts," he said. "But right now it will keep my head from exploding."

* * *

Even with the coffee, Christina slept on and off through the morning and into the early afternoon—adrenaline crash, most likely, from her trauma. He didn't want to disturb her or leave her alone, so he found quiet things to keep himself occupied. It was his day to fetch Small Lee when school let out, and then he'd promised Auntie he'd watch him until she returned from bridge club. When Christina woke next, at about two, he gave her the option of staying behind or coming with him. She put on her sneakers.

Rain threatened, and Devon grabbed his umbrella before leaving the apartment, but he and Christina made it to Small Lee's school well before the skies broke and just as the doors spilled children into the courtyard. Shirttails already flapping free of his pants, Small Lee broke into a run when he saw the two of them waiting.

"It's the juggling lady!" Before Devon could correct him, the boy added, "What's wrong with your face? Did you fall down?"

"Lee Song. We don't say—"

"It's all right," Christina said. "I had a little accident, but I'm okay. Your uncle even checked to make sure."

"And we call her Miss Christina, by the way," Devon said gently.

"I'm sorry. I forgot."

"We're good." Devon rested a hand on the boy's shoulder.

"Now let's go home before we get drenched."

"Is Miss Christina coming with us?"

Devon fought a grin. "I already asked her. But tell you a secret? I think it would be an extra special nice thing if you invited her, too."

Small Lee spun toward her. "Please, Miss Christina, will you please come home with us? We'll have snacks and play blanket fort. Please?"

Christina hooked up an eyebrow.

"We always play blanket fort when it rains." Small Lee skipped circles around them as they walked. "It's fun."

* * *

Devon rummaged through Auntie's cupboards, eventually deciding on tomato soup and grilled cheese sandwiches.

"Impressive," Christina said as he set the platter on the table. "You can check for broken bones and whip up culinary delights."

Lee Song's nose wrinkled. "Cue-linn..."

"Cu-lin-ar-y," she said. "That means things about food."

Devon slid a glance in her direction, mouth tight, eyebrows scrunched together. She'd seen a similar expression on his nephew's face when he concentrated hard on his juggling lessons. The doctor didn't say much while they ate, but he didn't get an opportunity—Lee Song chattered away about school and what he'd learned and the friends he was making.

When they'd finished eating, Devon put the dishes in the sink and asked the boy to go wash his hands. After he'd left the room, Devon pulled Christina aside. "If you don't want to play, that's fine."

"If it's his favorite rainy-day game—"

"Let me tell you about his favorite rainy-day game. We set up all the furniture and cushions in the living room like fort walls and drape blankets across the top. If you're someone who would prefer not to be in a situation like that..."

"Oh." Christina's gaze dropped, then she offered him what she hoped was a brave smile. "Well, I can always sneak out the back door and tend to the arsenal, right?"

* * *

Small Lee liberated the cushions from the sofas and chairs while Devon moved the furniture. He contemplated a modification of their usual arrangement, a rough circular pattern, to accommodate their guest. Auntie would have a fit if she saw the condition of her living room, but he could handle her. Especially if he helped clean up afterward and fixed her a glass of iced tea.

As he repositioned one of the pair of tall ladder-back chairs they normally used as tent poles, he grinned at the amusement tilting the left side of Christina's mouth. "You really never did this when you were a kid?"

She shook her head. "I guess we weren't a blanket fort house. My mom would have had three levels of conniptions if I started messing with her precious interior decorating. You'd think we were royalty or something."

"Faster, we have to build it faster!" Small Lee demanded.

Before Devon could remind his nephew about being patient, Christina jumped in to help, following the boy's instructions. He worried that she might be overexerting herself following her injuries, but woe to the person who told her what she could and couldn't do.

Soon all the cushions were arranged against the furniture and the blankets draped over the tent poles. And in the sanctity of their fortress, lit by one of Auntie's table lamps, they shared stories and jokes, read and colored, for most of what remained of the afternoon.

Devon snuck glances at Christina—while she did funny character voices when she read, negotiated the sharing of crayons, and told his nephew how much she'd loved going to Faneuil Hall when she was a little girl. She seemed fine. No overt claustrophobia symptoms, no panic attacks. But he'd seen how well she could mask her emotions. There was a bit of make-believe in magic, and Devon surmised that she was as good as the jackass she worked for, if not better.

"And how is Miss Christina liking our spectacular fort?" Devon asked.

"It's a wicked awesome fort," she said. "And cozy. In a nice way. It's like learning a really cool secret about the two of you. Thank you for inviting me, Lee Song."

"You're welcome," he said, and asked for another story.

* * *

Auntie's mouth fell open when she walked in. Devon met her eye and held a finger to his lips. The blanket roof had mostly fallen away; they'd all agreed that it was too warm and stuffy to be completely covered up. Lee Song had fallen asleep in Christina's lap during *If You Give a Mouse a Cookie*, and, only a few minutes earlier, she'd snoozed out as well, the angle of her head giving Auntie a clear view of the contusion. Devon wiggled free and took the shopping bags and umbrella from his aunt's arms, then gestured that they should speak in Uncle's office. When he closed the door, she rounded on him, eyes blazing.

"Has this been reported? Is she still with that…that sociopath?"

"She had an accident during rehearsal," Devon said. "I didn't feel anything beyond a contusion. Although I suspect his lack of care with her contributed to the injury."

"You aren't taking Lee Song to his shows any longer, is that true? The poor child had nightmares for a week."

Devon still felt horrible about that. "He misses her juggling lessons, though. She's very good with him and he adores her. If I'm not around and he needs a sitter, perhaps you and Uncle would consider her."

Her brow furrowed and she slashed the air between them. "Not if *he* comes within a hundred yards of this building."

He held up his hands. "Preaching to the choir."

She eyeballed him a moment and gave a knowing nod. "And how are things with Gwen?"

Matching her gesture, he said, "If you're asking because you want to know if I have feelings for her, then the answer is that I'm a grown man, and I don't have to tell you."

"Dae Soon." His Korean name was soft on her lips and she smoothed the hair from his forehead in a decidedly maternal way that made his stomach pitch. "Please be careful."

* * *

Mimi invited her to stay for coffee after dinner, but Christina felt she'd already worn out her welcome and the Park family living room.

Plus the way the woman kept lifting those uber-sympathetic glances to her cheek made her squirmy. After declining as graciously as she knew how, after promising a special juggling lesson to make up for his no longer being allowed to come to their shows, Christina said goodbye to Lee Song. Devon offered her a lift home, but Christina insisted he do no more than walk her to the best place to catch a Green Line train.

It had stopped raining by then, and swirls of fog danced around their feet. The sidewalks glistened, streetlights glinting off them. She regretted leaving the Rowes Wharf enclave; Mimi Park was a good and caring person, Lee Song totally adorable, and Devon was a decent guy; she hadn't seen too many of them lately. He didn't require endless explanations, and she felt safe with him. Although that could simply be a hangover from the comfort and medical care he'd given her. Once she returned to her own nest, she'd probably toughen over again.

Too soon, they reached the Haymarket stop. "You have my number?"

Christina resisted the easy joke about "having his number" and simply nodded.

"Be safe," he said, and for a moment looked like he was thinking about kissing the top of her head. Something a brother would do. She might have appreciated that. Christina liked the idea of having a brother. A guy she could tease and have fun with. Who would beat up bad boyfriends and snarl down bullies and always have her back, no matter what kind of stupid shit she got up to. She could damned well take care of herself and had for years. But how different, how odd, and how nice it would be to have someone watching out for her—well, other than Herbert, who was a kick-ass, stand-up guy but old enough to be her grandfather. With Devon, it felt more like being cocooned in couch cushions and soft blankets and solidarity.

"Blanket fort safe," she said, and he grinned at her before saying goodnight. As she gingerly took to the stairs, the stiffness beginning to peak earlier than he'd predicted, she felt his eyes on her until she was gone from his view.

After transferring to a B train at Kenmore Station, Christina settled into an empty twofer, feeling suddenly exhausted, and pulled out her phone. She'd kept it off on purpose, to let Ralph know she was not a piece of his equipment, that he could not make her dance in his palm like his handkerchief.

When she turned it on, she was not surprised to find a lack of messages. That was Ralph telling her he had no interest in her games, because he only wanted to play those of his own invention. To reassure herself that she indeed had Dr. Devon's number, she checked her contact list. And there he was. No name, no picture. That first day Ralph started going on about Houdini and the lottery numbers, she wrote it off as a quirky magician thing. But the first time he'd vanished on her, she'd circled her wagons. Maybe she was being paranoid, but she'd changed the password on her phone and stitched a secret lining in her purse.

Which had been in Ralph's truck for five days. Her stomach constricted and she shivered. Hand shaking, she dug into her purse, pushing aside her wallet, hairbrush, lipstick, wiggling a finger into the opening. She let out her breath when she discovered her bounty, as it were, was still intact. Her emergency escape plan: forty bucks, a credit card she rarely used, and the ripped piece of handbill upon which Devon had written his phone number. The money would be more than enough for cab fare to get to the owner of those digits and the credit card for whatever she might need afterward. She stared at the slip of paper. Something wasn't right. Had she folded the corner like that? Or had Ralph? Was this a signal to let her know he'd been there? Her stomach pinched tighter. Immediately she began punching buttons, pulling up the credit card company's website and putting in her password for the card. No new activity. And would she like to sign up for white-glove protection service, insuring her credit card purchases against breakage or loss? No, thank you.

As the T was nearing her stop, she sent a text to Devon reminding him to be safe, too. She hesitated a moment and then added "please." If Ralph had seen that number, she had a horrible feeling Dr. Devon Park would need more protection than a blanket fort could provide.

* * *

When he returned, Auntie had already given Small Lee his bath, but there was still time for Uncle Devon to read bedtime stories. After two, the boy settled into gentle slumber. Devon tiptoed out, leaving the door open a few inches, the way his nephew preferred it, and met Uncle Doctor in his study.

"He's had a busy day," Uncle said.

"Me, too." Devon sank into the comfortable chair next to Uncle's desk, where he'd been perusing medical journals online.

"So I heard."

Of course, Auntie had told him; the hardness of his glare made it plain.

"You're playing with fire, Dae Soon. You know what happens to people who play with fire."

Devon rolled his eyes. "If you'd seen that contusion, you might have done the same—"

"Yes, you're probably right. But she attracts trouble. I don't want trouble around my family. We've had enough."

Devon's fingers tightened into the padded arms of the chair. "As if I would put my own flesh and blood in danger."

"Intentionally, no. But you're a young man with a lot of time on his hands. As I'd feared, it's an invitation to lazy thinking."

He bolted from the chair toward the door.

"Dae Soon, stop."

But Devon kept going. Out of his office, down the stairs, and into the night.

29

Instead of the solitude Christina had hoped for upon her arrival, she was greeted by a tumble of suitcases and backpacks in the living room. And a note from her world-traveling roomies: *Home! But going out to meet friends. Sorry about the mess.*

She sighed. At least their second wind bought her time to chill out before two pairs of alarmed eyes questioned the state of her face. And the kitchen. And their plants. Her muscles craved a hot shower, but something more primal shouted that impulse down. Not that Devon's mattress hadn't been comfortable, but she needed the sanctuary of her own bed. An idle thought crept in that Devon's mattress might be more comfortable with him in it, and her heart beat a little faster.

Stop that. We have work to do.

Christina pulled the blanket over her head, trying to replicate the feel of that warm, sweet space in Mrs. Park's living room. It wasn't the same, of course, but it helped focus her thinking. She'd promised to meet Ralph for rehearsal in the morning, and she needed to work out how she was going to play it. Straight-up professional, she decided—the only way. No mention of where she'd gone or whom she'd been with.

And definitely no mention of what Ralph might have found in her purse.

But could she do anything about the claustrophobia? It would have to be a Band-Aid solution; she knew that. Several websites, and several therapists over the years, had warned her that it could take time. And, according to those same therapists, more money than she could afford. Yoga breathing sometimes helped. It had helped her during her first trial with Ralph. Could it help now? After what he'd done? And coming up, coupling the memory of what he'd done with performing the trick before an audience?

She needed a practical application in a controlled, Ralph-free environment. Fortunately that was only a few feet away.

Among the shoes and out-of-season storage in her closet, Christina carved out a space just large enough for her body. Her pulse galloped at the mere thought of what came next. But she had to. She had to try. A full-length winter coat waited at the ready. She pulled the door closed until the dark smothered her. Inching the coat up to simulate the burlap sack. Pressing her wrists into a pair of stage cuffs she'd bought from Herbert. Her chest tightened and her breath came in short bursts. *Count,* she urged herself. *Count to a hundred. One…two…shoulders relaxed…three…four…five…deep breath, let it out slow…*

She felt her chest opening up, and the small window of relief gave her a glimmer of confidence that she could do this, that it wouldn't be so bad.

Then something scurried up her leg. It took a few minutes to realize that the screaming was coming from her own mouth. And that among the several people yelling in Haitian from outside her apartment, one was opening her door.

* * *

Call the police, call the police. Polis. It was one of the few words Christina knew in Haitian, but she couldn't come up with the right combination to tell them not to call, other than waving her arms around and telling them no, no, no. Of course she realized how it must have looked. Shut in the closet, handcuffed, screaming, giant bruises on her face and body—of course they must have thought she'd been attacked and beaten. Finally it dawned on her to violate the magician's code and show them that the handcuffs were stage fakes.

"Look." She held up her wrists, clicked them out. "Not real."

This didn't convince them. "Please," she said. "No police. I'm a magician. I was practicing a trick." Holy lexicon. She had no idea what the Haitian word was for "magician." She should have spent more time with the women on the stoop.

"*Magicien,*" she said. It was French, and she knew part of Haitian Creole was based on French, so it felt like a decent shot.

Two of the men exchanged a dark look.

"The magician," one of them said with a sneer as he gestured toward her cheek. "*Majisyen.* He did this to you?"

Um. Apparently they'd been paying more attention to her

comings and goings than she'd thought.

"Well, sort of." She touched her face. "This was an accident. From a couple days ago." She pointed to the closet. "This, today, was me practicing part of my act. Until a mouse ran up my leg. *Souris?*" She shuddered. "At least I hope it was just a souris."

"Souris?" This started another uproar and two of the women turned on the man, who threw up his hands in defeat and promised to call an exterminator.

"Okay," Christina said finally. "Thank you so much for your quick response. It's nice to know I have good neighbors. And that apparently one of you has a key. You rock. But I think I can take it from here."

When they finally left, Christina made a cup of tea and huddled up tight in her window, watching the big curve of Commonwealth, trying to convince herself that when the rubber met the road, or the assistant met the small, airless box and the mean majisyen, she'd be able to handle herself better than this little test run. She had to.

* * *

Ralph sucked a breath through his teeth when he saw the bruise. "That'll take a lot of makeup. I didn't think—wait." He disappeared a moment and returned with arnica gel. Unscrewed the cap and held the tube out to her, then said, "Maybe I should let you do that."

She snatched it from him and stalked off to the bathroom. "Steady, chiquita, you can handle him," she told her reflection as she dotted the cool gel across her cheekbone. When she came out, two cups of tea sat on the kitchen table and he urged her to sit. It seemed so deceptively innocuous. And yet the box where he had attacked her sat not twenty feet from the table.

For a long, horrible moment, he worked his hands together. "Look," he finally said, his face unconvinced of how it should comport itself. "Some things happened the other day. We said some things, did some things. But I'm willing to overlook it and move on."

You're willing to overlook it! After you— "Fine."

"Fine." He sipped his tea.

"A contract is a contract, after all."

"Indeed it is."

"And we're professionals."

"That we are."

"Fine."

Silence balanced precariously on the smell of mold that permeated the building after a day or two of rain. It mixed with the pine scent of the box that was already jumbling up her stomach. She took another gulp of her tea to steady herself. Even the fact of Ralph breathing next to her felt too close for comfort. In a few minutes, he would be touching her; in a space that small, in a transfer that quick, there was no way it could be performed without contact, without trust on some level. She could act, right? That was part of being a magician, part of being a waitress, selling herself, selling the goods? She didn't walk away with more tips than Desiree for nothing.

Desiree. Bitch. For all she knew, Ralph was still sleeping with her. Touching her. Her skin bunched with gooseflesh at the thought. *Down. Breathe.*

"Okay." Ralph rubbed his palms together. "Ready, Teen. Sorry. Christina. Let's go."

* * *

The first time, the dry run-through, was the toughest. She kept replaying Herbert in her head: mind over matter. She let Ralph clip the cuffs on her wrists. On his cue, she stepped into the box, directly over the gathered-up bag at the bottom. She focused on her breath as he pulled the sack over her head, so she wouldn't be overwhelmed by the darkness and the stench of sweat and fear that had soaked into the fabric. A tap on her shoulder meant down, into the box, pressed against the edge. Leaving room for him to land from above.

"Okay, Teen. On my count in ten...nine..."

She did what was required of her. Out of the cuffs. Out of the bag. Readying herself to release the hatch and rise up while he came down.

"Three...two...spring!"

And after a couple of terrifying moments, it went smooth as silk, she on top like a salmon swimming upstream and he in the box, scrambling back into the bag and cuffs for the big reveal.

She exhaled the adrenaline rush of relief and smiled, more to herself than to Ralph, as he congratulated them on a good start.

If she focused on the moves, the tasks, the cues, she did well. When other thoughts intruded, she shoved them away. By the afternoon, they'd added the music, some lame power-pop from the seventies, and a little patter, which they were working to refine. That required adjournment to the kitchen and more tea. He tapped the end of his Houdini-blessed pen against a pad. Apparently the well had run dry and frustration wrinkled his forehead. Then he brightened. "Spontaneous," he said.

The word landed like a boulder in the pit of her stomach. Oh, good God. No. She could not do "spontaneous" with him now. No sudden gusts of gravity. Not when she was trying so hard to control her reactions.

"It kicked ass for us in Faneuil Hall," he said. "Let's go back to what worked. Take the street inside, so to speak."

It worked because he wasn't sleeping with someone else then, and he wasn't a major asshole and hadn't slammed her into a box and locked her in.

"I don't think—"

"We gotta sell this, Teen. If we look like a couple of stiffs out there, hell. No one's gonna remember us."

She huffed out her frustration. "Fine. Spontaneous."

It could be great. Or it could be the biggest disaster on the Eastern Seaboard.

"Great. Problem solved. Dinner?" An expression she knew well lit his eyes. He was kidding, right? The indigo heat intensified. He wasn't kidding.

"Oh. I sort of have…plans."

"Plans."

Crap. She knew she shouldn't have said that.

"Plans like, with your boyfriend. Those kind of plans?"

The gears whirred. The pen tapped. *Cool. Stay cool.* "I don't know what you're talking about."

"You were with him yesterday, weren't you? That's why you weren't answering your phone?"

"I wasn't answering my phone because I didn't want to talk to you. In case your memory is short, you locked me in a goddamned crate."

"For your own good! You were freaking out. I thought it would, you know, calm you down. Like they do to dogs."

Dogs? She sighed and rubbed the back of her neck. "Whatever. Done. Over. I just want to do this show and…" He challenged her to continue. She raised her palms in frustration as she blurted out, "Leave. Okay. Yeah. I just want to do this show and leave."

"Leave."

"Look. We have a contract; I'll honor the contract. But I can't…Ralph. This is killing me. It was fun in the beginning. We had fun, it was a blast, but now? I hate that it's come to this, but every time I look at you, I want to punch you in the face."

"That's cold, Teeny."

"Need I remind you? You. Locked. Me. In. A. Crate."

"I had to! I thought you were going to hurt yourself."

"Yeah. Good thing that didn't happen."

"I didn't think you'd fall on your face."

"Right. Because I'm a cat and I land on my feet, right?"

"Usually. Usually you do. You're very graceful."

"And I'm supposed to do what with that exactly?"

"Say thank you?"

She let out a loud groan. He was…grinning at her. "I don't even want to know what's going through your mind right now." The grin spread into his eyes. "Okay," she said. "Now I do. And I'm leaving."

"Too bad. It would have been fun."

"Goodbye, Ralph."

He pointed at her, his expression turning serious. "Rehearsal tomorrow morning. Ten o'clock. Don't be late."

30

"Gwen."

"Mmm?"

Devon turned on his side so he could see her face. "Can we talk?"

"Um. Yeah. Sure." She shoved back her hair, pulled herself up on one elbow, and ran a finger along his tattoo. "What do you want to talk about?"

He shrugged. He didn't have more of a game plan than getting her to slow down for a minute. "We just…lately we don't talk much."

"Park."

"I know. Busy."

"You know what it's like."

"Yeah, but—"

"I'm here now, so let's talk."

But the sudden pressure of that fumbled up his words. It was so much easier when they walked together, when her sharp eyes weren't challenging him.

"Any interesting cases?"

She smirked.

"What?"

"I'm not gonna be your surgery porn."

"What the—?"

"I knew this would happen. It's like your little face is pressed up to the window."

"Gwen."

"Pathetic, Park." She rolled out of bed, plucking up her clothes. "Either get back in or get out, but this halfway shit is gonna kill you. I know it's killing me." He made a grab for her arm. "I'm already late."

"Gwen."

"Gotta go."

"Stop."

She turned, buttoning the fly of her jeans. "Problem?"

"Yes, problem." He pushed himself up. "You and me.

Problem."

"Hey. I'm not on leave, okay? It must be nice to be the princeling of Boston surgery and be able to take time off, but I can't."

The words hung like the echo after a sharp slap.

"Oh, God, I'm sorry." Gwen stepped toward him. "Park. Devon. I'm sorry."

He put up a hand. "No. You're right. Go."

* * *

The front door slammed. Gwen's car cranked over after two tries, muffler like a motorboat, and she sped away. Devon lay in her bed until he could no longer hear her. Only then did he get up, dress, and begin the long, slow walk to the Newton T station, during which he dissected the corpse their relationship had become. Knowing in his still-beating heart that except for the recriminations and the blame and the drinking, it was essentially over. And probably had been for a while. So he continued his autopsy in the bar he and his roommates frequented in Central Square. Two beers later, it began to dawn on him that his reason for leaving Mass General was not, as he'd feared, the beginning of the end of him and Gwen, but a moment of clarity, of perspective about the inequality of their friendship. He'd grown so comfortable with being called upon when needed—as a handy sex partner or someone to pick up a check—that he hadn't considered any other options. He hadn't considered that he deserved better.

Thomas the Tank came in fresh off his shift and joined Devon for his third beer, and a shot, because the clarity was still breathing and he wanted to drown it.

"You remember the one about the frog?"

"The one that turned into a prince?" Thomas smirked. "Why, you got warts?"

"Frog in the soup pot," Devon said. "Frog hops into a pot of water. Thinks, this isn't so bad. In fact, it's rather pleasant. And slowly, the temperature is raised. A little warm, thinks the frog, but still nice and relaxing. Soon and without his knowledge, because the increments have been so small and he has adjusted to each, he is soup."

"How many of those have you had?"

"I don't want to be soup."

"None of us does, mate. Circle of life, though. We all end up cooked."

Devon leaned back and sighed. "No. Not the way I meant. It's—"

"Much as I'd love to stay and get all existential with you," Thomas said, "I got a girl expecting me. You okay to get back home?"

Devon nodded. "Fine."

Thomas made a slashing gesture to the bartender. *Sure, cut me off. Might as well. I'm already soup.*

He wasn't aware of how long he'd sat, sipping on a glass of water that had arrived at his table. But eventually the room stopped swirling and he craved his own bed. Devon tossed a couple of bills on the counter and headed down the block toward home.

* * *

He'd never been more relieved to have the place to himself. With Thomas off to his girlfriend's and his other roommate still at the hospital, that left him free to continue his ruminations undisturbed. He yanked off his shirt as he stumbled through the living area toward his bedroom. When he opened the door, he sucked in a breath and jumped back.

Someone was sitting on his bed.

For a second he thought it was Lee, the sense-memory brought on by the alcohol, as it sometimes did. The man-specter was about the size and shape of Lee: short, compact, features sharp in the shadows from the streetlight.

But then he knew.

"Nice ink," the magician said. "Bet it drives the ladies wild."

"How did you get in here?"

The man shook his head, making a *tsk*-ing noise. "Flimsy locks. You should know better in a neighborhood like this."

"You broke in to my apartment?"

He rubbed the fingers of one hand together. "I like to keep in practice."

"If you don't leave, I'm calling the police."

The man lifted his palms, his fatuous smile making Devon itch to fling him out bodily. "Easy, Doc. I just wanted to talk."

"Talk." Devon crossed his arms over his chest. "Then leave."

"All right. See, I have a little problem. I don't like people taking what's mine. I'm rather protective of what's mine."

Devon cocked an eyebrow. "Surely you didn't just commit a felony over three beanbags."

"It's more like a misdemeanor, but come on, a trained sheepdog could have popped your locks with a credit card. And no. This is not about the beanbags."

Devon pulled himself up to his full height, thrusting out his chest. The man answered the challenge, his thick muscles making him look taller somehow. "You don't want to fight me, kid," he said.

"That won't be necessary if you leave."

"It won't be necessary if you keep your hands off what's mine."

"I haven't…and she's not your property."

"In a metaphorical and metaphysical sense, yes. She is."

The words jumbled up in his head. "How did you even find me?"

He laughed. "God, you crack me up. I can find anybody. Anytime I want to. Until now, I hadn't wanted to. You seemed harmless enough." He paused. "Nice school your little sneak thief goes to, by the way. Bet that costs a mint."

That, he understood. Devon shot across the distance between them and grabbed the man's collar. "Touch him and die."

"Whoa, easy there. Just making an observation. A guy can make an observation, can't he?"

"Not when it involves my family."

"It's settled, then. You don't mess with mine, I don't mess with yours."

"If you hadn't injured her," Devon growled, "she wouldn't have come to me. For medical care, mind you."

"For a little bruise?"

"Her cheekbone could have been broken. Fortunately for you, it wasn't."

"Did you kiss the boo-boo better?"

"Get out of my house."

The magician let out a weary sigh as if he'd been the one detained too long. "Well. I guess I'll be moving along now. Things to see, people to do, small children to delight with my legerdemain."

"Yes. And here's hoping we don't meet again."

"Oh, you hurt my feelings. And I was just starting to have some respect for you, Doctor. Or should I say Doctor Gangbanger?"

"*Out!*" He also snarled a few choice words in Korean.

Chuckling under his breath, the magician finally took his leave. Devon slammed the deadbolt, stalked back to his room, and threw himself onto the mattress.

"What have you done?"

Devon leaped straight off the bed. Kwang Lee's voice. He had to stop drinking. "What have I done? This is your fault. Call her, you said. At least find out her name, you said."

The laugh. The laugh pierced him.

31

Stage rehearsal consisted mainly of carting the Metamorphosis and their other props from the truck into the theater, union guys working with Ralph to block out the set, Ralph telling them they were wrong, a couple of arguments, and Ralph stalking away to cool off. Christina should have left him alone. Let him talk to Harry or do whatever he did to get his bearings. But God knew how long that would take, and eleven more acts had to work out their bugs, too, before tomorrow night. He needed a dose of reality and he needed it soon.

She found him pacing in the wings and caught his arm on his return lap. "Mr. Magnificent, a word?"

"Not now."

She drew her hands back. "Okay, when? We're on the clock. You want to get bumped tomorrow? All these people backing the showcase, who could give us decent gigs, who could get us to goddamn Vegas, you want their first impression to be a guy who's a pain in the ass to work with?"

"Like it matters." He meted out a dramatic sigh and cast his eyes to the rafters. "You want out of the act. You don't want to come with me to Vegas. So it doesn't matter."

Chew the scenery on someone else's time. "Oh, no you don't. You're doing this show. We're doing this show. What comes next...let's talk about that later, okay? We haven't worked this hard to bail now." She hooked a thumb over her shoulder. "So you're gonna get back out there and tell the stage manager how you want the lighting. And it damned well better make me look pretty."

"Don't need lighting for that." The sad smile and the depth of his indigo gaze attempted to reel her in. Pathetic. She almost felt sorry for him. Okay. A little sorry for him. Damn it.

She softened her voice. "Can we...just take care of this right now?"

"Fine." He dropped his shoulders. "But the way things are going, when we get the ticket tomorrow, you'd better keep it in your purse for good luck."

"Don't I always?"

* * *

"Why can't I go see Miss Christina's special show?"

Wanting to give his nephew a less frightening answer than *I don't want you anywhere near that sociopath she works with,* Devon glanced up at the swirl of drugged-looking sea creatures in the New England Aquarium's big tank. Nothing came to him—no surprise with all he'd had to drink the previous night that his mind was limping along in second gear—so as they ascended the circular walkway, he settled for an adult cop-out. "It's going to run past your bedtime."

"Not fair," he said.

"Rules are sometimes not fair."

"When I grow up, I'll make the rules."

"Yes," Devon said. "You will. And I'm sure they'll be very good, wise rules."

"Will there be juggling?"

"No, I don't think so."

"Fire-eaters?"

"Maybe."

He pouted. "Totally not fair."

"Another time, I'll take you to see fire-eaters."

This brightened the boy some. He was quiet for a while because they'd reached the top, and Edmond, the big sea turtle, paddled over and popped his head up as if to greet them. Then Small Lee said, "Uncle Dev, is Miss Christina your girlfriend?"

A different set of totally-not-fair rules stabbed at Devon's gut. "No, we're only regular friends. Miss Christina already has a boyfriend."

"But she can have more than one! Auntie Sook has three; I heard Grandmimi say so."

"Auntie Sook is—" Devon stopped himself before accidentally giving his nephew a big word he didn't feel like explaining. "Different," he added.

"Why?"

"Well, it's just her way. Like Grandmimi plays bridge. Like Uncle Doctor reads his newspaper before he goes to work. Auntie Sook has a lot of boyfriends. Miss Christina prefers to have only one." Bastard.

Devon relished the thought of pushing the magician into the tank on a day when the sharks didn't look so well fed. What kind of cretin breaks into a person's home and threatens his family? He'd considered calling the cops after the man left, but whom would they have believed? Devon, whose breath at the time had been flammable, or the trickster who'd disappeared into the night? And might filing a report only serve to make Christina's life more difficult? He still wasn't sure what to do, except keep a careful watch on his nephew.

"Wasn't Doctor Gwen your girlfriend once a long time ago?"

Joka, you're killing me today, with the questions. He was relieved to have a new topic, but why couldn't it have been something simple, like how to perform neonatal aortic valve replacement surgery? "She was my sort-of girlfriend."

Small Lee's nose wrinkled. "What is sorted girlfriend?"

Devon grinned despite the emotion clawing up his chest. *Sorted girlfriend.* Like it was all figured out and settled. A man grew to a certain age, a certain station in life, and he was handed an appropriate partner. *There. Done. No others.* Like the penguins downstairs in their chilly habitat, mated for life.

"Uncle Dev, what is sorted girlfriend?"

"Sorry. *Sort-of* girlfriend. Another not-fair grown-up rule." Okay, he could have done a better job of that. He tapped a finger to his chin and studied the motion of Edmond's flippers while he thought of what to say. "Doctor Gwen is very busy studying how to fix people's brains. It's important work, and it's really hard to learn. You thought *I* was at the hospital a lot before my vacation? What she does takes hours and hours a day. Way longer even than Uncle Doctor is at his job."

"That's way long," Small Lee agreed.

"It is. This is why 'sort-of,' because I could only see Doctor Gwen sometimes, when she didn't have to work." Yes, neurosurgery was demanding and yes, he respected that. He'd just wanted respect in return. Maybe, like she so frequently reminded him, bearing the Park name had given him some advantages. But it also carried a heavy burden and often required him to work even harder to prove himself. It wasn't right, though, that he'd needed to keep proving himself to her. And perhaps that was both their faults.

"Is that why Doctor Gwen never played blanket fort?"

"Too busy for blanket fort."

The boy blinked up at Devon as if he'd just said there were three suns and two moons. "But we have the best blanket fort in the world!"

"I know." He smiled, remembering all the hours he'd played with his brother in the wreckage of their mother's living room when they were little. The rainy Saturday afternoon he first taught his nephew how to arrange the couch cushions and make a tent out of Auntie's spare linens, racing toy cars over the shadowed carpet and each other. And of Small Lee dozing in Christina's lap. "Best blanket fort ever."

* * *

Lee Song entertained the family through dinner with his story about the secret life of Edmond the sea turtle, and what he did when the people left the aquarium at the end of the day. Devon toyed with the leftover food on his plate, but Auntie was not fooled.

"Dae Soon, you're all right? You look flushed."

"Fine," he said. "Didn't sleep much last night."

Uncle lifted an eyebrow. One of his many diagnostic talents was detecting misbehavior on the faces of his nephews.

"I'm fine," Devon repeated. In no way, shape, or form would he tell his aunt and uncle about last night's surprise visitor. Or that he'd had a couple more beers after the man had left.

Auntie leaned closer and pressed a hand to his arm. "You don't look well at all. Why don't you lie down on the couch for a while? I'll make tea."

"I appreciate your concern, but as I said—"

"Mimi, leave the boy alone." Devon flipped his gaze toward the head of the table. Uncle was taking his side? No. The man was smirking. "The hangover is probably punishment enough."

"What's hangover?" piped the small voice next to Devon.

"You'll learn when you're older," Uncle said.

"I don't make a habit of this," Devon grumbled.

"He's just teasing you." Auntie shot a look of displeasure at her husband, then gave Devon a loving smile tinged with concern. "We know that you don't. But if there's anything you'd like to talk about…"

How he wanted to. But he couldn't. He couldn't make them worry. And he absolutely would not do anything to scare his nephew.

Uncle leveled a gaze at him. "But if it's about that girl—"

The hiss of his uncle's Korean name from his sweet aunt's lips made Devon flinch. It was about that girl. Ultimately. Probably. At least about the miscreant she allowed to touch her body, the sociopath responsible for all those bruises, all that pain. It involved Devon now, his family, and he could not let this madness continue.

"Dae Soon." Auntie's eyes widened in alarm. "Where are you going?"

"Out. You're right. I'm not feeling well, and I need some air."

32

Twenty-four hours. Twenty-four hours and she would be done with him. She already had her bus ticket and several hundred dollars in cash. She'd written a check for the next month's expenses and put it in an envelope with a note for her roommates, promising to call later and explain. She also had a plan. Herbert had come through; he knew a couple in New York who ran a real magic club. In exchange for waitressing and odd jobs, they offered a spare room and the opportunity to learn. This time, she'd be doing it right—as an apprentice, not an assistant, in a place where no one knew her as Ed McNulty's girl. Her nerves hummed at the idea of it—with excitement and dread. Starting over would be tough. The work would be damned hard, the hours long. But she'd been working her ass off and what had it gotten her so far? All tied up with Reynaldo the Magnificent in more ways than she should have ever allowed.

It had taken nearly all her mental strength to get through that day's rehearsals, keeping her emotions so tightly wound that even yoga, a long, hot shower, and a pep-talk call from Herbert hadn't helped. Every other second she tried to convince herself that running away wasn't cowardly. What she had up her sleeve amounted to self-preservation, some much-needed perspective, and a healthy dose of common sense. God knew what would happen if Ralph caught a whiff of what she was up to. And maybe, one day, from a safe distance, she could explain.

Or not.

Christina curled up in her window with a cup of chamomile tea, leaned her head against the cool glass pane, and gazed out toward Cambridge. It was miles away and blocked by many buildings, but she imagined she could see Devon's apartment. *He'll be fine.* Probably better off without her. He'd find something awesome to do with his life, marry some nice girl, and make a bunch of cousins for Lee Song. Happily ever after.

She tried more yoga breathing, forcing calm into her body and running through the plan one more time, searching for the trapdoors, the exposed angles, anything that could give her away.

Then her phone rang. It was the number she'd memorized.

"Are you home?" he said without preamble or waiting for her to answer. "I'm on my way over."

"House calls now, Doctor Devon? Are you putting this on my bill?"

"This isn't funny!" His voice climbed half an octave. "A man breaking into my apartment and threatening my family is not funny!"

Her stomach pitched. *Ralph*.

"Yeah," Devon said, and she heard him suck in a breath. "Not funny. I'll be there in ten minutes."

* * *

She buzzed him up and, heart slamming around in her chest, waited at the door. When she heard footsteps approaching, she pressed her palms against the wood as if the gesture could calm the coming storm. She'd brought this on him. Whatever Ralph had done, whatever he had threatened to visit upon this nice guy and his beautiful family, it was all on her. Unable to stand the guilt a second longer, she whipped open the door just as he raised his fist to pound on it. The last time she'd seen Devon, she'd carried home the memory of the sweet, brotherly concern on his face. Now his furrowed brow and tense jaw eviscerated her, and she had to turn away.

"God, I don't know how to—what to say—I'm so sorry. He didn't...*hurt* you, did he?"

His response was a jumble of English and Korean. She caught something to the effect that "hurt" was relative and if anything happened to his nephew, they'd find pieces of a magician in the shark tank at the aquarium.

"I think I know how he found you."

Still staring daggers at her, he reached an arm behind him to close the door as she grabbed her phone and tapped his number into a search-engine bar. His name popped up. It probably hadn't taken too much sleuthing to figure out where he lived. After all, Christina had tracked him down easily enough.

Devon almost spat the words. "He broke into your phone?"

"Doubtful he'd know how. Lock tumblers, mechanical things, he can work them in his sleep. Technology, not so much. Searching on your number is probably as computer savvy as he's ever gotten. I think…that time when he left me stranded at Faneuil Hall? He had my purse in his truck." She told him about the secret lining. And the secrets she had stashed there.

Her words softened his features until only a slight frown remained. "So I was your get out of jail free card? So to speak?"

"Wasn't that your intention?" She shot him a rueful smile. "To rescue me, my doctor in shining scrubs?"

A blush feathered up his cheeks. "I—it was an impulse, but yes, I think so."

"I'm leaving." Before he could reply, she added, "After the show." Then she explained. The theater had a back exit. She'd already planned the streets she'd turn down to get to the yoga studio, where she'd retrieve her purse, stashed beforehand in a kit locker she'd rented, and then go to the bus station.

The intensity gathering in his eyes looked like a preamble to a plea to come with her. She shook her head before he could ask, and he pressed his lips together as if he already knew how she would answer.

"Then let me help you," he said. "Somehow? I'll send money. My uncle probably has connections in New York. At least let me make sure you get to the bus safely."

So sweet. She couldn't hold back a smile of regret as she cupped a hand to his cheek, surprised at the rough stubble poking through the smooth skin.

He leaned closer and whispered her name, the sound more magical than any flourish or illusion she'd ever known, and damn how it made her want to cry over the possibility of never hearing it again. Or see eyes looking at her like she held all the cards, all the answers. She licked her lower lip in response to the quickening of his breath. What could it hurt? One taste? One kiss? One chance to lie in his arms before she left?

Christina couldn't do that to him, or to herself. It would be awful and selfish and unfair. If a guy had treated her like that, she'd want to kick him in the balls. Repeatedly. She would get on a bus and find him and kick him some more. Just on principle.

But then he said her name again. And that wasn't fair, either. It floated on such a soft breath that it melded into the pulsing of the blood in her veins and crawled through the cracks in the walls she'd constructed around her heart. He reached down to cradle the back of her neck in warmth at the same moment she curled a hand around his right—unmarked—shoulder. At the touch he gave her a shy grin, which drifted closer, his soft mouth the last thing she saw before she closed her eyes and tilted her head, awaiting him. His lips brushed hers and found their way home with such tenderness, she could think of nothing but letting him take away her pain. As her legs began to quiver, his palm slid down her back, gathering her into a circle of sweet safety, her own blanket fort.

No. She was leaving. She couldn't let this happen.

Christina pushed away, unable to chance more than a glimpse into his softening face.

"I can't," she said.

"Yeah." His chin dropped toward his chest. "I know."

His Adam's apple bobbed as he pressed his lips together and slowly lifted his gaze to hers.

"I'm sorry," Christina said. "I never thought he'd—"

"Hey." He brushed his fingertips across her jawline and she had to swallow hard not to show how badly she wanted to drag him off to her room. "I'll be fine. We'll be fine. It's you I'm worried about. Even though I should probably have not done what I just did, you'll still let me help you?"

She grinned up at him and couldn't resist brushing a hand through his hair and stealing one last sweet kiss. "Doctor Devon, you drive a hard bargain."

33

Freshly shaven and still buttoning his shirt, Devon came out of his room. Thomas the Tank, flopped on the sofa in front of a football game, mocked him with an exaggerated wolf whistle.

"No company tonight?"

"She's on late shift. So what's up with you?" Thomas squinted. "Is that...you got that fancy-boy goop in your hair? Oh, man. Gwen will laugh her arse off."

"Who says it's for Gwen?"

"Interesting. Out of the soup pot, are we?"

Ignoring the comment, Devon thought about the spare ticket Christina had given him. "Give it away or sell it or bring Mimi, whatever," she'd said. Those were her last words before kissing him again, and every cell of his body ached that he had to leave, but the scent and feel of her cloaked him like armor all the way home and beyond. Until this moment, he'd planned to go to the showcase solo. It seemed simpler, given what she needed him to do. But Thomas was awfully large, had been one hell of a rugby player in undergrad, and Devon felt no shame in asking his huge friend to tag along.

"Do you like magic?"

"Fine enough, more so if there are pretty girls involved."

Just as Devon had thought. He held up the tickets. "Well, get dressed then."

* * *

The theater was general admission; a few seats were roped off up front. Devon assumed those were for people who might be scouting the acts. He tried to find two seats on an aisle, not too far from the stage. In his head he calculated how quickly he could be up the side stairs and behind the curtain.

When they settled into their plush accommodations, Thomas scanned the program. "A regular talent show going on here."

"Something like that." He hadn't told Thomas what was really going on. Although he probably would remember Christina, and when he saw the two of them on stage, he might gather why Devon had been so keen on coming. He hated to lie but thought it a good idea to give his roommate some sort of pretext to explain why he'd be leaving at the end of her act. "Hey, there's a chance I'll have to duck out at some point. My nephew's been having nightmares, so lately we've been talking a little if he can't fall back to sleep."

"Poor little bugger," Thomas said as Devon set his phone to vibrate and stuck it in his pocket. "I'd be having nightmares, too, if my great-uncle were Park Senior. How'd you manage?"

"I don't live with him anymore, for one. And for two, he's not so bad. Strict, yes, but occasionally he surprises me."

The lights flashed and a few moments later, a man who apparently was serving as the master of ceremonies came out and told them what they were about to see.

"If this sucks, Park, you're buying shots after."

Devon nodded without taking his eyes from the stage. Maybe he had imagined the vision, a case of wishful thinking, but he thought he saw a tumble of strawberry-blond curls flash from the side of the curtain.

* * *

While the first of five comedians on the program did his thing and did it badly, Christina rubbed her damp palms together, trying to quell her nerves. Ralph, leaning against a wall backstage, winged a towel at her. She nabbed it on the fly—it smelled like the hand cream he used to keep magic apparatus from snagging on any rough spots on his skin. Then she moved closer, because it would look unusual not to be in the same vicinity as her partner before they went on. If he knew or suspected anything about what she was up to, his face held its own counsel.

"Listen to that." Ralph cocked his head toward the stage. "Crickets. Poor bastard."

"Yeah, right." Her voice cracked. She cleared her throat.

"You good?" It was what he said to her before every show, and she gave him a nod. "Spontaneous," he added.

Holy shit. "About that—"

"Too late," he said, his voice light. "We've already planned out all our spontaneity. Can't change it now."

"Where's the box?"

"It's safe. Now. But I should tell you. There was a problem."

"What kind of problem?"

"Damage. Sons of bitches, moving it around like it's Aunt Ida's hope chest." To her widening eyes, he said, "Relax. My guy fixed us up. Had a prototype he tooled together. Works fine. While you were out having your frappacappa whatever, we tested it up and down."

She was aware of a couple of the other performers staring at them and dropped her tone. "Anything I need to know?"

"Not much." He examined his nails. "This one's a little smaller."

Her stomach quivered. "How much smaller?"

"You'll barely notice."

"I gotta see it."

"No access from here. Hey, it shouldn't matter, right? Since you've licked that claustrophobia thing."

She squinted at him. Did he know? Was he faking that look of innocence?

"Yeah," she said. "No problem."

Three more acts before they went on. A singer. A comedian. And another magician. When she saw the rundown, she almost freaked. Ralph had only smirked and said, "Please. I've seen him. All sizzle, no steak. We'll look that much better by comparison."

It was of little comfort, especially after Ralph had told her about the box. *Can't think about that now.* In an attempt to calm her nerves, she paced in the small backstage prep area, making chitchat with some of the other talent, unable at one point to restrain herself from taking a peek out into the audience. It was only through the tiniest of slivers at the edge of the stage, and she knew she had to be quick about it or one of the managers would be shooing her away. She couldn't really see a whole lot. She'd imagined, years before, that when she did her first show, her father would be front and center, cheering her on. Maybe even on stage, part of her act. She knew Sal and Rosa wouldn't be out there; Rosa was back in the hospital for more tests. When Ralph thought she was out having a coffee and a chill, Christina was stashing her things in her locker at the yoga studio and on the phone with Sal, making sure they were okay. She vowed to check in later and reassured him that she didn't mind that the restaurant would be closed for a few days, because Rosa was what mattered. It twisted her guts up that she couldn't tell them more. Later, she promised herself. Then she felt a tap on her shoulder and a voice growled, "Move it, Red."

"Sorry," Christina whispered back. "Just trying to see…"

And as she let the curtain slip, she thought she saw a familiar face, and a familiar shock of black hair.

She returned to where Ralph was standing. He gave her a last-minute once-over, tugged a bit at her costume here and there. It pissed her off, but she mashed down her instinct to throw off his hands. Okay, she did it once, just for appearance's sake. She didn't want him to think she was acting strangely. Or that she was freaking out down to her toes.

"Teeny." He grinned as he shook his head. "God, you're so sexy when your feathers are ruffled. I'm gonna miss that."

"Ralph…"

He stuck out his jaw and tapped a finger against his cheek.

"Reynaldo," she said, making a little bow.

"That's better. Okay. Listen fast. A couple guys will bring the box on stage. We come out, like we practiced, all smiles and flourish. I start the patter, and we're off to the races. Whatever I do, just go with it."

Go with it. Her father had said that to her, too. She hadn't really known what it meant then. How could he have expected a ten-year-old to understand all that stuff so fast? It wasn't her fault. But that hardly mattered now. She took in a few deep breaths, closed her eyes, imagined blanket forts instead of suffocating little boxes, and the warmth of Devon's body instead of the clank of the cuffs and scratchy hug of the burlap sack. On that last thought, she tried hard not to smile. He was out there. He'd kept his promise. He'd cover her, getting her to the bus station, hopefully fast enough so that Ralph, who of course would stay for the accolades, would not couple Devon's presence with Christina's disappearance.

And then she'd never see either of them again.

* * *

She tried not to listen to the magician doing his routine. But it was hard not to. He was loud as hell, so over the top he made the chatty Mr. Magnificent seem like a mime. Ralph, meanwhile, rolled his eyes and said he was going out for some air. Christina, afraid that stepping out of the venue would also bring her thoughts out of the space, stayed behind, doing her deep breathing and running through the sequence in her head. *Intro...display the box...get prepped and put in...cover locked down tight...random audience member check...music swells...more spontaneous whatever from Ralph...*

As Mr. Wonderful was accepting his polite applause for a reveal that didn't live up to what he'd promised, Ralph stepped back in. Just a few minutes until they went on. Ralph peered from the wings as the previous act's accoutrements were cleared, giving her the play-by-play as if to comfort himself.

"...there goes the last of his set, and...we're up. This way, Miss McNulty." She froze, the muscles of her belly, held tightly by the corset, quivering. In a light voice, he added, close to her ear, "The hair color is way hot, but I can't help but wonder how you'd look as a brunette. You should consider going back to it. Might really get a rise out of Doctor Gangbanger. You make such a cute couple. Love conquering all that youthful damage; a Hallmark moment if I ever saw one. I could just cry, if I knew how." When she couldn't get her feet moving for a moment, he grinned at her and made a little shooing motion with his hands. "Come on, Teeny. Let's go have some fun."

* * *

The breath stuck in Christina's chest. When she stepped onto the stage, all her senses began to blend and swirl together: the too-sparkly lights, the lame seventies music, the applause welcoming their arrival, the MC's introduction. Her heartbeat joined in, thundering over all of it. Feeling like she was about to faint, she forced some air into her lungs. She knew she only had one choice: ignore what Ralph had said. Ignore whatever he knew, how he'd come about it, and do the show they'd trained to do. But why, oh fuck why, spring this on her right before the biggest moment of their lives? Sabotaging her performance was screwed up enough, but his own opportunity as

234 • *A Sudden Gust of Gravity*

well? By making sure his partner had that always-professional deer-in-the-headlights look?

No bandwidth to think about that now. Just do the show.

Ralph waved and bowed; she followed his lead, the silent partner. He began to tell the story of the illusion. Like a lot of his magic, the patter was based on myths or fairy tales. Most had to do with star-crossed lovers or spells of betrayal; redemption came in the reveal. But she didn't even hear the actual words anymore, not through the filter of her intense focus to stay vertical and poised, and the feeling she was about to throw up. Only the rise and fall of his voice came over her, the cues for when she was to step forward for the cuffs. When to get in the box.

"...And the fair maiden was forcibly and against her will bound..."

It was the cue to thrust out her wrists, but... *Forcibly and against her will?* That wasn't in the script. Before she could react, he caught her glance and yanked her forward, nearly taking her off her feet and, using far more vigor than they had in rehearsals, clamped the cuffs down. They were a different color—gold, not silver. Had a different shape. They felt wrong. Were they also borrowed from the prototype maker? She didn't dare test their strength, not until she was safely stowed from the audience's eyes.

His fingers crushed into her elbow. "...then, enchanted by the wizard's spell, imprisoned in a cage of her own making..."

She matched his lugubrious pace, taking heavy, slope-shouldered steps to the box. Then chanced a peek down at where the sack pooled at the bottom. That didn't look like burlap. It looked like bright-white canvas, thick and impenetrable. Her pulse hammered against her ears. When she'd reached the edge and didn't step in immediately, he gave her a shove, big enough to be seen in the back row.

Her gut clenched and she could almost smell the cigarettes and stale breath of her father's box. Ralph's hand gripping her forearm tight enough to make her bite at the inside of her lip, she stepped over the edge. And he went on about her imprisonment as he pulled the canvas up over her head and shoved her down into the small, dark space.

*　*　*

Thomas had recognized Christina from the start. As the magician pushed her toward the box, he leaned toward Devon. "Drama's a bit over the top, don't you think, with the Harry Potter stories and such? And is this all part of the act, the way that fuckwit pushes her around?"

"I presume." Though each impact made Devon want to rush the stage and pummel him.

"No wonder all the contusions. Right mess she was, the day she came by. Wouldn't let me look at her, said she wanted to wait for you."

"She said that? Verbatim?" Devon sucked in a breath when the man shoved down on the top of her head like a cop manhandling a suspect into a squad car.

"I don't remember word for word, but it was pretty clear she was warm for your stethoscope. Damned if I know why."

Devon's phone vibrated against his chest.

The text was from Auntie Mimi's number. Words garbled and spelling atrocious, the AutoCorrect making a hash of it. He got the gist, though.

A man had tried to break into Lee Song's bedroom window.

Devon jumped out of his seat. "Watch her. When the act is done, meet her backstage and do what she needs. Please," he hissed, and rushed out to call Auntie.

*　*　*

The lid thumped down loud enough to cover her gasp at the sudden noise. The rattle of the lock was the next cue, but for a second she could not make herself move. *Get out get out get out* kept flying through her mind, but it was like she was paralyzed.

She swallowed.

Breathe.

Next he'd ask for a volunteer to come on stage to make sure the lock was real and the box sturdy. Of course they both were. They didn't need an audience plant to make that determination.

She knew what she had to do. Okay. Her mind settled enough to start.

First, out of the cuffs. Then, out of the bag. Set them up so he could flip them on quickly. Back up to the side of the box and wait for the next cue to drop the hatch.

Cuffs. She flicked her wrists. Nothing. She pulled. Nothing. Heat flashed through her; sweat beaded at the back of her neck.

Fuck, why couldn't she get out of them? They were stage cuffs. They didn't need a key, just a trick to unlatch them. But what was the trick? Did he even know? Did he assume they all worked the same way? Could he have—were they real handcuffs? *You fucking bastard. Okay. You can do this.* Her hands were small. Maybe small enough to… *slow, deep breaths.*

As he nattered on with his audience volunteer, Christina wedged the cuffs between her thighs, tucked her left thumb in and rolled the hand inward, making it as narrow as possible. By wiggling and pulling, she was able to work a hand out, but not without some painful scrapes. Occupational hazard, but the sucker was off. Easy enough now to get the other hand out.

The outer lock rattled, echoing inside Christina's head. "As you can hear, that's on good and tight, isn't that right, good sir?"

She couldn't hear his response.

"And that's a good, solid box?"

Thump. Thump, thump, thump.

The voices retreated. Christina assumed he was walking him back to his seat. Giving her time to do what came next.

Out of the bag. Harder this time, because the box was so small. Good thing his awful music was so loud. But how the hell would they make the transfer? Not her job to worry about that. Just to do her part.

Clearly, they were no longer a team.

The music swelled. Perfect timing, because she whacked herself a few times on the sides of that very sturdy box attempting to get out of the bag. Something stung her leg and she sucked in a breath to keep from yelping. And in flinching away from that impact, another sharp pain jabbed her arm.

She felt warm liquid seeping along her thigh. Fucking screw tips—the illusion guy should have sanded them off. Maybe there wasn't time. She didn't want to think that Ralph had left them there on purpose.

After a few more scrapes, she had the bag and locks where Ralph would need them. He was winding up his patter, and then she heard the cue word that he was about to get on top of the box and signal the stagehand to make with the dry ice machine and the flash-and-dazzle light show, laying out a huge puff of colorful fog that would hide their transfer. She pressed her body as flat as she could against the side, making room for him to land.

But where was Ralph? Her breathing hitched and her heart raced. Panic shot down her arms, numbing her fingertips.

No. No. No. Breathe.

She saw her father's dead, unseeing gaze. All of a sudden the weight of a man of Ralph's size landed atop the crate. On impact, she jerked sideways, racked with pain as her ankle turned and a screw tip sliced inches up her calf.

And the hatch fell.

She shot out a hand to protect herself, but it wasn't fast enough to stop the unfamiliar and much too thick slab of wood from bashing her in the temple.

34

It was too far to run, and Devon knew he'd never get a cab, so when Aunt Mimi didn't pick up, he dashed around parked cars and through traffic to get to the Kenmore T station.

A quick, fumbled text went unanswered.

Uncle's number went straight to voice mail.

He cursed his uncle's decision to dispense with their landline in favor of cells. Still clutching his phone, he swiped his pass through the turnstile and nearly knocked over a couple of people as he raced for the waiting inbound train. He'd just beaten the slide of the doors, and as the train rattled off, he grabbed the pole, trying to catch his breath.

Trying to think.

Trying all the numbers again.

Nothing.

Nobody.

In desperation, he tried Mrs. Sook—another recorded message. He would kill that man—and Devon was certain the magician was behind this. He'd squash him like an insect. If he harmed one hair on Lee Song's head…Hippocratic oath out the window, big time. He attempted to calm himself enough to be useful, but his racing heart pounded in his head and all he could see was that tiny little face.

* * *

"Holy Christmas." The soft words vibrated through Christina's head. "Teeny."

Fingers tapped on her cheek, and she thought she was responding, but nothing came out.

"Teen." A harsh whisper. A clatter of metal against wood against the thump of horrible, horrible music.

"Wha—?" She blinked. A blanket of white vapor flowed through the hatch. It was all she could see. Every nerve in her body hit the alarm. A scream built in her throat and a hand clapped over her mouth.

Ralph. Dry ice. Not smoke. No fire.

"Get up," the voice said. "Get out."

Her tongue felt thick, her chest heaving with effort. "You…trying…to kill me or something?"

"Can the drama. Get up. Ten seconds and they're gonna blow our cover away."

She squeezed her eyes shut. Shook her head. Shaking it clear. Right. She knew this. She had to get up. Out. Complete the trick. She had to. Grappling for the edges of the box, she counted down in her head.

Eight. Wincing at the pain.

Seven. Both hands braced on the top. Woozy at the blood trailing down her forearm.

Six. Finding her feet beneath her. One, gone to sleep, twisted at the ankle.

Five. Push. *Goddamn* it.

Four. Fuck, leg hurts. Ignore it. You're stronger than that.

Three. Head up. Shoulders up. *Push!* Mind over matter.

Two. Bracing wobbling feet over the hatch so Ralph could swing it closed from beneath.

One. Hit the pose.

Hold.

Beneath the music, the fans whirred. The vapor whooshed away. Stage lights glinted purple, blue, and gold through the swirling fog.

Hold.

One whoop from the audience, joined by another, and applause.

Atop the crate, she took a bow, nearly stumbling when she straightened, then put up a finger and smiled at the crowd as if to say, *You ain't seen nothing yet.*

In time with the music, Christina leaped to the stage, landed on her bad ankle and with all her strength bit back the yowl that wanted to escape. With a flourish she gestured to the crate, unlocked the top, and pulled it open.

A figure rose, encased in the white canvas sack, now covered with old-fashioned travel stickers. She released the drawstring. Standing in the box, wrists firmly cuffed and mouth gagged by a colorful bandanna, was a stagehand in Ralph's costume.

After a few bows the pair ran off. Leaving the stage empty for

Ralph's eventual and triumphant return: handcuffed and bagged in one of the armoires dressing their set.

Christina never got to see Ralph's reemergence. Because as soon as she cleared the stage, her legs collapsed beneath her. She didn't know how long she lay there, staring at the lights, unable to pull in a breath, face after face peering down at her in alarm, yelling to each other about what should be done. From the din came a loud male voice, a familiar accent, telling them he was a doctor and to give the lady some air.

"Hey," he said softly. A face she recognized. "Christina, gorgeous, stay with me. You lost some blood and got one scary-looking knot on your noggin, but stay with me now. Ambulance is on the way. You're gonna be fine."

I know. She couldn't make her mouth say the words; instead she started to laugh with what little air she could grapple into her body.

Fuck you, she thought at the throbbing pain in her temple and her arm and in her twisted leg. At the rips in her costume, at the warm, sticky blood trickling down her limbs and onto the floor. *Fuck all of it.*

I did it. I kicked this thing's ass.

* * *

"Come on, come on," Devon muttered. The train had pulled into Haymarket but the doors weren't opening fast enough. From there he could make the half-mile at a run, so he sprinted up the stairs, dodging knots of pedestrians bound for the Quincy Market nightlife, and took off toward Atlantic Avenue, the loud club music swirling off behind him.

When he finally reached the condo he bashed at the doorbell. Auntie's voice, spouting off a string of Korean irritation, made him gasp in relief that she was home and, hopefully, all right.

She flung open the door, and when he saw her thin, worried face, he threw his arms around her. "Where is he?" Devon sputtered, still catching his breath. "Is he okay?"

"What? Who? Dae Soon. What's wrong?"

"Lee Song. Where is he? Your text…the man at the window?"

"He's in his room." She followed him. "And what text? What

man? I don't—"

Devon broke for the back hallway. "Joka?"

"Uncle Dev!"

He'd padded to the doorway in his pajamas. His eyes were bright and his hair skewed every which way. The child was one of the most beautiful sights he'd ever seen. He grabbed his nephew up and held him close, kissing the top of his head.

"Is Miss Christina's show over? Will you read me a story? Ow. Too tight hug."

"Sorry. Yeah. Okay. Let's read a story."

He set Small Lee down, gave his hand a little squeeze, and led him back into his room. The light over the window assured him that Auntie had set the alarm.

"Dae Soon, I'm waiting. What the devil…?"

"I thought—" He didn't know what he'd thought. If she hadn't texted him, if there was nothing wrong, who could…? His eyes narrowed. Maybe it was someone who knew more about technology than he'd admitted to. But he didn't want to scare his nephew. Or Auntie. "I just wanted to say goodnight."

She wasn't convinced, but after a long squint at him, she backed down. The boy jumped into bed and Devon sat in the chair next to it.

"Which one would you like?"

Small Lee asked for *Horton Hears a Who*. But as Devon was reaching for the book, his phone vibrated, and he gulped when he saw the text from Thomas. "Joka. I'm so sorry. I have to go."

* * *

Thomas met him in the lobby of the emergency department and pressed a temporary ID into his hand. "So they don't give you a hard time for not being family. Pays to have friends in low places." Thomas took him back, and Devon swallowed hard when he saw Christina, employing his training at not letting the patient's condition show on his face. Man, she looked like hell. A wicked lump on her temple. Contusions wherever he could bear to glance. A huge bandage ran the length of her forearm. A resident was addressing what looked like a major gash on her right calf. And the way her left leg was propped and stabilized, something bad had happened there, too.

Devon peered over the resident's shoulder, evaluating his suturing technique. Thomas tapped him on the arm. "Let's allow the man to do his job, shall we? She's tanked on painkillers. Come outside, we'll talk."

Thomas gave him the rundown. No concussion, but they wanted to watch her. Three large incisions required closing. "The ankle's sprained. And ten to one the left tibia's broken. Rudy's coming up to take her to X-ray once they get her stitched."

"What the hell happened?"

"Buggered if I know, except that trick looked a little dodgy. By the time I caught up with her, she'd passed out in the wings."

"And the magician?" He couldn't keep the snarl out of his voice.

"God knows. But something tells me he's bound to show up here like a bad penny."

"No doubt. She was trying to get out of town. At least that was the plan. Maybe he found out."

The Tank Engine's mouth went slack. "That wanker," he muttered, along with a few more colorful words. "I'll tell the desk."

35

The break in Christina's leg required surgery and a pin, and her medical team wanted to monitor the head injury, so they admitted her for a few days. Rosa, her own tests complete and all negative, came by and they played gin rummy. Devon fetched coffee and ran interference, generally keeping himself busy. Herbert brought flowers. So did her roommates, who stayed for a brief, curated version of events, because they were on their way to somewhere else. Thomas came up from radiology and sat with them and watched a Red Sox game until a nurse chased him out.

Ralph had still not materialized. But his lack of presence loomed large. She felt it when Herbert leaned over and asked, sotto voce, if she wanted him to fetch some friends and a baseball bat. She felt it when Devon shifted uncomfortably in his chair and asked her, his voice stiff and careful, if there was anyone else she wanted him to call.

She shook her head and watched his face, the play of light across his downcast features. "This is going to be weird, isn't it?"

"Weird...how?"

Christina cocked an eyebrow at him.

"Right." Devon's shoulders sagged.

"Are you sorry? Would you have kissed me if I hadn't told you I was leaving?"

"Hypotheticals. Let's just concentrate on your recovery for now," he said, but the brief smile in his eyes and the six shades of pink on his cheeks tipped his hand.

Then another thought drifted up. "Did I—?" Christina swallowed the dryness from her throat, and he helped her with a glass of water. "Did I give you the locker key when they admitted me?" Before the show, she'd hid it in her costume.

"Um, no. Not that I remember. I can go over to the yoga studio, talk to the manager, explain what happened."

"Nah, it'll probably turn up. Maybe one of the orderlies has it. Anyway, not like I can go anywhere for a while."

"Oh." The flush reclaimed his face. "Right. About that. When you're released, how will you manage in your apartment, with that unreliable elevator and roommates who are hardly ever around?"

"I'll get by. That's what crutches are for, right?"

"Aunt Mimi would love to have you." He pulled himself up straighter in the chair. "For as long as you want to stay, I mean. And Lee Song made me promise to ask you to save him space to draw something on your cast."

"I'm a blank slate." She nodded toward her leg. "And that's really sweet of her, but…"

"Yeah, I know. Weird. Just something to consider."

* * *

Much as Christina enjoyed the company, except the ones who bathed her with pitiful looks, she felt relieved when the loudspeaker announced the end of visiting hours. A hospital ward wasn't exactly Superman's fortress of solitude, but at least she could get a bit of rest. Sleep wasn't happening, though.

She blamed the upending of her routine, the medication schedule, and the abrupt break in her physical activity for leaving her in this state. And, of course, the injuries.

The nurse dimmed the lights and said she'd come by soon with her nighttime dose, which at least promised a break from consciousness. Until then, she closed her eyes and attempted a few slow yoga breaths, wincing when the expansion of her lungs touched the pain—bruised ribs from where the hard underwiring of the costume had crushed into her. The depth she could achieve varied hour by hour, depending on the level of happy juice in her system, and finally she found a balance.

On her eight-count exhale, she felt his presence. Her eyes flew open and she grabbed the call button.

Ralph, sitting in her bedside chair looking more comfortable than he had a right to be, held up his hands. "Hey, I come in peace."

Even in the shadows, she caught the contrition on his face. Still, she kept a finger hovered over the alarm. "Nice of you to show up at all."

His softening gaze roamed the damage. "I didn't know it was this bad. I went looking for you after the show, but you were gone.

Figured you were somewhere getting stitched up and you wouldn't want to see me."

"Two for two. Congratulations." But his story didn't smell right. How could he have missed the ambulance? The crowd of people hovering over her, Thomas leading the charge? Her brain wasn't working fast enough to connect the dots, though, so she let it drop. When Ralph lingered on her bare shoulder, she hitched the oversized hospital gown and pulled the blanket up to her neck.

"For what it's worth, I'm sorry. I didn't mean for this to happen."

"Yeah? What *did* you mean? You changed the box—"

"I swear to you, that was not the box I test-drove that afternoon. Hey, I had to work with that inferior piece of crap, too. Bastards. If I ever find out who—"

"—and the cuffs and the bag."

"All in the box. All gear I'd never seen before."

Blood pulsed harder into her temples, throbbing extra pain into everything she'd injured, but she didn't care. "That shit you pulled about my past? What the fuck were you thinking? Seriously? Telling me that right before we went on?"

He shrugged. "It's called showmanship. Maybe you've heard of it?"

"Please do explain. You're not even supposed to be here. And if I don't like what you say, I swear I'm whaling on this button and two hundred pounds of mean nurse is gonna toss your ass into the Charles."

"Aw, where's the love, Teen?"

She held up the call pad. "Talk."

"Fine." He huffed out a sigh. "You ever watched *Psycho?* Remember how Janet Leigh screamed? It freaked everyone out because that wasn't acting. It was real. Hitchcock didn't tell her, but he had the shower set to freezing. To get a more natural reaction."

"Seriously." She narrowed her eyes at him. "That story's a fake, made up by some bored back-lot tour guides, probably to squeeze a few bucks out of the tourists."

"Still a good story."

"Still a lie. So you trampled into my past to make me scream like Janet Leigh?"

He dropped his gaze to his entwined fingers before meeting her eye. "I had some...information tucked away, in case of an emergency. I felt for ya, Teen. Helluva tough break, you being just a kid."

He could have left Devon out of it. It was one thing to violate her privacy, but someone else's? Although for the doctor's safety, she bit back the words.

"But I had mad respect for you," he said. "Because you took whatever I threw at you."

"All this...and locking me in a crate, that was some kind of test?" She nearly hit the button. "You fucking heartless bastard, get out of here before I—"

Ralph raised his hands. "Okay. I deserve that. But I was thinking of our act. Just hear me out. Please?"

Something in his tone pulled her back. "Again. Talk."

"You were getting overconfident," he said. "I figured if you had the psychic energy to pick away at me, at us, it meant you already had the sub-trunk in the can. I was afraid it would look too staged when we performed."

"Hence the spontaneity."

"Kinda what I was going for, yeah."

Forgetting about the pain line, she tugged in a breath and winced. "I do have some acting talent, you know. You could have just said to work it like I was freaking out."

Half his mouth crooked into a grin. "Nothing gets the adrenaline pumping like real live fear."

"It could have totally screwed up the act, left you with a zombie out there. How did you know all that adrenaline wouldn't freeze me cold?"

"Because you're good."

She opened her mouth but couldn't get anything to come out. He thought—

"Yeah. I said it. Meant it, too. When I saw you through the hatch, I swore you wouldn't..." Ralph swallowed. "Well, Christina Louise Davenport McNulty, or whatever the hell your name is, you proved me wrong. You got up. You keep getting up."

Still she could not form words.

He dropped his voice. "You're too good to be stuck being

someone's assistant."

Again, she wondered if she'd heard him right. Or maybe he was just blowing smoke to keep her from suing his ass or throttling him as soon as she was physically able.

"And, well." He nodded toward her leg. "Looks like you're gonna be down for the count for a while, and I need to keep working. Got four gigs lined up thanks to that showcase. So I'm firing you. I'm releasing you from your contract."

She cut her eyes toward him. Her amended deal had been sweetened with a ladder of bonuses, from agreeing to sign on, to how much work resulted directly from the show. None of which he'd paid her for yet.

"You'll get what I still owe you, don't worry about that."

"Sixty-forty."

He shook his head. "Let's make it fifty-five forty-five. For your troubles. And because I still have top billing."

"Fifty-fifty and I don't haul your ass into court for negligence."

"Hey, I got screwed over, too. The box…" He fell back against the chair. "Fine."

"In writing."

"Fine," he said, a little sharper.

Damn, she wanted her painkillers. As she was thinking about pounding on the button just to get a dose, he said, "The numbers hit on Saturday, did you know that?"

"Ralph. Really?"

"I had a feeling. With us having the show and all. Okay, it's not millions. There were a bunch of winners, and I'll probably only net high five figures, but it's enough. I'm making plans. Big plans."

She was about to say that forty—no, now forty-five percent of the money was hers. That she'd put in her time, signed the damned agreements, hung out at the convenience store a lot of Saturday mornings with him and his Houdini-blessed writing implement waiting for the clock to strike ten. But then she realized it would only keep her tied to Reynaldo the Magnificent. Knowing him, he'd set her up on some kind of installment plan instead of a clean split. Lottery winnings aside, he was offering her an out, and she was taking it. She'd be crazy not to. "Crap. The ticket. It's in my purse." His brows lifted ever so slightly. "It's…safe," she added.

"I'm sure it is," he said.

The pain was getting worse, and she squeezed her eyes shut and sighed. "I'll get it to you."

"I'm sure you will."

She tried a few more breaths. And when her lids fluttered open, the chair was empty. A nurse stood in the entrance, shooting a glare down the hallway.

"You okay?" she said.

Christina shrugged. "Yes. No."

The nurse gave her a gentle smile and pressed a hand to her shoulder. "We'll up that dosage some, put you out for the night."

"Thank you. One thing, though. In my stuff, when I came in? Did anyone find a key? Like a small locker key?"

"Everything would have been put in this cupboard, here." The nurse opened it, peered in, and fluffed a hand through what remained of her costume. "Just some clothing…"

"There's a pocket."

"Right. Got it. There's a T-pass…nope. No key. Sorry, Christina. I'll ask at the lost and found in the ER, but usually they're good about keeping the personal possessions with the person."

She sighed. Then suspicion snaked through her. Dammit. Her phone was in that purse, too. "Could you help me with something else? I need to send a text."

* * *

Herbert came by early the next morning with two mochaccinos. They smelled so good she could have kissed him. He taught her a new card trick, which went a long way toward settling her nerves, especially after she'd told him about Ralph's visit.

He agreed with her suspicions.

"Yeah, anything he offers I'd definitely get in writing. Notarized and witnessed and maybe with a vital organ for collateral. But what you're thinking definitely sounds like his speed. You were leaving the act, and him, so he wanted to give you a hard time about it. Found the key in your costume while you two were doing the transfer in the box, then he made off with the goods just to rub it in your face."

"The minute it started making sense, I got a message to Devon.

He said the yoga studio was closed by the time he got over there, but he was going to stop in when they opened. Should be here any minute."

She tried the trick again and Herbert corrected her technique. Then he leaned closer to her and said, "You know, it's still not too late for me to have him killed."

"Who, Devon?" She lifted her eyebrows at him.

He grinned back. "You like the kid, huh?"

"He doesn't make me want to hurl."

"Yeah. Just what I thought when I met my wife."

"Herbert."

"Miss Christina." He gave her a gentle smile and waved a hand. "Run the trick again."

A few minutes later, Devon was in the doorway, an expression on his face that made her drop the cards.

He sat on the edge of the bed and handed her the bag. She collected it but couldn't take her eyes from him. "I told the manager you'd lost your key." Anger and worry tightened his words. "Then he pulled an envelope from beneath the counter and asked me for identification. He said that if it matched the name on the envelope, he could help me."

The blood drained from Christina's face. Dammit. There was the flaw in her plan. Well, besides the illusion going sideways. Ralph was all buddied up with the yoga studio manager. Maybe he helped Ralph scout particularly flexible and attractive contenders. Probably sold the guy a line of bullshit that Christina stole from him, like his last assistant, and he'd come to claim what was his. So if the manager saw him opening her locker, a locker that he'd told Ralph she'd suddenly rented after taking classes there for years, of course he wouldn't question what the magician had been after. Herbert cleared the cards away one step ahead of Christina's diving into her purse. "It's gone," she said. "Bus ticket, credit cards, phone, all my cash…that bastard." And, of course, the lottery stub. Perhaps the only thing he'd intended taking. The rest of it was probably just to piss her off.

Devon's mouth pressed tight. "And once again he took your phone."

"At least this time he left the keys."

His eyes sharpened and he smiled. "Good. You'll probably want something to wear when you're discharged, right?"

"Um, probably a good idea?"

"I'd be happy to get that for you. Right now would work, if you don't mind."

She handed him her key chain. "If it's no trouble. But Devon—"

"No trouble. I have Auntie's car today. I promised to do some errands for her." He leaned over and kissed the top of her head. "This won't take long."

He left and she stared after him, wondering what the hell was up and if she should call Thomas to keep him from whatever kind of trouble he looked far too eager to start.

"Apparently you don't make the kid hurl, either," Herbert said.

"Shut up and deal."

"Brought the wrong deck for poker."

"Rosa left hers in the drawer."

He started reaching for it but instead pulled a smartphone from his pocket. "Hey. Almost forgot." He swiped a thumb across the screen and showed her a picture. Christina took the phone from him, brought it close to her face. She was standing on top of the godforsaken crate like a rock star. Purple fog swirled around the base of it, licking up to her feet. She had one hand crooked behind her head, one pointing straight up in triumph.

"Look at you," Herbert said. "Standing up there torn to shreds with a sprained ankle and a broken leg. Like the goddamn queen of hearts, excuse my language. You don't need him. And you know what? You never did."

Her hands began to tremble with the knowledge of it. "You're right." She imagined her own top billing. The Amazing Christina. Queen of Hearts.

"Do you mind if I send this to my mother?"

He took the phone back and selected a different image. "Use this one instead. Less blood. I know you don't exactly see eye to eye with your mother about the magic thing, but there's no sense killing the woman."

"Good point." Silence fell between them as she tapped in her mother's email address and a quick message promising to call. "Are there more?"

"Yes," he said.

"And…can I see them?"

Herbert pulled in a long breath.

She swallowed. "What, are they really bad?"

"In a manner of speaking." He gestured that she should scroll back a few images. There were a few more of her on top of the box, a couple before she'd been put inside. Then—

"That's Ralph." She squinted. "Backstage? What the hell's he doing? Herbert, when did you—"

"Something didn't add up when we talked on the phone, night before the show. So a little voice told me to drop by the theater early, see what was what for myself." His mouth tightened. "Now it's starting to make sense, given what you just said. Tell me again what he claimed happened with the set."

Christina's heart-rate monitor sped up so fast she thought a nurse would be flying in the door any second. When her voice finally worked, it was so small. "He…said one of the workers damaged it. Which was why his illusion guy had to bring in a new prototype. It was a little smaller, but we would just have to work with it. Then when Ralph was here, he said someone sabotaged us…that box we got stuck with wasn't the prototype at all." She swiped back a couple shots. And there was an image of Ralph, placing what looked like a clump of white fabric inside the box.

"Zoom in," Herbert said.

She did. And sucked in a breath so fast she busted through the pain line and grabbed her ribs. Clutched in Ralph's hands was definitely the white bag she'd been inside. On top of the mound of white sailcloth sat the gold cuffs that had been clamped around her wrists. *Bastard.* "He said…he claimed he didn't know how that stuff got swapped with ours. Damn it, I could kill that son of a bitch."

"Take a number."

"But why the hell would he—?"

He set a hand lightly on her arm, his voice gentle. "Okay. They've been pumping you with a lot of goofy juice in here, so let me walk you through it. During his little visit, he told you the new box was a complete surprise to him, too, right?"

"Yeah."

"So you'd think you were both operating under the same disadvantage."

A hot fist of anger punched her stomach as the threads began coming together, but the fuzz of the painkillers kept them from fully connecting. She rubbed her temples. "Herbert. How long were you back there?"

"Long enough to watch him and the stagehand fellow he hired put that set through its paces a few times. Including giving him a key for those cuffs."

Damn it. Well, that explained how the stagehand got into them. She'd been wondering about that. So they got to practice and she'd come in cold. "And let me guess. There was no damage to the original box. There was no 'prototype.' Just the final, totally unsafe box we used on stage. And a pair of real handcuffs."

He took a long look at her face. "Maybe this is a little too much for you all at once. In your state."

Her eyes narrowed. "Herbert. Tell me."

He hesitated. "Just because I believe in getting my facts straight, I might have made a call to Reynaldo the Asinine's illusion designer. A gentleman I've known for many years, by the by. And he might have sung like a canary. Not just his ethical concerns about a little switcheroo his client asked him to pull—which he refused, by the way."

"So I guess he got someone else to do it."

"No doubt. Anyway, thanks to this generous friend, I'm also privy to a couple of potentially useful facts about upcoming shows that, mind you, don't involve splitting his take with an assistant." He waved a hand. "These useful facts include contacts for union people and bookers and such. But you didn't hear that from me." Herbert pulled a piece of paper from his shirt pocket. "Now. Given all that, I'm leaving this in your capable hands to do with it what you think best."

She fumbled it open and turned a questioning look on Herbert.

He pointed. "It's the designer's phone number. I have a strong hunch he'd be very happy to speak with you." Herbert then leaned back, one side of his mouth lifted into a smirk. "There's a lesson for you, Miss Christina. If you want to buy someone's silence, don't forget to pay him."

36

Devon saw the tailgate of the pickup from halfway down the block. His mind had been whirring too fast during the drive to make a plan, and now his stomach joined in the battle. One question jumped to the top of the heap. He yanked the Volvo to the curb and strode toward the magician, who was placing what looked like a cardboard box into the back of the truck. The words were almost out of his mouth until he saw that fatuous smirk.

"Well. Just my luck. There's a doctor in the house."

"Shut up."

"Put it away, Doc. I'm not interested."

"I want that phone."

"Beg pardon?"

Devon shoved out a hand. "Cell phone."

"Don't have one. Don't believe in them. Technology is destroying the delicate balance of interpersonal human relations. Plus, the causal link between radiation and various kinds of cancer hasn't completely been disproven. But I don't have to tell a doctor that, do I?"

He could have punched him just so he'd stop talking. "Christina's cell phone. And the rest of what you took from her."

"Still don't know what you're rattling on about, but make it snappy, all right? I gotta get on the road while I'm still young."

"You stole her money. You hacked her phone to make a threat to my family. That's illegal. Therefore that phone is evidence, and I'll turn it over to the authorities. I know you have it because who else would have put my name on that envelope? Who else would know that she'd send me to collect her things from her locker?"

The man tilted his head and pressed his lips together before continuing to load the truck.

Devon added, "Didn't you hear a word I said?"

"I heard some pretty serious accusations. Damn crazy ones, too. All right." He shrugged. "I admit to retrieving a certain bit of property that the lady decreed was rightfully mine. But that's it. Women's purses scare the crap out of me, tell you the truth. Never know what's in those things. Nevertheless. I don't have her phone, don't even own my own phone, let alone a computer, and if you think I even know how to hack into one of those idiotic things, well, I don't know what you're smoking."

"Maybe you got someone else to do it."

"Maybe you better get out of my face while you still have one."

Devon crossed his arms over his chest and glared.

The magician flashed him a savage grin. "Oh, that's right. You guys take that oath. 'First, do no harm' or some such. You'd never touch me."

"I'm on leave," Devon growled.

"Go on." The magician tapped his jaw. "Pop me one. Right here. Oh, I can smell how bad you want to. What? You think acting like a big tough guy, that's gonna make Teeny hot?"

"I swear you'd better stop talking right now…"

The man hiked an eyebrow. "I could give you a few pointers…draw you a map of her special little places, if you like. Make it real simple for you."

"Enough!" He grabbed the magician's shirt and shoved him against the passenger side door, pinning him there.

"All right. I get it." He put his palms up. "She's all yours. I'm not fighting you over her. I'm not in the mood. And I don't feel like messing my hair up over some ball-busting little bitch who tried to play me for a sucker. She'll do the same to you. Who knows, she might be working you right now."

Devon shoved him harder. If he could push him right through the truck, it would vastly improve his day.

"You want to search me, you and your authorities? Get a warrant. Now back off, man, or I'm gonna lodge my own complaints about harassment, and tell you the truth, I'm getting a little cranky about having my personal space invaded."

"As if I'm going to walk away. The minute I turn the corner you'll be gone."

"Damn, you're smart. All that higher education did you a world of good, huh?"

"Shut up."

"But you know what they say. You can take the boy out of the gang, but you can't take the gang out of the boy." He smirked.

"Or…at least one boy."

Devon's jaw tightened, and his fist clamped so hard around the man's shirt that he swore his knuckles might snap. Boring into the magician's eyes, he dropped his voice. "You know the advantage in joining a gang like that? They look out for their own. Like family. I'm certain, given the loss of my brother, they'd be more than happy to do me a favor, if I asked. One phone call, and they'd find you. In fact, I can promise you that. Lie to me all you want, but if I even suspect that you're bothering any of us, I will make that call. Doesn't matter where you go, where you hide. And I can guarantee that they'll mess up more than your hair. I've seen their work. It's not very nice." He paused, mentally apologizing to his uncle and the entire medical community for what he planned to say next. "Here's some interesting information about the small intestine. It's about twenty feet long. And it works a lot better when it's inside your abdominal cavity. As opposed to lying in a stinking pile on the sidewalk."

The smirk froze on the man's face.

Devon was about to go on, wondering how far he could push this performance without straining credulity, but in his mind he saw his brother. Surely he might understand the impulse to protect Lee Song, might even admire Devon's acting skills. But this was no way to honor Lee's memory, pretending to be like the men his brother looked up to, like the men he fought—violence perpetuating violence. He released the magician with one last shove to try to sell the point harder, then backed off.

The man laughed, although a film of sweat shone on his forehead. "I knew you wouldn't touch me. Wouldn't want to hurt your delicate little doctor hands."

"Stop talking before I change my mind," Devon said. "You're a small, pathetic man. Anyone who would endanger a child or hurt a woman to prove a point is small. Pathetic. A coward." He swept an arm across the space between them. "Go ahead. Leave. If you have the phone, don't have the phone, I don't care anymore. But if you mess with my family again, if you mess with Christina, I will have no qualms about hitting that number. Or finding you myself and hurting my delicate little doctor hands." Pulling his final card, Devon shoved a finger toward the serpent on his bicep. "If you think I earned this for just showing up, you'd be dead wrong."

Then he turned and walked back to the Volvo. He'd gotten as far as the second parking meter when the magician sputtered an insult to Devon's manhood. He should have known that the man was also the type of coward who needed the last word. But Devon steeled himself not to look back, not to respond.

Besides, he'd promised his aunt an oil change.

37

Rosa knelt at Christina's feet and helped wriggle the modified pink yoga pants over her cast. A bit of gray had begun to creep into her boss's roots, and Christina resisted the urge to smooth a hand over the woman's hair, tell her to stop worrying about the restaurant and take care of herself. But Christina was part of the problem, leaving Rosa and Sal not only stressed but down another waitress.

"Are you guys going to be all right?" Christina asked.

"Pfft." Rosa made a dismissive gesture, pushed against the mattress for leverage, and sat beside her on the bed. "A little bump in the road, we'll be fine. Like you, we're strong. We survive."

She had to find a way to survive, too. Six weeks in this thing would mean a ton of lost income. Fortunately, the check she'd left her roommates would cover the upcoming month, but that had wiped out a big chunk of her savings. Her mother had offered to help her, but Christina would prefer it didn't come to that. "You'll— if I want to come back...?"

"Honey. Like I say." She pressed a palm against Christina's cheek. "You're our girl. You want to come back, we'll always make room. If life has another plan for you, that's okay, too. We only want you happy."

Christina grinned.

"There you go," Rosa said. "Happy. Wait." She tucked a curl behind Christina's ear. "Now you're happy *and* pretty. Shame we had to cut those pants. They're so cute."

Christina looked down at the inch or two of bare skin between the top of the cast and the bottom of the pant leg. "At least it's still summer." She peered out the window. "It is still summer, isn't it? Feels like I've been in here for weeks."

"Not so bad." Rosa smiled. "And it's a beautiful day. You'll see, when you get those papers and they let you go. What did that nurse say, another hour?"

"At least."

"I'll get you a little bite to eat, then. It won't be my cooking, but it'll be better than they serve here."

Rosa grabbed her bag and was halfway out the door when Christina stopped her. "Hey, could I borrow your phone?"

"Sure, honey." She fished it out and handed it to her.

"And if you see Devon on your way out, could you, uh, take him with you?"

Rosa's lips pursed.

"It'll be okay. I promise."

After a brief glare of warning, Rosa relented. Christina counted to five and then punched in the digits.

Herbert was right about the man's eagerness to talk to her. He sounded like a really nice guy; he even asked about her injuries. Then they got down to business. She took a few notes, and he gave her the jackpot: confirmation that even though Mr. Magnificent had blown out of town, there was a way to reach him. Via the cell phone number that the designer had been using to contact Ralph for at least the last six months—which looked nothing like the number he'd used to text her.

Bastard.

Christina thanked the designer and promised to stay in touch. She decided to save her next call for later. When she had more time.

And more privacy.

Because that conversation wasn't going to be happy or pretty.

38

The low beams of late-afternoon sunshine made Devon feel slow and languid. So did curling up next to Christina on his aunt's sofa. Sometimes he worried that this was just a dream, and he'd wake to discover she'd refused Auntie's invitation. But there sat the lovely juggling girl, and at her feet, his nephew frowned in concentration while he added his latest masterpiece to the plaster cast. "Joka, it'll be a shame to lose such beautiful artwork when the cast is removed."

Small Lee glanced up with a frown, as if he hadn't expected this result.

"No worries." Christina pulled her new phone from a pocket. "It's all here. We can even print out enough copies for everyone's refrigerators."

"Did you take a picture of my superhero dragon?" The boy pointed it out, on the lower outside of Christina's shin.

"Of course." She aimed the device at it. "Let's get another one just in case." Glancing down the length of her leg, Devon admired her existing decorations. Herbert had written, "When I said break a leg I was only kidding." She'd been gifted with a small and surprisingly delicate hummingbird from Uncle Park, who tut-tutted everyone's surprise that he knew how to draw. Rosa had signed with "My brave girl" in Italian: *La mia ragazza coraggiosa*. Auntie Mimi penned a few Korean characters and claimed it would be bad luck to tell what it meant. And Small Lee was currently working on his third contribution. He'd already drawn Batman and was putting the finishing touches on Edmond the sea turtle's shell.

"You're going to leave room for Uncle Devon, aren't you?" Christina asked.

He pushed a little index finger against a vertical path on the opposite side of her shin. "It goes here. We have black and silver markers and a pink one for the tongue."

Auntie came around from the kitchen with a platter of sandwiches and caught a whiff of what they were doing. "No. Dae Soon, you're not putting that on her. It's bad enough that you wear it."

He scrambled up and took the tray from her hands. "Auntie."

After examining his face a moment, the concern in her eyes softened. "At least hers will only be temporary."

"We'll take pictures," Devon said. "And put them on the refrigerator."

"Troublemaker. Now you're teasing me. But when your uncle comes home, he won't be amused. You know how he feels about that...thing."

"Actually, Mimi, it was my idea," Christina said. "I thought it would be a nice tribute to your nephew. Dae Soon told me that in your family's tradition, the snake represents good luck and protection from evil."

Devon's breath caught and a shiver slid down his belly. She'd never called him by his Korean name before. From Uncle's mouth it was punishment. From Auntie's, a maternal caress. From Christina it was something else entirely. He felt braver when she said it, more worthy. Her face glinted with mischief. "Or it intends to offer me an apple," she added. "I'm not sure."

"Then you should have made him get this snake," Auntie said to Devon.

"As if he ever listened to me." He set the tray on the coffee table and Small Lee abandoned his artistic pursuits in favor of peanut butter. Devon returned to the kitchen to fetch him a glass of milk, and iced tea for Auntie and Christina. As he rummaged up drinks, he said, "Did I ever tell you about the time I tried to get him to wear a tie for school picture day?"

"Secret brother story!" Small Lee yelped with his mouth full and quickly hid his chewing behind his hand. "I want to hear!"

"I thought I was being so smart." Devon set the milk before his nephew. The boy took it in both hands and cuddled up to Christina in the space Devon had just vacated. *Hmm, you are very like your father.* "Every year it was a big argument to get him to dress up nice. But that year, I said, no tie needed, it's casual picture day."

"Because you thought he'd do the opposite?" Christina said.

"Always," Devon groaned. "Almost. When we left for school, he wore a T-shirt and jeans, like he did every day. I figured, oh well, lost that fight. But when I went to the auditorium at picture-taking time, I heard all this laughter. And there was my brother, wearing his tie.

And his gym shorts. And nothing else."

Small Lee dissolved into a fit of giggles. Christina grabbed his milk so he wouldn't spill. "Did they take the picture?" she asked.

"Nope. The principal sent him home." Devon grinned. "Our mother was so mad it was ten minutes before she could speak anything but Korean."

In his peripheral vision, he saw that Auntie had slipped into the guest bath. She threw the fan switch, which did little to hide her sobbing. Christina touched his arm, and he turned to her, planning to offer reassurance or at least some comfort, but her eyes were so soft that a lump formed in his throat.

"I feel bad sometimes when we talk about him," Christina said. "I don't like to upset her. Or your uncle."

Devon swallowed. "I feel bad when we don't talk about him. It's like we're trying to *not* remember. I want to remember." He said a few words to Small Lee, and the boy nodded with excitement and ran off to his room. "Take your time and pick your favorite—make that two—and bring them back to Miss Christina, okay?"

He reclaimed his spot on the couch, and before he could think himself out of the impulse in their serendipitous moment of solitude, he leaned close and kissed her. Her lips smiled against his as if she'd been waiting for him to make the next move, but knowing his nephew would be back any second, he cut it short. "Thank you," he said.

"Damn. Thank *you*. So what did I do to deserve that? I'll make sure I keep doing it."

"I just appreciate that you're helping to keep him alive. My brother was funny and loyal and stubborn and everyone loved him. He died doing a really stupid, foolhardy thing that left a child without a father. But that doesn't mean he deserves being altogether forgotten."

"That's...that's beautiful."

He thought of kissing her again, but then the bathroom fan switched off. "Wish it were as easy to set right as a broken leg."

Christina's eyebrows shot up. "Easy? You think this has been easy? You try peeing sitting down five times a day with a million pounds of plaster on your leg."

"Poorly chosen metaphor," he said. "I'm sorry."

"It's a beautifully decorated million pounds of plaster, but still." A series of rustles and thumps came from Small Lee's room. "What did you send him off to do?"

"Secret mission."

But when he came bombing back into the living room, a lightweight quilt trailing behind him like a superhero cape, nearly knocking Auntie over in the process, his cover was blown.

"Special blanket fort!" Small Lee cried out. Devon grabbed him around the waist, lifted him up, and set him on his lap before he could get anywhere close to landing on Christina.

"Lee Song, what did we talk about on the way home from school?"

"Being very careful around Miss Christina so she can get all the way better?"

"Yes. And what else?"

Small Lee looked like he was thinking especially hard. Devon prompted him with a whisper in his ear. Then, leaving Devon with the blanket and the two books he'd selected, he eased off the couch and walked up to Auntie Mimi.

"Grandmimi?"

"Yes, my polite young man?"

"Will you please come play in our blanket fort?"

Her brows rose and she peered toward her sofas and chairs.

"No cushions involved," Devon said. "This is the modified version so nobody has to get on the floor if they don't want to."

"And so we don't wreck your living room," Christina added. "Well. As much as we usually do."

"I'll play," she said, her face serious. "There is one condition."

Devon put his hands up in surrender. "Okay. I won't draw the snake on her cast."

"That's between the two of you; I'm tired of arguing about it. But as for this condition?" She rubbed a hand into Small Lee's hair. "I get to read the first story."

* * *

Devon was four pages into the second story when Uncle Doctor's key turned in the lock. Mimi bolted up at the sound and started picking her way out of what remained of their blanket canopy.

Big brown eyes pleaded with her. "Grandmimi, stay."

"Someone has to get dinner on."

Devon followed. "I'll help you."

Christina reached for her crutches, wanting to do something useful that involved getting off the sofa, but Lee Song tugged at her hand.

"You can finish the story."

"No way, buddy." She set the book in her lap. "*We* can finish the story."

"Never a dull moment here lately," the elder Park said as he shut the door behind him.

"We're learning to read bigger words," Lee Song said.

"So I see. Miss Christina's using her time here well. And when you're done with today's lesson, you can sort out your mail." Uncle Park set a bundle of letters onto the coffee table, all forwarded from her apartment. "I guess somebody forgot to bring it in."

"Sorry," Devon said over his shoulder. "We were having an interesting discussion on the way home from school and I forgot."

Christina leaned forward. Among the letters was a padded envelope addressed to Christina Louise McNulty. There was no return address and the postmark had been smeared, but it was clear enough that even Lee Song could have spelled out Las Vegas. Her heart dropped into her stomach. "Devon…"

He was by her side in an instant, asked his nephew to go help Auntie, and gestured for the package.

"I've got this," she said. "I think." She pulled the tab and, holding her breath, tipped the contents onto the table. Out slid a brand-new packet of juggling scarves. A thin oblong box. And a cascade of what looked like…money orders?

Devon caught one before it sailed off the edge. "What the…? A thousand bucks? How many of them are there? Why—?" He grabbed another, and another. "It looks like they're all from different post offices."

Christina could only stare at the bounty before her. The call had gone straight to voice mail, but the threat she'd left upon it, followed up with Herbert's photo, had apparently worked. He'd done it. He'd paid her. He'd been a dick about it, but he'd done it.

While Devon was going through the money orders, frowning, a little piece of paper fluttered free. She recognized Ralph's scrawl: *47/53. My final offer.*

Devon glared at it. "Is that some kind of code? Is he still messing with you? I'll—"

"Down, Lancelot." She grinned up at him and snuck her hand into his. "Maybe Houdini told him to grow a conscience."

He tossed her a skeptical glance. "Yeah. Somehow I'm having a hard time believing he gave this up of his own free will." When Christina winked at him, he shook his head. "I'm not sure I want to know what happened to change his mind, but remind me never to get on your bad side."

"I don't know," Christina said. "I think Houdini and I might have had a little help. Doctor Devon, that oil change took an awfully long time."

His cheeks flushed adorably. "They were crowded. Then I had to go to your apartment and find you something to wear."

The outfit that had apparently taken him so long to choose was sitting in a pile of clean laundry atop her dresser, and she was about to goad him further when Mimi said, "What is the meaning of this?"

Devon busied himself with gathering up the slips and Lee Song inched closer, probably curious about what was in the package that had all the grown-ups clustered around it, dumbfounded.

"I'll venture a guess that it's my hazard pay." Then under her breath, Christina said, "If it's not fraudulent." She wouldn't be at all surprised if the money orders were fakes. Or written with some kind of long-lasting disappearing ink. Before anyone could ask more questions she didn't feel like answering, she made sure the boy's eyes were on her, and then she opened the bag of scarves. "Mimi, Doctor Park? With your permission, I'd like to give this to Lee Song." She fluttered one out. "Look! Juggling toys you can play with in the house."

The misdirection was apparently a success, at least with the youngest member of the household, who took the scarf from her and repeatedly tossed it over his head, letting it float to the carpet. "I'll teach you after dinner."

"Reading lessons and toys that won't hurt Grandmimi's nice things?" Dr. Park actually grinned. "Young lady, this boy might never let you leave."

She sensed Devon beside her, his outrage melting, and had a feeling that boy wouldn't let her get too far, either. Which set her stomach wobbling again.

The latest scarf toss lighted on the coffee table. When Lee Song plucked it up, he pointed to the box. "What's this, did you get more presents?"

In the excitement, Christina had almost forgotten about the other item in the envelope, and slid what looked like a black velvet jewelry box from a cardboard sleeve.

She dropped it as if it were on fire. "I can't." The money, should it prove real, was more than enough compensation. She'd earned it, for what he'd put her through. If he'd done something stupid and bought her an expensive piece of fluff, it would just be too much. Like she owed him. And she didn't want that in her head.

"For goodness' sake, I'll do it." Mimi lifted the lid and Christina turned away. "Is that…real Swarovski crystal? They're very pretty, but dear, I don't think those sticks will be long enough to hold your hair in place."

Christina chanced a look, and her throat tightened. The Jumping Gems. Just like her father's. "They're not for your hair." She swallowed, picked one up and ran a finger along the ebony wood, then smiled. "Ladies and gentlemen. Watch this."

* * *

Logic dictated that a Las Vegas postmark and a payoff meant the magician truly had disappeared from their lives, but a voice of worry in Devon's gut told him something different. Mainly that voice nattered on with what the cretin had said about Christina, the accusation that she was probably working him. He gazed down at her, snuggled against his shoulder, the light from the television flickering on her face. Ever since they met, and especially over the last couple of months, he'd been growing ever more entranced with her, not just by her strength but by the real, vulnerable woman beneath her walls of steel and sarcasm, and he didn't believe she'd been acting.

The show went to commercial and she leaned in for a kiss. He was happy to oblige. With Auntie and Uncle at the theater and Lee Song asleep, he felt like a teenager home alone with his first girlfriend. Like that teenager, he burned to do more than kiss, and the way she trailed her fingertips along the small of his back made him forget his name. He had to stay in control, though. There were her injuries to consider, and with the disruption in the household routine, his nephew had developed a habit of waking up an hour or two after bedtime and wanting a glass of water or reassurance that everything was okay in his world.

But Devon couldn't stop himself from worrying about his own world, and the intentions of the small, sweet woman in his arms. How could he even ask such a thing? *Are you using me? Am I just a rest stop before your next adventure?* Every way he worded it in his head sounded petulant and insulting.

And then, maybe sensing something amiss, she eased away. The width of her pupils darkened the remaining green iris to a startling depth that made his heart race and his jeans even more uncomfortable. He brushed a curl from her temple, buying a moment to regroup.

"What's wrong?" she said.

"Nothing."

"Can't kid a kidder." She ran a finger over the furrow between his brows. "This always gives you up."

"I'm that transparent?"

"From the minute I saw you."

"I'm disappointed. Here I'd hoped to be all manly and mysterious."

She slid a palm up his chest and shoulder, lighting on his jaw. "Manly, hell yeah. Mysterious, um, no. At least not to me."

The opening felt right. "You, on the other hand..."

"Women are supposed to be mysterious. It's how Scheherazade won over the king. It's why you wait for the veils to drop."

He grinned at the image, the memory of the day she caught him in her circle of juggling scarves. The colorful squares were sitting on the coffee table; Lee Song had been playing with them earlier. He snagged the red one, looped it around her shoulders and used it to tug her closer. Her eyes sparked with mischief. "This is interesting," she said. "Tell me more."

"Christina…" She gazed up at him and heat rushed through his body. "It would be really helpful now if you didn't look at me that way."

"What way?"

"Well…that."

"You can hardly blame me. I get to spend hours a day with a sweet, sexy guy—and his family. Not that I don't adore them or appreciate what you've done for me. But it's kind of driving me crazy."

He softened his hold on the scarf ends, releasing her. "Is that, uh, a good kind of crazy?"

"Best kind of crazy."

"But you'll be leaving us."

She shrugged a shoulder. "Well, yeah. I kind of imagine that after I get my cast off, your aunt and uncle would like their lives back."

"But will you be leaving Boston?" He rushed on, not wanting to hear her say the words yet. "Before the show. You had a job waiting for you in New York. Is that just on hold until you're physically able?"

"I can't imagine they'd hold it for me. A busy club in Manhattan can't afford to be down a waitress for long."

He swallowed. "But there's probably something else out there for you. Another club, another show, another—"

"Devon."

"You've been working so hard. You were on your way—"

"Hey, slow down. I just had the shit kicked out of me, okay? I need a little time to regroup."

"Before you leave." He sank back against the cushions.

"Damn it, will you let me talk?"

He held up his hands.

"New York was an escape route. He snapped and I had to get scarce, for my safety but mainly yours and Lee Song's. Herbert offered an out and I grabbed for it."

Devon's mind raced back to the evening in her apartment. In that muddle of emotions—the anger about the threats, the fear for his nephew's safety, his distress that he couldn't do more to help, not to mention the end of Gwen—had he missed the bigger picture?

That once again, the damsel could damn well rescue herself? And maybe him, too?

"And now that he's gone"—Christina tugged in a breath—"I have more options. Look, I don't know the future. I'm not married to the idea of New York. Or even leaving Boston. I just knew I needed to be far away from him."

His throat suddenly dry, Devon took a measure of her face. The soft, raw openness suggested sincerity. But he had to make sure. "Were you...are you...was I just convenient?"

She glared so long he thought she might scorch him. "Convenient? *Convenient?* You of all people should know—" She waved a hand across her face as if to cancel out her last statement. "Okay, Mr. Convenient. Answer my question right now. In my apartment. Did you kiss me because you thought you'd never see me again?"

"No."

"No?"

"I kissed you because I'd just broken up with my girlfriend—"

Her eyes widened. "I'm a rebound? You accuse me of playing you when you're a rebounder?"

"You didn't let me finish. *She* was playing me. And it had essentially been over for a while, all but the final nail in the coffin. But I thought I'd found someone who liked me for me. And I was kind of freaking out about losing her before I could tell her...how I felt."

That silenced her. He reached for her hand, cupping it like a warm, small animal between his palms.

She shook her head. "Don't. Don't you dare."

"Christina?" She pulled away, right into the opposite corner of the sofa. If not for the cast, she might have curled herself into a ball.

"It's so easy, isn't it?" Her voice broke. "It's so easy to tell someone you love them. People do it all the time. But I've seen what happens. Look what happened to my parents. They loved each other once. Bam, poof, all gone. And Ralph? He had the fucking nerve to—"

"Hey." He said the word so loud he was afraid he'd wake Lee Song, and he softened his tone. "Different guy, here. Completely unfair comparison. And no, it's not easy. For the record? I don't think I ever told Gwen, or any woman, that I loved her. Maybe because it's hard. Or I never felt that...whatever. Probably why it didn't work. But when I'm with you...when I think about you...when I look into your eyes and even when you're making fun of me, all I know for sure is that I don't want to be with anyone else. Call it what you want. Now, if you need to leave, at least I'll know I tried to do something about it."

Other than a softening of her mouth and a tilt of her head that threatened to melt the rest of him into mush, she had no reply to that. After a few moments, though, she slid a few inches toward him. "I'm sorry about your girlfriend."

"Sort-of girlfriend."

She scooted a little closer. "You do deserve better."

"You're right. I do."

"Did Lee Song like her?"

"She wouldn't play blanket fort. What do you think?"

By now Christina was near enough to set a hand on his leg. She leaned her head on his shoulder, and he worked an arm around her. Her pulse pounded against him, and he willed his own heart not to hammer its way out of his chest. "I think...I think you deserve someone who would play blanket fort. It's only fair."

"Yes, I think so."

She sniffed. "I'll need some time."

"Fortunately, I have a lot of that right now."

"Good." The breeze must have picked up; the jingle of mast lines from the harbor bled into the silence. "I want to be that person you deserve, Dae Soon."

The way she breathed those two syllables dissolved what remained of his doubts. She snaked her arms around his neck, and he lost himself in the sweetness of her mouth and the heat of her body against his, so lost that he hadn't even realized Auntie and Uncle had come home until he heard the door close. They backed away from each other, not soon enough, based on Auntie's blush and Uncle's lifted brow. Christina apologized with delightful charm, and they were gracious because they adored her, too. Devon was certain he'd get an earful from his uncle later, that he should be more responsible and circumspect when Lee Song could have wandered into the living room at any time. But for now they said nothing on the subject and bid Devon and Christina good night. Which meant it was time for Devon to go back to his apartment. He gave her one last kiss and wished her sweet dreams.

Stupid house rules, he thought as he returned to Cambridge, dreading the Christina-less agony of his lonely bed. But it was not his house, there was an impressionable five-year-old child to consider, and his aunt and uncle were doing a very kind thing to allow Christina to stay there during her convalescence.

And she loved him. She might not have said those exact words, but he knew it to be true; he felt it in the marrow of his bones, and for the first time in a long while, Devon Park was happy.

39

Refusing to let her spend her new, and quite legitimate, nest egg on a medical procedure he could perform himself, Uncle Park removed Christina's stitches at Aunt Mimi's kitchen table. But when it was time for the cast to come off, Devon escorted her to the outpatient care clinic attached to Mass General.

Thomas the Tank came by to offer his congratulations on her coming-out day. He hadn't seen the masterpiece the plaster had become, so he spent a few moments admiring it. When he saw the snake and learned who had drawn it, he nudged Devon's shoulder. "Oh, you're soup now, boyo."

"Medical jargon?" Christina asked.

"Something like that," Devon said.

"Think they'll be able to see me this century?" Her mouth twitched and she shifted in her seat. "The itching under this thing is making me insane."

"Does kind of look like a pileup in here," Thomas said. "Sorry, love."

Devon offered to get coffee. Thomas stuck a five in Devon's shirt pocket. "I take it like my women, Park. Hot and bitter. Go on, then. I'll be more than happy to babysit your girlfriend."

As he walked away, he heard Christina giving Thomas a good-natured cursing out for the babysitting remark, and Devon couldn't help a grin. He loved her spirit. He also loved hearing someone call her his girlfriend. It sounded almost as good as his Korean name on Christina's lips. Not "sort-of girlfriend." Not "sometimes-girlfriend." But a word without any qualifiers. He could get used to that.

The walk to the nearest cafeteria took him past familiar hallways, and his pulse quickened when he saw the arrows to the emergency department. When Christina had been brought in after the show, he'd put on his mental blinders and done what he'd had to do, but it had been damn near impossible not to think about what it had been like to work there. How it could be slow one second and crazy the next. How some days, patients were not people. They were charts and procedures and diagnoses and room numbers. Some of his colleagues had thrived in that environment. Not him. Clearly not him.

"Excuse me, young man?"

He stopped to focus on the voice that had broken through his thoughts. It belonged to an older woman. Her rheumy eyes darted as if she'd just had a fright, and her breathing sounded labored. "Yes? Can I help?"

"I can't find my husband."

"Is he in emergency? Because it's right down that hall."

"I don't know if that was it."

"What's his name? We can ask someone to look it up, find out where they've taken him."

It took a long time for her to remember, and he surmised that the stress could be having its way with her cognitive function. So he escorted her to the nearest help desk, punched up reception, and after a brief conversation, discovered that the man had just been transferred to an ICU upstairs.

"May I take you there?" he asked, and she nodded. When they reached the proper floor and he left her at the nurses' station, he promised himself to stop in before he took Christina home. Just to make sure she was all right.

As he was heading back to the elevator, it struck him that of all the people in the hallway downstairs the distraught woman could have asked for assistance, several of whom wore scrubs or other hospital garb, she had stopped him. Why, he didn't know. But it made him happy to be someone who could offer comfort. That part, he did miss. He missed it terribly. Surgery was not the right fit for him, he knew that now, but something else in the field awaited him. Whether that would be working directly with patients, in family care, or with at-risk kids, he wasn't sure yet. Only that he wanted to return to medicine, complete his training, and then see where he was needed.

And Christina was the first person he wanted to tell. Devon punched up her number, but apparently Thomas had commandeered her phone, because he said, "Sorry, mate, you had your chance. She's mine now." Then he faked a demonic laugh and handed the cell back to her.

"Your roommate is...disturbing, but I like that about him. And where are you? Roasting the beans?"

"Got distracted." The elevator doors whooshed open on the first floor.

"Well, get un-distracted, because they just said ten minutes until I get the saw."

"I finally get to watch someone saw you in half?"

"Was that a joke, Dae Soon?"

Grinning at the lovely sound, he picked up his step. "Please. That's Doctor Dae Soon."

"Really? Devon. You're going back?"

"Yeah. I am. I really am."

He heard Christina telling his roommate. Thomas gave up his best rugby cheer and said something about all of them being soup.

Best kind of soup.

40

"Well. Christina, Queen of Hearts." Herbert shot her a grin and nodded to her leg as she climbed the last few stairs into the shop. "Lost a little weight since I saw you last."

"Freedom is a wonderful thing. And crutches suck." She set two coffees and her father's magic case on the counter.

Catching him eyeballing it, she said, "Doing a little redecorating since I moved back into my place. And I thought you might like the Ed McNulty collection, or at least what's salvageable."

He flipped the latches and let out a low whistle. "This is a bit of history." He pulled out a silver cup, tested its heft, and turned it around in the light. "Craftsmanship. Don't often see 'em this nice anymore."

"Those were actually my grandfather's."

"You do come to magic honest, huh. You sure you don't want to hang on to any of this? Can't say that it's worth much, dollar-wise, but for sentimental value?" He hitched a brow at her. "Right," he said. "Understood."

She sipped her coffee and watched him ferret through the items, separating out the perishables—the crumbling red sponge balls and decaying rubber thumb tips—from the hard goods. "Wand's not too worse for wear." He gave it a twirl and up popped a small bouquet of red silk roses, which he handed to her. "For you, my good woman."

Christina closed her fingers around the base of the wand and brushed the silky blooms against her chin. Remembering how her father had surprised her with this trick. "Okay," she said with a sigh. "I'll keep this one."

"Thought you might."

"If you haven't already, could you please thank your friends in New York for the offer?"

"Already done. They're good people. Keep 'em in your back pocket, if you know what I'm saying."

She nodded. "Something else I wanted to show you." She pulled out the Jumping Gems.

"Well. That's one classy piece. But you're breaking my heart.

You could have bought that here."

"It was a gift."

"Hmm. A little 'sorry I robbed you blind and tried to kill you' present?"

"Twisted, huh."

"Still a nice bit of equipment. You remember how to work it?"

"Passable, but I could use some refinement."

He set her father's case beneath the counter. "Then you've come to the right place. Can't have my apprentice out there looking sloppy."

She grinned at him. "Herbert?"

He shrugged. "Just an idea. I get those once in a while. Can't afford to pay you, and I don't mess with the big illusions, but if you're looking to hone your close-up chops like the big kids, I'd be more than happy to teach you everything that's still knocking around in my head. Well, that I haven't taught you already."

Her smile broadened. She liked the sound of that. And with her cut from the lottery winnings, safely invested thanks to advice from Uncle Park, she could get by for a while, supplementing with a few shifts at the restaurant when Rosa and Sal needed her.

"I've, uh, also been thinking about redecorating," Herbert said. "Some decent space in that back room. Nice high ceiling, too. If you catch my drift."

"Juggling lessons?"

"Profit center. And that, I will pay you for—a set price per student that we'll agree on, if you're interested. Gets customers in here and sells equipment." Herbert crooked a thumb over his shoulder toward the storeroom. "It's a little messy now, but come, take a look. Dream a little."

In her mind she already saw a bright, sunny room full of giggling kids, tossing beanbags around. Then the picture expanded. Maybe she could apply to perform in the Marketplace herself next summer and invite some of her best pupils to join her. Her earnings would be based on her efforts, not what someone else thought she was worth. Or wasn't worth.

And she'd be an apprentice to one of the best magicians she knew. Not an assistant, making someone else look good, but learning and growing at her own pace.

His smile faltered. "Or just think about it."

"It sounds amazing, Herbert. You caught me by surprise, is all."

She was about to say more but the door chime caught her attention. So did the little giggling voice that promised to be quiet, and her heart did a happy-dance when she saw the two Park men shuffling up the stairs.

"I hope we're not interrupting. School let out early, and when I told my nephew Christina would be here for her magic lesson…"

"Not interrupting in the slightest." Herbert extended his hand across the counter and Devon shook it. "Nice to see you again, Doctor."

"Please, Devon is fine. And this young man is Lee Song, very much interested in magic and especially juggling."

"Then you've come at exactly the right time," Christina said. "Follow me."

As she could have predicted, Lee Song vibrated with ideas, and told Herbert, his new best friend, every one. She hung back, taking a rough measure of the space, smiling at the boy's enthusiasm. She leaned toward Devon. "I could make him my assistant. What do you think?"

"I think he'd love it. He'd take payment in peanut butter sandwiches and blanket fort hours."

"I can work with that. How'd the interview go?" His grin said it all. "Doctor Devon, they're taking you back?"

"Even better. There's an opening in the pediatrics program. The hours will be tough and I'll be playing catch-up for a while, but it's…where I need to be. Where I *want* to be."

She grabbed him into a hug, then kissed him.

"Hey," Herbert said. "No canoodling in the magic store."

Christina shot him a dirty look.

"Okay, for you guys I'll make an exception."

"What's 'can-noodle'?" Lee Song asked.

"That right there," Herbert said. "Gettin' all smoochy and stuff."

Devon pulled back and landed a final smooch on her forehead. "We should probably get going. Don't want to break the rules. Or explain more big words."

"Wait. Before you go…" She dashed to the front counter and rummaged through her father's case, coming back with a second wand. Kneeling before Devon's nephew, she flourished it like she'd seen Herbert do, and up popped a bouquet of yellow roses. The boy gasped, eyes widening with his grin. "A little present for Grandmimi."

"Thank you, Miss Christina."

"You're welcome, Lee Song."

When they left, she grabbed three juggling balls from the display case and joined Herbert in the storeroom. "Watch it there, hotshot, until I make some room for ya."

"It'll be fine," she said. "I'm a professional, after all, and someone has to test the equipment."

"You break it, you bought it."

She made a face at him and ran one of the balls down her arm, let it skim across her shoulders and into her waiting hand, then went right into a three-ball cascade. It had been a while, but her muscles remembered.

Her body remembered.

Her soul remembered.

On her fourth rotation, she tossed the ball high and twirled. When she stopped and reached out, the ball kissed her palm, and for her audience of one, she bowed.

THANK YOU FOR READING

Thank you for taking the time to read *A Sudden Gust of Gravity*. I would love to hear from you! Won't you please consider telling your friends or posting a review? Word of mouth is an author's best friend and greatly appreciated.

Want to hear about new book releases, special offers, and events? Please sign up for my mailing list at http://laurieboris.com/mailing-list/.

ACKNOWLEDGMENTS

Writing is usually a solitary act, but shaping up a manuscript for publication can take a village, a few meltdowns, and a whole lot of coffee. I'd like to tip my hat to the following fabulous people who helped me along the way.

Thank you to Bette Moskowitz, Mare Leonard, Anne McGrath, Ann Cappozzolli, and Heather McIntosh for the early critiquing.

Thank you to Tom De Poto for the first look and the honest assessment. We might have to get that key to the executive washroom gold-plated.

Magician Steven Max Droge read an early draft of this manuscript on many, many train rides, after which he educated me on the finer points of the craft and told me some great stories. Dr. Gerda Maissel took time from her busy schedule to give me a consult on Devon's residency.

I'm grateful for the eagle eyes of Yvonne Hertzberger, Melissa Bowersock, Lynne Cantwell, Erin McGowan, Jen Daniele, Leland Dirks, Cindi Jackson, and Amy Redd-Greiner. Beta readers are gold.

David Antrobus, uber-editor, did his usual amazing job of sanding off my screw tips.

Rich Meyer of Quantum Formatting worked his magic as well; he does such great work.

I'd also like to thank Ey Wade, Nicole Storey, Books Untamed, and the DB Collective for support and general mayhem; Sean Sweeney for the technical assist at the buzzer; and Elena Ahmadi Gestoso for fixing my Spanish, because in school I only learned enough of the language to get myself into trouble.

Thank you to my blended, extended family for always being on my team. And last but never least, I'm grateful to my husband for the lovely cover, for his great feedback, and for still not running away screaming after all these years of being married to a writer.

A LITTLE ABOUT LAURIE

Laurie Boris has been writing fiction for over twenty-five years and is the award-winning author of six novels. When not playing with the universe of imaginary people in her head, she's a freelance copyeditor and enjoys baseball, reading, and avoiding housework. She lives in New York's lovely Hudson Valley with her husband, Paul Blumstein, a commercial illustrator and web designer.

Connect with me online:
Website: http://laurieboris.com
Amazon Author Page: http://www.amazon.com/author/laurieboris
Facebook: http://www.facebook.com/laurie.boris.author
Twitter: http://www.twitter.com/LaurieBoris

LAURIE'S OTHER FICTION

In the Name of Love: Stories about Revenge, Redemption, and Rebirth (Flash-fiction anthology)
A lonely neighbor tries to melt a widow's reluctant heart. Bullying brothers threaten to spoil a young girl's Halloween. Left at the altar once, a woman takes a gamble on a second chance. These are just a few in a collection of thirty short and shorter stories about growing up, growing older, moving out, moving on, revenge, redemption, and love in all its shades of bittersweet pain and joy.

The Picture of Cool (Book One, Trager Family Secrets)
Television producer Charlie Trager spends his days working with beautiful women on a daytime talk show. But underneath his cool façade, there's a hollow spot in his heart, waiting for the right man to ease his loneliness. Then he meets the show's next guest, a handsome young politician with a bad case of nerves—and a secret that could turn both their lives upside down. (Short novella: 14,000 words)

Don't Tell Anyone (Book Two, Trager Family Secrets)
Liza's mother-in-law once called her a godless hippie raised by wolves. Now, after five years of marriage to her elder son, five years of disapproval and spite, the family accidentally learns that Estelle has a fatal illness. And Estelle comes to her with an impossible request. A horrified Liza refuses but keeps the question from her husband and his brother. As the three children urge Estelle to consider treatment, their complicated weave of family secrets and lies begins to unravel. Can they hold their own lives together long enough to help Estelle with hers? (Winner, The Kindle Book Review's 2013 Best Indie Books Award and indieBRAG medallion recipient. May be read as a standalone story.)

Playing Charlie Cool (Book Three, Trager Family Secrets)
Television producer Charlie Trager knows he's lucky to have a successful career and good friends and family who support him. The man he loves, however, is not so lucky. Joshua Goldberg suffers the

spite of an ex-wife gunning to keep him from their two children…and maybe Charlie. Determined not to let Joshua go, Charlie crafts a scheme that could remove the obstacles to their relationship…or destroy their love forever. (Note: May be read as a standalone story, but if you'd like to know how Joshua and Charlie met, you might want to read *The Picture of Cool* first.)

Sliding Past Vertical

Sarah loves Boston. The feeling isn't mutual. After a run of bad luck, she moves back to the college town where best friend Emerson lives. Still in love with her, he'd dreamed of her return. But well-meaning Sarah's hasty decisions often end in disaster, so Emerson's dream may become a nightmare.

Drawing Breath

Art teacher Daniel Benedetto has cystic fibrosis. At thirty-four, he's already outlived his doctor's "expiration date," but that doesn't stop him from giving all he can to his students and his work. When he takes on Caitlin, his landlady's daughter, as a private student, the budding teen painter watches in torment as other people, especially women, treat Daniel like a freak because of his condition. To Caitlin, Daniel is not a disease, not someone to pity or take care of but someone to care for, a friend, and her first real crush. Convinced one of those women is about to hurt him, Caitlin makes one very bad decision. (Finalist, 2013 Next Generation Indie Book Awards.)

The Joke's on Me

When a mudslide plummets her hopes, her home, and her entire collection of impractical footwear into the Pacific, former actress and stand-up comic Frankie Goldberg takes the only possession she has left—a cherry red Corvette convertible—and drives east to her family's bed and breakfast in Woodstock, New York. This begins a journey into the family she left behind, the family she joked about in her act. But the joke's on Frankie. While she was doing impressions of her slightly menopausal Jewish mother and her sister the serial divorcee, her family was slowly leaving her. And maybe that joke is just too new to be funny. Travel along with fearless Frankie as she puzzles through the eternal dilemma of coming back home to find that nothing is where you left it. (*The Joke's on Me* placed as a finalist in the 2012 Beach Books Festival.)

* * *

LAURIE'S OTHER BOOKS

First Chapters (Contributing Author)
Indies Unlimited: Author's Snarkopaedia Volume 1 (Contributing Author)
Indies Unlimited: Tutorials and Tools for Prospering in a Digital World (Contributing Author)
Indies Unlimited: 2012 Flash Fiction Anthology (Contributing Author)
Indies Unlimited: 2014 Flash Fiction Anthology (Contributing Author)
Boo! (Contributing Author)
Boo! Volume Two (Contributing Author)
Boo! Volume Three (Contributing Author)

Made in the USA
Middletown, DE
09 January 2016